20
5|03
6|03

The Warrior's Way

Zane punched the wall again in his rage. His great clan—joined with the filthy freebirths of the Draconis Combine! To force any Nova Cat to interact with them was only asking for trouble. Zane wondered if the Khan was actually plotting the destruction of the newly formed Zeta Galaxy. Then, in a sudden flash of understanding, he saw the truth.

Though every Nova Cat warrior was honor bound to obey the will of his Khan, there were times when a warrior's path might diverge from that of his Clan. His doubts did not make him any less a Nova Cat. His duty lay in showing others the error of their thinking so that all might return to the way of the Clan. In that moment, Zane vowed he would make that happen by becoming an example of a true Nova Cat warrior.

For the first time in a long while, Zane smiled to himself. Today was the beginning of a new path for him—a new path for all the Nova Cats.

They simply did not know it yet. . . .

PATH OF
GLORY

Randall N. Bills

A ROC BOOK

ROC
Published by New American Library, a division of
Penguin Putnam Inc., 375 Hudson Street,
New York, New York 10014, U.S.A.
Penguin Books Ltd, 27 Wrights Lane,
London W8 5TZ, England
Penguin Books Australia Ltd, Ringwood,
Victoria, Australia
Penguin Books Canada Ltd, 10 Alcorn Avenue,
Toronto, Ontario, Canada M4V 3B2
Penguin Books (N.Z.) Ltd, 182–190 Wairau Road,
Auckland 10, New Zealand

Penguin Books Ltd, Registered Offices:
Harmondsworth, Middlesex, England

First published by Roc, an imprint of New American Library,
a division of Penguin Putnam Inc.

First Printing, December 2000
10 9 8 7 6 5 4 3 2 1

Series Editor: Donna Ippolito
Mechanical Drawings: Duane Loose and the FASA art department
Cover art by Fred Gambino

To Virgil, Erde, Tara—no matter the name you might wear, you are the breath of my life. Thank you for burning your wings with mine as we dare fly too close to the sun.

Acknowledgments

Though this list is long, without these people in my life, I would not be who I am and this book would not have come to pass, making my dreams reality. Unfortunately, I know I will forget some deserving of mention; I apologize in advance.

To my family: Jay and Shirley, for their supreme example and unwavering devotion to God; my brothers and sisters Keith (and Michelle), Lisa (and Ralph), Craig (and Gayla), Kevin (and Trina), and Suzanne (and Mark), for their love, friendship, and endless support; to my brother Kevin—my twin, my best friend, my role model . . . thanks!

To my "other" families: Barbie and Leroy Liddle and Lola and Alan Dean—when another set of parents was needed, you were there for me.

To my new family: Arlene and Ron Stalzer for always being there; Alan and Carol Lewis for letting me join their daughter in marriage; Christy, David, Geoff, and Jennifer for putting up with "the goatee guy."

To all my teachers—school, church, and in life—who have taught me so much.

To the original seven: Chad "God" Dean, Tony "White Truffle" Liddle, Denby "The Man" Cluff, Jeff "Highlander" Morgan, Scott "Druid" Crandall, and Manu "Cow" Sharma—we started this journey half a lifetime ago and much to my astonishment, it appears that there is no end in sight. More brothers than friends, thanks for all the Verners, Pringles, rock 'n' roll, chocolate bunnies, gaming into the early morning hours, and memories that have given me endless stories for the telling.

To those friends who have joined the ride since it began—Dan "Flake" Grendell, Steve "Xai" Pitcher, Troy "Trashborn" Allen, Michael Jackson, Larry Yanez, Jared and Heather Cluff (not even among friends would many have done as much as you, Heather, thanks!), Angie Dean, Kate Liddle, Tracy Cluff, Jeff Mink, Jim "bob" and Brook Lloyd, Jessie and Jaime Foster, Gavin and Emily Duckworth, Jason and Kathy Hardy, Vance and Kim Mellon (you'll get "culture" into me yet!), the Daemon Horde (you know you who are), the BC Legion (for those not mentioned above!), MechForce United Kingdom (you all gave me a home across "the pond")—from Arizona to Illinois to England, you have added richness to my life and more.

To those authors who have given me words of encouragement, raised the bar for me to achieve, and have become good friends in their own right: Loren (and lest I forget, Heather) Coleman, Christoffer "Bones" Trossen, Chris Hartford, Michael Stackpole, and Jason Hardy.

To the FASA staff, past and present: Bryan Nystul, Mike and Sharon Mulvihill, Robert Boyle, Mort Weisman, L. Ross Babcock III, Mike and Stacy Nielsen, Jim Nelson, John Bridegroom, Fred Hooper, Rett Kipp, Joel and Tammy Biske, Diane Piron-Gelman, and Jill Lucas (wherever you are, I hope you realize your part in getting this book finished—thanks!), for your friendship and allowing me to work with such a talented group of individuals.

To Donna Ippolito at FASA for giving me this chance and putting up with my tardiness and to Annalise Raziq for working hard to make sure my first novel was readable.

To all the friends I have had through the years—those mentioned and those not—though I hope you already know it, for me, there is nothing I treasure more than your friendship.

And finally, to my own family, Tara Suzanne and Bryn Kevin, who give their love unconditionally and provide the support I need to keep going every day.

Prologue

Jova Plateau
Hoard
Kerensky Cluster, Clan Space
13 May 3060

The cataclysmic explosion flared like a supernova across Jova Plateau, washing the early morning darkness in a false dawn of tortured reds and angry yellows. The battle raging across the plateau seemed to freeze for an instant as the blast spent its terrible energies and the glow faded.

Then the night was torn asunder once more. The howl of rapid-fire cannons sent tracers spinning through the dark sky, PPCs spewed deadly bolts of energy, and lasers speared the dark with coherent light. Smoke and dust were churned into the air, illuminated only by the relentless firing of weapons. All was madness across the battlefield.

"Galaxy Commander, was that the *Chronicle*?" came an almost panicked cry over the commline. Tirill Nostra, who was already trying to raise the WarShip on the commline, recognized the voice of Star Colonel Bel.

"Neg," he said, then abruptly cut the connection. It was too devastating to think that Kappa Galaxy's WarShip had been destroyed in the blast that had just lit up the sky over Hoard. Without the *Chronicle*, the Galaxy would be hunted into extinction. The only reason they had not already been swept from the field was that the other Clans could not help fighting among themselves even as they pursued his force.

"*Chronicle*," he said for the dozenth time, "this is Galaxy Commander Tirill Nostra of Kappa Galaxy. Respond, repeat, respond." Even if the WarShip was unharmed, the explosion could have caused an ionization of the upper atmosphere that would nullify any attempts at communication for long minutes.

He tried again and again, but no response came back. The best he could do now was continue to fight, whether or not the WarShip had been snuffed out. If his Galaxy could buy the Nova Cat civilian population enough time, they might still escape off-planet. Protected by the *Chronicle*, they would make the long journey from the Clan homeworlds to the Inner Sphere.

That was a victory for which Tirill Nostra would gladly give his life. He was a warrior genetically bred and raised for the single great purpose of serving his Clan. He might die fighting, but his Clan would live on.

Then another voice came over his earpiece. "The

Star Adders will miss their WarShip, quiaff?" Tirill immediately recognized the exultant voice of Star Commodore Sel Bravos, the *Chronicle*'s commander.

He let out a long sigh of relief. The *Chronicle* had destroyed the *Star Fire* and was still intact! The Nova Cat civilians would escape even if it meant every warrior in Kappa Galaxy died to make it happen.

Another of his officers reported in next. "Galaxy Commander, the Hell's Horses have joined the fight."

"Savashri," Tirill cursed savagely. The Hell's Horses Twelfth Mechanized Cavalry Cluster had arrived five days ago, but had held back till now. Perhaps their joining in now proved that the rumors of a burgeoning alliance between the Horses and the Wolves were true. The First Wolf Lancers had dogged Star Colonel Bel's Fourth Garrison Cluster till late last night, ceasing only when the Ice Hellions' Forty-fifth Striker Irregulars had suddenly attacked *them*. The bitter hatred between the two Clans was long-standing.

He shook his head to clear his mind. All that was meaningless compared to the magnitude of what was happening to his Clan. The Nova Cats were being driven from their homeworlds, and Tirill Nostra must protect the civilians of Hoard, no matter what had brought his Clan to this dark pass.

It had all started seven days before when the Star Adder Eleventh Armored Cavalry Squadron and their 417th Adder Sentinels had suddenly left their enclaves to attack Kappa Galaxy. The Ice Hellions soon joined the fight, and two days later Clan Wolf and Clan Hell's Horses forces were also on Hoard.

In a shocking disregard of *zellbrigen*—the traditional rules of war—the attacking Clans had concentrated their fire. All forty-five warriors of the Forty-ninth Garrison Cluster were wiped out under such overwhelming force.

From reports that came in via HPG, he learned that the Nova Cat enclaves on Barcella, Circe, Brim, Gatekeeper, and Delios were also under attack by the other Clans. The only exception was Bearclaw. No one knew what was happening there because all attempts at communication had failed. Meanwhile his Galaxy had fought long and hard just to survive, though they still did not understand why this was happening.

The truth, when he learned it, was horrifying.

Tirill had finally gotten the story out of Star Colonel Eliza Talasko of the Star Adders Eleventh Armored Cavalry Squadron after several days of fighting had almost destroyed the Seventeenth Garrison Cluster and left his own Fourth Garrison Cluster dangerously weak. Talasko spared him nothing, and he raged inwardly as he listened. Even now he could hardly believe what she had told him—that the Nova Cats on Strana Mechty had fought on the side of the Inner Sphere!

She said that the Inner Sphere had arrived in the homeworlds a month ago, then virtually exterminated the Smoke Jaguars. They went next to Strana Mechty to challenge the remaining Clans to a Trial of Refusal. If the Clans lost, they would end their invasion of the Inner Sphere.

In a devastating turn of fate, the Clans were defeated and both Nova Cat Khans perished in the fighting. Talasko told him that the Grand Council had convened a few days later and voted to Abjure the Nova Cats, casting them out forever. The Council had given them a month to depart, but no word ever reached the Nova Cat enclaves elsewhere in the homeworlds.

Outraged at the Nova Cat betrayal, the other Clans had not honored the grace period and began to attack the Nova Cats within days of the Abjurment. Now, a week after the fighting on Hoard had begun, Tirill Nostra was amazed that his Galaxy had survived even this long against the fury of the other Clans. They could not hold out much longer.

He opened a commline to issue the orders that would surely seal the fate of his Galaxy. Tirill Nostra smiled to himself. He did not fear death.

Clan Nova Cat would live on.

GHOST BEAR DOMINION
DRACONIS COMBINE BORDER

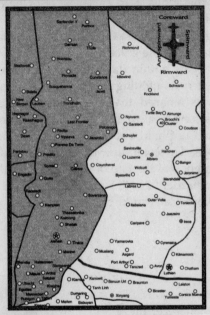

Coreward

Antispinward

Spinward

Rimward

Sanbender V
Pjanhou
Damian
Thule
Richmond
Holmsno
Pinnacle
Constance
Idlewind
Schwartz
Skallsvoll
Susquehanna
Janett
Rockland
Bixbie
New Bergen
Leoben
Trondheim
Nyovarn
Turtle Bay
Almunge
Hrafnagtar
RasalHague
Last Frontier
Garstedt
Brocchi's Cluster
Coudoux
Redfio
Polcenigo
Schuyler
Dawn
Vipaava
Jezersko
Pomme De Terre
Savinsville
Hanover
Fairfield
Predlita
Luzerne
Albero
Bangor
Engadin
Spital
Colmar
Courcheval
Wolcott
Marshdale
Jeronimo
Gunzburg
Radstadt
Byesville
Labrea
Klempten
Bovarzane
Theodora
Outer Volta
Tomiiner
Kaesong
Itabaiana
Juazeiro
Irece
Sholan
Asheim
Thalka
Caripare
Maienei
Yamarovka
Cyrenaica
Musang
Asgard
Kamamock
Reindar
Halberstam
Stampaltz
Port Arthur
Tarazed
Avon
Luthien
Chatham
Mtuais
Ardoz
Setubel
Klamia
Kanowit
Baruun Urt
Braunton
Laiston
Utrecht
Kreuzberg
Egadias
Meinander
Tanh Linh
Bicester
Corsica Nueva
Rubigson
Meiten
Dumaring
Babuyan
Xinyang
Yumesta

**DETAIL OF THE
INNER SPHERE
3062**

LEGEND

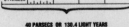

8 PARSECS

40 PARSECS OR 130.4 LIGHT YEARS
SCALE: 1/8 INCH = 1 PARSEC = 3.26
LIGHT YEARS = 19,164,277,850,000 STATUTE MILES

MAXIMUM JUMP: APPROXIMATELY 30 LIGHT YEARS
FOR NAVIGATIONAL PURPOSES USE 9 PARSECS = 29.34 LY

© 3062 COMSTAR CARTOGRAPHIC CORPS

1

Battle Cruiser SLS Severen Leroux
Zenith Jump Point, Irece System
Draconis Combine
12 June 3061

Warning klaxons began to peal along the corridors
of the WarShip *Severen Leroux* as it hung suspended
in space, some two billion five hundred million kilometers from Irece, the world it was set to protect.
Startled, Star Admiral Jan Jorgensson looked up
quickly from her deskwork and stabbed at the inter-
com mounted on the bulkhead.

"Star Commodore Antila, what is the meaning of
this?" she growled into the speaker. She hadn't ordered
a readiness drill, nor had her important visitor arrived.

"Our sensors have picked up an infrared radiation
spike nearby, Star Admiral. We are detecting another
ship jumping into the system."

"What! Our visitor isn't expected for another several hours."

"That is why I took the precaution of calculating all possible scenarios, Star Admiral. The probabilities for the vessel's arrival in-system range from twenty-two seconds to as much as eighteen minutes or more. The eighteen-minute ETA is less than one percent, and it would have to be a *Potemkin* Class WarShip loaded with a full complement of DropShips. I do not think the Diamond Sharks have decided to test our resolve by invading the Draconis Combine, quineg?"

"Neg, Star Commodore. I do not. The Diamond Sharks are our only allies among the Clans since the Abjurment." It had been more than a year, but Jan Jorgensson could only now say the word without flinching.

"There are many possible reasons why the merchant Clan might decide we are best conquered."

"Possible, Star Commodore," she cut in, "but not probable." This was not the moment for one of her verbal duels with Antila, who was meticulously thorough. "Our guest is in transit as we speak, and no intruder is going to interfere with his reception. We show no incoming ships logged for this date, and you were wise to sound the alarm. Deploy one Star of aerospace fighters immediately and hold the second in readiness. Launch the *Sacred Rite* as well, and prepare *Promised Vision* for launch as soon as the unknown ship arrives in-system. I am on my way to the bridge right now."

Jorgensson moved quickly—or as quickly as possible wearing the magnetic boots needed to stay on her feet in zero gravity. The hatch whirred open, and she began to make her way down the long, gray corridor toward the bridge. Below, the burning yellow-white ball of gas that was Irece's F8 class star burned at the heart of the system like a beacon.

When the mystery ship appeared exactly two hundred and forty seconds after the infrared radiation spike first appeared, Jan Jorgensson had just reached the bridge. In the void of space, some ten thousand meters off the prow of the *Severen Leroux*, the emergence wave of an incoming vessel split the dark. The spindly shape blurred into existence, arriving almost instantaneously from some other star system light years away.

Antila glanced over at her. "Star Admiral, our aerospace fighters and the *Sacred Rite* have already begun a burn toward the ship."

Jorgensson heard the note of pride in his voice and shared it. She and her crew had won the *Noruff* Class DropShip away from the Steel Vipers in a Trial of Possession that had been one of their finest moments. So pleased was Khan Leroux to acquire this swift and deadly DropShip that he had allowed Jorgensson to name it. The *Sacred Rite* was the only ship of its kind in the entire Nova Cat Touman.

"Have a look," Antila said, gesturing toward the holotank in the center of the bridge.

Jorgensson gazed at the laser-generated, three-dimensional image of a *Monolith* Class JumpShip hovering in clear detail over the tank. The largest JumpShip in service with either the Clans or the Inner Sphere, a *Monolith*'s seven hundred-fifty-meter length could carry up to nine DropShips. This particular vessel had obviously seen some vicious fighting. Pockmarked craters and smooth, blackened troughs from autocannon and laser fire covered almost every meter of its hull. Even the DropShips docked around the *Monolith*'s cargo section showed the scars of the battle. At least one had lost several decks to the explosive decompression caused by a hit.

Only eight DropShips were docked to the vessel. What had once been the ninth docking arm was now a fused mass of metallic parts. Even more shocking was that the entire stern of the *Monolith* was simply gone. The place where the ship's critical parts had once been—the jump-sail array, the drive-charging system, the station-keeping drive—was now a gaping maw. Jorgensson wondered how in the name of Kerensky the ship had survived the jump.

"Magnify the extreme forward prow," she said, eyes glued to a spot on the blackened armor plating where she had glimpsed an insignia.

One of the technicians tapped a command into the holotank's console, and the sound of the keystroke was abnormally loud in the dead silence of the bridge. The three-dimensional image of the *Monolith* seemed to zoom toward her, and she experienced the momentary sensation of falling into it. Someone gasped as one side of the hull became visible. Though much of it was scorched and burned away, there was no mistaking the eyes of a nova cat peering from the Clan emblem.

Jorgensson was stunned. "Star Commodore, scramble the second Star of fighters immediately and launch both *Promised Vision* and *Promised Sight*." She was outraged at the sight of a Nova Cat ship so devastated.

"With the station-keeping drive destroyed, we must stabilize the ship as quickly as possible before she begins to succumb to our star's gravitational pull. We must also send an immediate message to Irece, with instructions to relay it on to the SLS *Faithful* stationed at the nadir jump point. Inform them of the *Monolith*'s arrival and instruct them to be prepared for possible hostile intrusion."

She thought of the DropShip on its way here. "Send that message to the *Nova Cat Alpha* as well."

Jorgensson walked slowly around the holotank, continuing her scrutiny of the ravaged vessel. "Have we been able to contact the ship yet?"

The communications tech glanced up briefly. "No, Star Admiral. If you look closely, you will see that the communications antennae on the prow seem to have been sheared away. We will not know more until we board her."

She turned to Antila. "Any thoughts on where the ship came from, Star Commodore?"

"Aye, Star Admiral," Antila said quickly. True to form, her second had calculated an answer even before she had asked. Though the trait was maddening sometimes, it had saved the lives of her and her crew on more than one occasion.

"Using the number of DropShips carried by the *Monolith*, along with the duration between the IR spike and the vessel's actual arrival time, I can say with ninety-five percent accuracy that the ship arrived from the Outer Volta system. Outer Volta is within one easy jump of three different worlds currently occupied by Combine troops. I do not discount the possibility that the Draconis Combine attacked the ship, but it is doubtful. The taboo against damaging JumpShips is still too ingrained in them. Pirates perhaps. But not Combine warriors.''

Jorgensson agreed with Antila—this wasn't the work of the Combine. But with her visitor arriving so soon, she could not take any chances. The *Monolith* had been virtually destroyed. If not by the Combine, then who?

''When will our DropShips rendezvous with the *Monolith*?'' she asked.

A new round of furious typing followed her question, and several moments passed without a response. ''They should make contact in less than five minutes,'' the technician answered.

Silence fell again as the waiting continued. Various techs moved from console to console, verifying the status of the *Monolith* as well as the progress of the *Severen Leroux*'s three DropShips and twenty aerospace fighters approaching the wreck of a starship floating before them on an endless sea of black.

Star Captain Lenardon waited as the DropShip *Sacred Vision* slowly maneuvered into position over the forward hull of the crippled ship. Though the *Sacred Vision* usually transported up to twelve 'Mechs, a Star of twenty-five Elementals were its only passengers today. The empty 'Mech bay loomed large around them, giving the power-armored troopers the look of giant insects with strange carapaces awaiting the command of their queen.

''Star Captain Lenardon,'' the voice of the DropShip

captain called over his helmet headset, "we are less than ten meters from the *Monolith*'s hull. We cannot maneuver any closer because the docking arms bar our way. You will have to drop from here. You understand, quiaff?"

"Aff," Lenardon said. He rotated his torso to the right and brought all the members of his Star into his field of vision through the V-shaped visor set into his helmet. He raised one armor-encased arm—the one ending in a wickedly shaped claw—and said, "Remember, this ship may be controlled by hostiles. Any sign of aggression or resistance is to be met with maximum force. We will occupy and take the ship as quickly as possible. Without its station-keeping drive, it has already moved from its original arrival point. We must stabilize it and learn who are the enemies that have struck at us."

Signaling with a downward slash of his arm, Lenardon turned and walked toward the 'Mech bay door that was already starting to open. The Elementals could as easily have used the man-sized hatch in the bulkhead, but it would have formed a choke point while each Elemental waited for the one in front of him to get through. Dropping from the 'Mech door was more dangerous, but it would permit the whole Star to reach the hull of the *Monolith* at once, providing a greater chance of success.

All twenty-five Elementals came to the edge of the gaping door, then leapt into the frigid blackness of deep space. Using maneuvering thrusters mounted in the back and legs of their power armor, they deftly closed with the mammoth ship below. With the agility and speed earned through years of zero-gravity duty, they made contact with the hull of the *Monolith*.

"Set the charges," Lenardon ordered, breaking the silence. With swift efficiency, a Point of five Elementals used their claw-mounted arms to remove a small package attached to each of their legs. While the rest of the Star spread out and hunkered down, the Point placed the packages against the hull of the ship.

"Detonation in fifteen seconds," one of them said over the commline, then they instantly scattered away.

The explosion was terrifying and effective. The shaped charges punched a hole into the outer bulkhead of the vessel, and the shock waves that shuddered down the hull threatened to dislodge the magnetic boots of the Elementals. Though this method of entry risked killing Nova Cats who might be aboard the JumpShip, it was the most effective way to eliminate any hostiles. Fortunately, the explosive decompression that followed produced only scraps of metal and no bodies, probably because the team had placed the charges over a seldom-used corridor.

Using the thrusters and enhanced strength of their battle armor, the twenty-five Elementals immediately began to move through the jagged rent even as pipes in the walls began to spray a tar-like black substance across the opening. The substance, known as HarJel, was used in WarShips and by Elementals to rapidly seal punctures and wounds. It was originally developed by Clan Diamond Shark, with whom the Nova Cats had a long-standing mercantile relationship.

That was how a portion of the Nova Cat JumpShip fleet had come to be outfitted with the substance.

Lenardon was the first through the hole, quickly taking in the situation as the cleaning agents of his visor sloughed off the HarJel that had sprayed onto his suit. Emergency back-up lights were on all along the corridor, indicating a complete loss of standard power. When the decompression occurred, emergency hatches had sealed off this section ten meters in both directions. With the skill and grace that only genetic breeding and several decades of battle-armor experience could bestow, Lenardon moved toward the left-hand hatch, knowing that a hundred meters down the other side of it was the bridge.

"Star Captain, we are through the gap," Point Commander Tol announced over the comm as Lenardon and two other Elementals took position facing the hatch. All three warriors raised their right arms, the ones ending in the muzzle of a small laser. After silently counting to ten—giving the HarJel time to completely seal the tear in the vessel's skin—the three warriors began to fire a low-powered, sustained burst of laser fire into the hatch at key points, slowly working their way across the metal. Because of the hulking size of the Elementals, the hole they were cutting was large, and other Elementals came forward to help cut to keep from overpowering the laser of any one power suit.

As the laser glow died, Lenardon lunged forward, slamming his right shoulder against the hatch. With a scream of tortured metal, the hatch bent inward, then suddenly tore completely free, slamming into the deck and sliding a short distance away. The laser-cutting had left smoke in the air on both sides of the hatch, and Lenardon saw several shadowy figures moving about in the haze as he entered the bridge. One had a weapon trained on him.

He activated his exterior speaker and spoke quickly to keep them from firing. "In the name of Khan Santin West and Clan Nova Cat, I, Star Captain Josef Lenardon, board this vessel and demand to know who controls it."

Several moments passed, an eternity, as more Elementals came through the hatch and fanned out to either side of him, ready to rush forward and eliminate any resistance. Slowly, the blurred figures approached, revealed now as stunned and haggard men in dirty but recognizable uniforms—Nova Cat uniforms. One of them looked like a warrior, while the rest appeared to be lower-caste ship's crew.

"I am Warrior Sal of Clan Nova Cat, and we control this ship," said the one with a rifle.

"How comes it that this ship has taken so much damage?" Lenardon asked. "Has the Draconis Combine suddenly decided that the Nova Cats are no longer welcome on their worlds?"

The warrior didn't answer.

"Who attacked you? Was it pirates?" Lenardon demanded.

"I do not understand what you are asking," Sal said. "We have just completed our journey from the Clan homeworlds. The damage—"

"What?" Lenardon barked. "That is not possible. The last refugees arrived almost two months ago."

"We became separated from the convoy bound for the Inner Sphere at Bearclaw, where the Snow Ravens and Hell's Horses attempted to destroy us," Sal said, his eyes growing distant. Slowly, he let the rifle slip from his slack hand, and it clattered to the deck, the sound echoing through the corridor.

Sal looked down at the weapon as though wondering how it had gotten there. "The convoy must have thought us lost, but we managed to escape to Circe. There we boarded as many warriors and lower-castemen as we could before resuming our journey to the Inner Sphere. The other Clans—they are the ones who tried to destroy the ship. We lost the stern during the last jump; the stress was finally too much."

Sal slowly sank to his knees, seeming blind to his surroundings as the memories moved across his inner vision.

Lenardon had been in the Inner Sphere during the Abjurment, but everyone had heard by now how the other Clans had driven the Nova Cats from the homeworlds, viciously wiping out three whole Galaxies in the process. This was the first time he had spoken face to face with any of the refugees, however.

Lenardon had fought in countless battles on numerous worlds spread across a thousand light-years, but he could never have imagined a Nova Cat warrior reduced to such a state as Sal. Staring at the slack-faced warrior, he could only wonder how his Clan could have fallen so far. Was it possible that the new path was not the right one?

2

Battle Cruiser SLS Severen Leroux
Zenith Jump Point, Irece System
Draconis Combine
13 June 3061

"The *Nova Cat Alpha* is docking as we speak, Star Admiral," came Antila's voice over her earpiece as Jan Jorgensson drifted down the ship's corridor using handholds mounted on the bulkheads to stay upright.

Her guest had finally arrived, and just when she had her hands full with the refugees of the *Dark Spine*. Seventeen hours had passed since the crippled JumpShip arrived in the Irece system. Seventeen hours of chaos, she thought, turning the final corner that would bring her to the hatch of Docking Collar Four.

With practiced ease, she used the leverage of a

handrail to make contact with the floor and engage her magnetic boots. Under normal circumstances, she would never have floated down the corridor, considering it undignified for one of her station. But these were hardly normal circumstances.

Her crew was already jumpy enough about their impending visit. Now they had to deal with the shock of finding still more refugees ravaged and driven from the Clan homeworlds.

Sounds on the far side of the airlock meant that her visitors were already boarding the *Severen Leroux*. Suddenly anxious, she ran a hand nervously down the front of her uniform, a habit she had yet to suppress. Though she'd been wearing the white knee-length coat and purple trousers of a Star League admiral for some time, she still had not fully adjusted to her new look. Particularly distasteful was the foppish hat.

With a hiss of adjusting atmospheres, the hatch swung open, and a giant of a man came drifting through it. Though short for an Elemental at just over two meters, he had the massive chest and arms that only Clan genetic breeding could produce. Adding to his striking appearance was his head of white hair and prominent salt and pepper mustache; most warriors never lived long enough for their hair to change color.

He floated effortlessly to a stop in front of Jorgensson, a sure sign of long experience in zero-gravity operations. Santin West, Khan of Clan Nova Cat, emanated power and authority.

"I, Star Admiral Jan Jorgensson, commander of the SLS *Severen Leroux*, welcome you aboard, my Khan," she said with great formality. "May your vision always guide us down the path."

The Khan acknowledged the ritual greeting with only a gruff nod. "Take me to the warriors," he said.

"This way, my Khan." Jorgensson would have leapt to do the bidding of any Khan of hers, but Santin West's commanding presence had her moving even before she realized it.

As they proceeded down the corridor, she marveled at how much she was still in awe of him, even though they had met before. As commander of all Nova Cat naval assets, her position was only two steps removed from the Khan's. Yet Santin West seemed to exist in a realm she could not enter, guided by a vision for the future of their Clan that she could not fully grasp. And that vision, far beyond any vote taken by the Clan Council, was what gave him his authority and why most Nova Cat warriors, including her, had gladly followed him after the Abjurment.

As they took the first turn, she glanced back at the airlock and saw several other warriors coming through the docking hatch. Their fumbling attempts to stay upright in zero-g contrasted strongly with the Khan's sure movements.

"Your last report indicated that the *Dark Spine* carried several thousand lower-castemen but only a handful of warriors," the Khan said. "Did a further search of the ship turn up any others?"

"No, my Khan. After an exhaustive search, we have accounted for a total of twenty-nine warriors—remnants from all three of our homeworld Galaxies." She felt a catch in her throat. The appalling waste of so many lives and so much equipment was a loss almost beyond comprehension.

As they continued down the corridor in silence, Jorgensson considered the enormous distance the Nova Cats had traveled as a Clan in the past several years. Their Khans had sided with the Inner Sphere against the other Clans in the Great Refusal, guided by visions that the destiny of the Nova Cats was tied to the new Star League. As a result the rest of the Clans had repudiated them and annihilated three Nova Cat Galaxies.

She could understand that her former Clansmen felt a sense of betrayal, but not how they could condone such waste. The Founder would be appalled to see what had become of his great vision. She almost missed a step as that thought was followed quickly by another. What would Nicholas Kerensky think of what the Nova Cats themselves had done? Would he too feel betrayed? Her hand flew up to the sacred Cameron Stars on her collar.

"Are you all right, Star Admiral?" the Khan asked, his deep voice booming in the emptiness.

"Yes, my Khan," she said quickly, embarrassed to be caught daydreaming in his presence. "We are almost there," she said as they rounded the final corner. At the end of the corridor a huge Elemental in full power armor stood hulking outside the hatch to the holding room. He pulled himself even taller as he saw them coming.

"Why are you keeping the refugee warriors under guard?" the Khan asked.

"There has been . . . an altercation between one of the warriors and my crew."

"And that is reason enough to contain twenty-eight other warriors, *quineg*? Because of the actions of one?"

"Neg, my Khan, but there was nothing else I could do." Jorgensson barely understood it herself. All Nova Cat warriors were aggressive, but what she had read in the report was unusual in the extreme.

"According to the reports of my crew, only one warrior was physically involved in the incident, but more than fifteen of the refugee warriors were present."

The Khan stopped and turned to look at her as they reached the hatch. "A Circle of Equals?"

"Yes, the warrior challenged my crewman to an unaugmented Trial of Grievance in the presence of the others. I am told that both fought well, but, in the end, my crewman triumphed."

"I fail to see what relevance that has to the situation, Star Admiral."

Jorgensson had heard that the Khan's temper was as violent as a combat drop into hostile territory, but that he considered such displays to be a serious weakness. She hoped there was truth in that rumor.

"My Khan," she said, "several other warriors attacked my crewman while he was still inside the Circle of Equals."

"What?" the Khan demanded.

She had been just as shocked by the reports. Any warrior who believed he had been dishonored personally or that the actions of a fellow warrior were dishonorable or dangerous to the Clan could call a Trial of Grievance. The Trial could be fought augmented in a 'Mech or power armor or it could be fought unaugmented—hand-to-hand. A Trial was always fought in a Circle of Equals whose radius could be as small as a few meters or as large as several kilometers. For the other warriors to have broken the Circle and attacked her crewman after he had won a Trial of Grievance was an unthinkable breach of tradition.

"They attacked and beat him severely," she continued. "Only the timely arrival of several Elementals prevented the death of my crewman."

Santin West stood there in the barren gray corridor, lost in thought. He stared beyond her down the corridor they had just traversed, seeming lost in thought.

"Then it is worse than I feared," he said softly to himself. He turned back to the hatch and gestured to the sentinel to undog it.

Puzzled by his words, Jorgensson followed her Khan into the room.

Zane looked around the large cabin that had been his prison for the last four hours. Five meters square, with two tables and several benches bolted to the deck, it had to be one of the largest on the WarShip. At the moment, however, it felt cramped and crowded with the twenty-eight other warriors who had also made the eight-month journey aboard the *Dark Spine.* He knew and respected every one of them, but right now would have preferred to be completely alone.

As he looked around at their dispirited faces, dark thoughts began to push their way into consciousness—images that usually only plagued his nightmares. He had managed to suppress them during the voyage from the homeworlds, but contact with the Inner Sphere Nova Cats—who he could never accept as his Clansmen—brought them rushing back with a vengeance. He closed his eyes and concentrated on restraining the fury that seemed to power the images.

Terrible darkness sows the seeds of effulgence, he chanted silently. The words were those of Sandra Rosse, the Nova Cats' most revered and mystical Khan, and the litany helped calm him and hold the demons of dreams and rage at bay. Several hundred heartbeats later, with a last, long exhale, he opened his eyes again.

A moment later he heard the hatch undog, then spin free and open. The next thing he saw was the giant figure of an Elemental, followed by the ship's commander. The arrival set off a wave of angry murmurs among the warriors, and Zane felt his rage boil up again. The Elemental's military insignia had changed, but no one could mistake the Khan of the Nova Cats.

Even more shocking than the insignia was the Khan's new uniform. To Zane it was a sacrilegious melding of the Star League Defense Force uniform and the one traditionally worn the Nova Cats. It was this—further proof of the corruption he believed was destroying his Clan—which enraged him most.

Though his heart hammered, Zane knew he must not let his anger overtake him. He closed his eyes briefly and silently chanted his phrase again. He might hate with all his heart the path the Nova Cats had chosen, but the figure standing before them was still his Khan. To oppose him now would be to die.

West was a warrior far beyond Zane's prowess, even without his size and strength as an Elemental. As the pounding in his ears lessened, Zane opened his eyes again.

The Khan stood there calmly, even as the murmuring in the room grew louder. Finally, he walked slowly forward and began to speak. His voice was deep and authoritative, demanding respect and attention.

"Warriors, I, Khan Santin West of Clan Nova Cat, welcome you to the Inner Sphere." He slowly looked around at all their faces. "Today is a day of rejoicing that you, our Clansmen, have found your way over black oceans to a new shore. A shore that holds a bright future for us."

Zane expected a new round of muttering from the other warriors, but none came. Glancing around quickly at their faces, he saw many looking almost spellbound by the Khan's commanding presence. It wasn't every day that a Khan paid a visit, but Zane still could not understand their meek surrender.

"You have survived what many have not," the Khan continued. "Generations ago, the Founder created twenty Clans to one day return to the Inner Sphere and reestablish the Star League. In that time, five of the original Clans have been annihilated, absorbed, or sundered. Clan Nova Cat might have ended up the same way, except that we have learned to read portents of things to come. By taking counsel from those signs, we are guided down our true path—a path that will allow us to flourish and become all that the Founder envisioned."

The Khan paused, letting the silence underscore the gravity of his words.

"Some of you may question whether we are truly walking the Way the Founder would have wished. If so, I do not consider such thoughts sedition for a Nova Cat. Our Khans have ever encouraged our warriors to look within to find their truth. The only danger is that other Nova Cat warriors may try to play on your doubts to turn you away from our current path."

Zane was shocked at the Khan's frankness. How could West admit to such grave discord among the Nova Cats? It was an error that would only strengthen the resolve of those who disagreed.

The Khan continued in his deep, resonant voice. "Though you follow me because I am your Khan, it is more important that you follow me because of your conviction that I am leading you down the path that best serves our Clan. You all know well the lines from our *Remembrance*:

> "Clansmen will follow their Khan,
> Proven to be the mightiest warrior.
> But Nova Cat warriors only follow a Khan
> With conviction born of personal vision.
> That Clan will surpass all others."

Zane and some others nodded, instantly recognizing the familiar words of Khan Sandra Rosse.

The Khan extended his huge arms in a gesture of openness. "That is why I will not demean you or the path we tread by demanding blind submission. Instead, I entreat you to find your own way by taking the Rite of the Vision so that you may freely join your will with ours.

"Until that time," West boomed, "you are warriors, and our Clan has need of your strength to ward us from our enemies. Orders have already been issued for the formation of a new Galaxy—Zeta Galaxy—within the next three weeks. It will be composed of those warriors who survived the devastation on our former homeworlds, which includes all of you. In the next few days you will travel to Irece to begin training with the new Galaxy. May your visions guide you."

With those words—the customary Nova Cat farewell—Khan West turned and went out through the hatch, again followed by Star Admiral Jorgensson. As the hatch closed, the warriors around Zane burst into excited discussion. He could sense the change in the air, the tension breaking as the others seemed moved by the words of their new Khan.

Zane remembered the look in Santin West's eyes as he spoke, a look of complete conviction that came only to one who has received a vision. Well, Zane was not so convinced. It was fine and good for Santin West to be guided by his own vision, but who was to say it was the one Zane or the rest of the Nova Cats should follow?

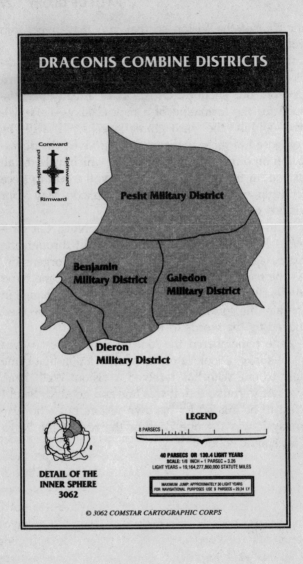

DRACONIS COMBINE DISTRICTS

Coreward
Anti-spinward
Spinward
Rimward

Pesht Military District

Benjamin
Military District

Galedon
Military District

Dieron
Military District

DETAIL OF THE
INNER SPHERE
3062

LEGEND

8 PARSECS

40 PARSECS OR 130.4 LIGHT YEARS
SCALE: 1/8 INCH = 1 PARSEC = 3.26
LIGHT YEARS = 19,164,277,860,000 STATUTE MILES

MAXIMUM JUMP: APPROXIMATELY 30 LIGHT YEARS
FOR NAVIGATIONAL PURPOSES USE 9 PARSECS = 29.34 LY

© 3062 COMSTAR CARTOGRAPHIC CORPS

3

New Circe, Yamarovka
Irece Prefecture
Draconis Combine
5 July 3062

With wild abandon, MechWarrior Zane pushed the throttle full forward on his 'Mech, sending his *Jenner* 2 careening along a firebreak road cut through the Yalleni Forest. Reaching a top of speed of over one hundred-fifty kilometers per hour, he knew it was foolhardy to navigate this treacherous road at such a pace. One misstep and he could twist an ankle actuator, but the hounding pursuit behind him outweighed the risk. He couldn't spare even a moment to check the bottom half of his viewscreen to see if the enemy 'Mech still followed. Instead, he stayed totally focused on the ground in front of him, hoping that his skill and luck would hold. Long seconds went by without the sound of weapons fire, the trees on either side blurring past and the dirt road like a flat, brown board before him.

Rejoicing that he had lost his dogged pursuer, he missed seeing the muddy discoloration in the road. With its next step, his *Jenner*'s massive foot sank almost a half-meter into soft dirt instead of hitting solid ground. The 'Mech lurched and stumbled, while Zane jerked his body backward in his seat in the wild hope that his neurohelmet would feed the action quickly enough to the gyro in his 'Mech's chest. Inside the helmet were neural receptors able to translate the inner ear's ability to balance to the gyro, which was what kept the ten-meter-tall machine on its feet and moving with fluidity.

But now the high-pitched whine of the gyro told a different story, and the machine slammed into the dirt with a booming echo. Zane was thrown forward so violently that his head smashed into the control console. The 'Mech bucked like a wild animal as it skidded across the ground.

When he came to, he was suspended facedown against his seat's restraining straps. He had no idea how long he had been out, which terrified him. He attempted to right his fallen machine, but that was hard to do in a 'Mech that mounted weapons where arms should be. Most warriors who piloted armless 'Mechs spent considerable time practicing the art of getting the machine back on its feet. On the battlefield, a 'Mech that could not get up from a fall was as dead as a tortoise on its back.

"Savashri," he cursed, checking the status display after he finally got the *Jenner* upright again. Only lightly armored to begin with, the 'Mech had taken a beating in its fall. The right weapon-arm had been torn away, and the right-side torso and leg had lost more than half their armor. Even more dismaying was the loss of the *Jenner*'s main armament, the extended-range large laser mounted in the right arm. Without it, his 'Mech was almost defenseless.

So much for surviving your first contact with the enemy unharmed, Zane thought bitterly. At this rate his 'Mech would end up destroyed without ever firing a single shot. Enraged and frustrated, he beat his fists against the control console. His hands began to bleed, but he couldn't stop, wouldn't stop.

His anger finally spent, he looked at his hands, which were bruised and bloody. The sight instantly cleared his mind. What was wrong with him? He was being pursued. This wasn't a time to indulge his rage. He had to figure out where his enemy was.

As though his thoughts were a signal, a lance of energy seared past his 'Mech, cutting into the forest to his right. The first tree it touched exploded as the laser beam super-heated the moisture trapped inside. Years of training took over, and Zane reacted without conscious thought. He pushed the throttle forward with a white-knuckled grip.

A glance at his secondary tactical screen revealed no sign of an enemy within range of his weapons. But the beam had originated from somewhere. Its angle precluded a strafe by an aerospace fighter, so it could only have been a ground attack.

Even before he could glance at his primary display, a stream of high-velocity autocannon rounds began to hammer the ground around his 'Mech, sending dirt geysers into the air. Zane immediately started weaving the *Jenner* side to side down the road, trying to make himself a more difficult target. He knew it would take only a single shell to tear off one of the *Jenner*'s legs.

A proximity alarm made him look sharply at another secondary screen. A second unit was on the road about a kilometer ahead of him—and it looked like a 'Mech. At his current speed, he would be within range of its weapons in mere seconds. He had only one option, an action as desperate as it was suicidal.

Without breaking the *Jenner*'s stride, he stomped down on his jump jet pedals, sending his 'Mech aloft on a plume of super-heated plasma. A jumping BattleMech might look like it was flying, but Zane knew it was more like a brick strapped to jet engines—a controlled fall at best. The *Jenner* 2 could lift to a height of two hundred-seventy meters, the greatest jump capability of any 'Mech ever designed. However, falling from two hundred-seventy meters in the air was tricky to control. Now that he'd launched himself blindly into a heavily forested area with an already damaged leg, he would need all his genetically engineered skills just to survive impact with the ground.

The *Jenner* gained altitude over the tree canopy, and Zane's worst fears were realized when he saw nothing but endless forest before him. Quickly gauging the terrain in front of him, he chose a spot that looked relatively promising. He hoped.

As the *Jenner* reached the apex of its jump and began to descend, he feathered the jump jets, bleeding off as much speed as possible before the machine plunged through the treetops. The reverberating howl of the jets could be heard even through the insulation and thick armor of his cockpit as they tried vainly to slow thirty-five tons of metal, myomer, and fusion engine.

Bracing for the terrifying impact, Zane and the *Jenner* plummeted through the forest canopy, the sound thunderous as the 'Mech crashed through trees, pulverizing branches and torching everything it passed over. Careening through the trees had created a slight list to the right, forcing Zane to set the *Jenner's* right foot down first. Even under normal conditions that would have ended in a fall. In the current situation, it spelled disaster.

Zane felt the 'Mech convulse as the entire right-hip actuator exploded under stresses it was never intended to bear and the rest of the leg was torn off in one huge piece. He cursed his luck, cursed the phantom enemies that hunted him, cursed his Clan for what they had become. He tensed for ultimate impact, and the inky dark rushed toward him as the *Jenner* slammed into the unforgiving ground.

Zane bolted upright, sweat-drenched and shaking. He sat there gasping for a few moments. Then he stumbled off his cot and slapped the wall light on the way to the small bathroom of the quarters to which he'd been assigned since the formation of Zeta Galaxy a year ago. Weak fluorescent light flooded the spartan room, illuminating whitewashed walls and a utilitarian metal bed, desk, and chair.

He depressed the button that started the cold water running, then splashed it liberally over his head and chest with both hands, trying to wash away the sweat and fear of his dreams. When he was done, he grasped the edge of the sink and leaned forward until his head rested against the polished metal sheet that served as a mirror. Chanting silently, he lost himself as rivulets of water ran down his body and pooled on the concrete floor at his feet.

He had thought the dream banished, but in the last few days it had returned. Every night the same. He was in his 'Mech, fleeing an unseen enemy in the Yalleni Forest of Bearclaw, just as he had done two years back. Rho Galaxy had been attacked by the Snow Ravens and Hell's Horses.

Because Bearclaw's hyperpulse generator was down while awaiting some parts for repair, the Galaxy was ignorant of events occurring elsewhere in Clan space. They had not heard about the Great Refusal or the betrayal their Khans had orchestrated in the Inner Sphere. Not until the Snow Ravens and the Horses ambushed and attacked them, throwing the ritualized order of battle to the four winds.

Zane had fled through the forest and been one of only nine warriors to escape the planet. To see his comrades slaughtered before his eyes for a crime they did not commit had brought him to the brink of despair. Only the enforced balm of comradeship and quiet contemplation during the long journey from the Kerensky Cluster to the Inner Sphere had pulled him back from the edge. Now he had no idea whether this recurring dream was pulling him away or, like a siren, drawing him to his own death.

Either way, he instinctively knew that this dream, this nightmare, was connected to his doubts and questions about the fact that the Nova Cats were now part of the Inner Sphere, colluding with the Draconis

Combine and the sham Star League. Yet the secret of the dream eluded him. Before Bearclaw, he would have sought the counsel of Oathmaster Biccon Winters, but he could no longer bring himself to trust her. She had too many ties to the Nova Cats' recent history. He would have to find the answer on his own.

His forehead still pressed against the mirror, Zane slowly came back to the present as he registered the muffled sounds of activity from the rest of the Zeta Command Compound. He lifted his head and peered at the blunt-nosed face framed by straight, short black hair that stared back at him from the mirror. Only the startling green of his eyes was distinctive. No Clan warrior cared much for his physical appearance, and Zane saw nothing special in his reflection. Like most of his kind, he took for granted the superb physique genetically bred to eliminate almost all body fat and honed by exercise to whipcord-strength.

All he could think of was that today was the day, and there was nothing he could do to stop what was coming.

Several weeks prior, Galaxy Commander Tirant Higall had announced that a new Cluster was being formed and that one of its three Trinaries would be drawn from Zeta Galaxy. That was unusual in forming a new unit; it was standard Nova Cat procedure to cull individual warriors from different units to lessén the strain on any single Galaxy or Cluster. Several days passed as the warriors of Zeta Galaxy speculated wildly about which Trinary would win the honor of joining the new Cluster.

When Zane heard the news that his own unit, Battle Trinary of the 37th Garrison Cluster, had been chosen, he felt a surge of joy for the first time in many, many months. Newly formed Clusters were always given top priority for combat-intensive missions. Surely, he would get the chance to restore the honor he felt had been lost when the Nova Cats cast their lot with the Inner Sphere.

In the week that followed, there was a marked improvement in the morale of the whole Trinary. For the first time since arriving on Yamarovka, Zane began to believe there was hope for him. But then had come the Galaxy Commander's second announcement. The new Cluster would not get a high-profile assignment—perhaps a raid into the Ghost Bear Dominion or a strike across the Dominion at the arrogant Hell's Horses. Instead, the Cluster that was to be his salvation was being formed to train alongside and fight war games with a unit from the Draconis Combine.

Stravag war games! The thought exploded in his mind, and he slammed his fist into the wall. Worse, against the same filthy freebirths who had seduced the Nova Cats into betraying the way of the Clans. Zane had already fought four Trials of Grievance to vent his frustration.

He went to the shower stall and savagely pulled open the door, which automatically turned on the water jets. The hot water stinging his skin usually calmed him, but today was the day he would meet his new Star Captain and the liaison for the Combine unit with whom they would be paired. It was bad enough that the Khan had ordered them to train against these freebirths. That he would make them *garrison* with the Eleventh Alshain Avengers was beyond reason. He felt like punching the wall again.

In the two years since the Nova Cats had come to the Inner Sphere, they had resided on worlds in the Draconis Combine, an enemy they had fought so many times during the invasion. Combine units were assigned to jointly garrison the worlds the Nova Cats occupied, and trouble had erupted almost immediately.

After three separate incidents, with a loss of life on both sides, the Combine's ruler had created the Irece Prefecture to give the Nova Cats their own territory to protect. Within its boundaries they would rule in the name of the Coordinator. All Combine forces were removed from worlds garrisoned by Nova Cat warriors.

It was against this backdrop that Zeta Provisional Galaxy was formed. True to his word, Khan West had assigned all the warriors who had survived the destruction of the homeworld Galaxies to the new unit. But most of them neither understood nor accepted the new path the Nova Cats had chosen. Morale was a serious problem plaguing the understrength and under-supplied Galaxy. And whereas the Clusters of most Galaxies were assigned to different worlds, the entire Zeta Galaxy was stationed here on Yamarovka, making them feel even more that they had been shoved aside and forgotten within their own Clan.

Zane pounded the wall once again. That Santin West would command any Nova Cat unit to deal with a dishonorable bunch like the Eleventh Alshain Avengers—the unit that, with no provocation, had attacked the Fourth Nova Cat Guards of Delta Galaxy—was simply further proof of West's corruption. To force any unit from Zeta Galaxy to interact with them was only asking for trouble. Zane wondered if the Khan was actually plotting the destruction of the Zeta Galaxy.

He quickly dried himself off and went to his clothes locker to get dressed. As he opened the door and saw the new Nova Cat uniform hanging there, it was with the same disgust he had felt every day since the first time he had laid eyes on it. He yanked the garment from its hanger and quickly pulled on the jacket and the trousers.

With a final tug on his sash, he strode toward the door without checking himself in the mirror. He knew what he would see. But something in that thought stopped him, and in a sudden flash of understanding he realized that neither the uniform nor the insignia defined him.

It was true that every Nova Cat warrior was honor bound to obey the will of his Khan, but there were times when a warrior's own path might diverge from that of his Clan. His doubts did not make him any less a Nova Cat. His duty lay in showing the others the error of their thinking so that all might return to the way of the Clan. In that moment, Zane vowed that he would make that happen by becoming an example of a true Nova Cat warrior.

He stepped through the door with one thought. Today was the beginning of a new path for him—a new path for all the Nova Cats. They simply did not know it yet.

4

Zeta Provisional Galaxy Command Compound
New Circe, Yamarovka
Irece Prefecture
Draconis Combine
5 July 3062

Zane strode through the halls of the Zeta Command Compound, his dress boots clacking against the ferro-crete like the distant reports of small-arms fire. Doors lined the corridors along both sides, stretching before and behind him like a mirror image repeating itself end-lessly into the visible distance. Dim light from overhead flourescents did nothing to relieve the drabness. There were no colors, no wall hangings, no bright signs. Such trappings served no useful purpose, and to the Clans, bred across dozens of generations to be utterly and un-conditionally provident, those amenities were a waste. It was better to put resources to more practical use.

He passed lower-castemen along the way, but ignored them as beneath his notice. When a warrior passed, he and the other exchanged the briefest of nods, recognition among equals. At the end of the interminable hallway was a pair of double-paned glass doors. Weak orange sunlight filtered through, sparkling off dust motes that swam in the air. Zane noted the dust, not surprised that the compound's freebirth laborers shirked their duty of keeping the building clean. He pushed open the doors and walked out into the early New Circe morning.

All around him were the sounds of marching feet, shouting men, the heavy thump of 'Mech footfalls, the banshee wail of hovercraft, the purring of internal combustion engines. The familiar clamor of a military base that was all he had known for more than a decade.

The long, rectangular building he had just left served as general quarters for most of the Nova Cats stationed in the compound. Connected to it by a series of covered walkways was the command and communication center—the C3—that was the cerebral cortex of Zeta Provisional Galaxy. Both buildings were located on a slight rise, with several flights of ferrocrete steps leading down to a grassy field that stretched out for five hundred meters below.

At the moment, the field was filled with warriors and lower-castemen going and coming from one place to another, vehicles rushing to and fro, and the glorious sight of a twelve-meter-tall OmniMech striding purposefully along the far right perimeter of the field. It was the Clan's newest and most powerful OmniMech, and the sight filled Zane with pride.

Though first produced in the homeworlds, the new Nova Cat capital of Irece was now turning out the design. Christened the *Nova Cat*, it was imbued with the spirit of its namesake. Though not the heaviest 'Mech at seventy tons, its sleek design was packed with immense firepower.

The field was bracketed on the other side by the mammoth structure of Zeta Galaxy's 'Mech storage and repair facility and the rapidly expanding spaceport. Its many-tiered buildings and a seemingly endless expanse of reinforced ferrocrete were surrounded by uninterrupted kilometers of razor-tipped, chain-link fence. Beyond the spaceport was the town of New Circe, also growing rapidly, spilling beyond its original boundaries. Zane thought angrily of all the free-births and Inner Sphere surats who were making the place so crowded. Why was his Clan permitting it?

A low, rumbling noise slowly penetrated his thoughts, and he looked up toward the familiar sound of an incoming DropShip. Hundreds of other eyes also turned skyward, straining to see identifying marks on the inbound vessel. Balanced on a tongue of flame, the tiny white speck soon came low enough for visual inspection, revealing the ovoid form of an *Overlord* Class DropShip. One of the largest military transports in common use, it could carry up to three full Trinaries of 'Mechs.

Zane knew the ship bore the emblem of the Draconis Combine, and it still made him ill to see the red crest of a rearing dragon in Nova Cat territory. It had been many months since any Draconis Combine Mustered Soldiery had entered Irece Prefecture, much less visited any of its worlds. What made the

arrival of this particular ship almost unforgivable
was that it was bringing with it the Eleventh Alshain Avengers.

"Zane, I see that our illustrious new Star Colonel
Jal Steiner is even now descending on a throne of
flame," boomed a voice from behind him, startling
Zane and triggering a flash of irritation. Turning, he
saw Star Commander Samuel, his immediate superior and the owner of that large voice. At just over
two meters and 180 kilograms. Samuel was of a monstrous size for a MechWarrior, and many Trinary
members joked that he was actually an Elemental
who'd been mistakenly placed in a MechWarrior
sibko.

"I see that you continue to find humor in the situation," Zane said, "even though our Clan's destruction is arriving at our own invitation."

Samuel smiled a huge grin that contained too
many teeth and seemed to split his face in half. "And
I see that you have once again gotten up on the
wrong side of your cot. Then again, I do not believe
you have a right side to your cot." His grin never
faltered, taking the edge off his words.

Zane had come to respect Samuel in the past few
months, which was fortunate—otherwise, the insult
would have demanded the immediate drawing of a
Circle of Equals.

Samuel apparently read the shadow that crossed
Zane's face. "Must we have the same discussion
every day?" he asked. "This is a beautiful dawn,
filled with sunlight that we rarely see, and no matter
what you think, we will be forming a new Cluster
this day."

The roar of the DropShip suddenly spiked in a thunderous crescendo, signaling the final approach as the crewmen bled off the last of the ship's velocity, preparing for touchdown. The noise hammered at the senses and made conversation impossible as Zane and Samuel descended the stairway toward the boxy, wheeled Indra infantry transport that had just pulled up at the bottom. It would take the members of Battle Trinary—the rest of whom were also converging on the vehicle—to the spaceport to meet their new commander and the DCMS liaison officer.

The Indra was designed to carry a Point of twenty-five Elemental infantry and gear, making it very comfortable for only fifteen warriors with no gear. Zane and Samuel moved quickly up the ramp and found seats next to Pela, Killian, and Geoff, the other members of their Star. Zane hated to admit it, but the dark-haired Pela was an even better *Jenner* pilot than he was, and she had bested him in combat on several occasions.

Once the last of the warriors had taken their seats, the Indra lurched forward and quickly accelerated to its maximum speed of eighty-six kilometers per hour. Within minutes it arrived at the spaceport, and its passengers disembarked onto the tarmac. The incoming DropShip was already settling into the landing pit when they got there. Main Door Four was opening, and a ramp extended toward the ground. Zane and the other fourteen warriors of his Star formed up at attention.

The ramp touched the ground with a loud clang, almost drowning out the sound coming from the darkened interior. Zane, however, had spent too

much time around 'Mechs not to recognize the whir-
ring of actuators and the heavy footfalls of a 'Mech
on the move. He would never have expected his new
commander to come marching out of the DropShip
in his 'Mech, but what could he expect from a warrior who had once been a member of Clan Cloud
Cobra?

The Nova Cats knew the power of dreams and
visions, which gave a mystical cast to their way of
thinking. The Cobras, however, had institutionalized
their beliefs into a religion. Zane thought it foolish
for them to try to define the indefinable, turning the
strength of their devotion into a weakness. Worse, he
had heard that Jal Steiner had converted his whole
former unit, the Xi Provisional Galaxy, to the Cloister
system. Just one more example of the corruption
eating away at the heart of the Nova Cats.

A *Shadow Cat* appeared at the top of the ramp, a
medium-weight OmniMech favored for Nova Cat
front-line Galaxies. It had back-canted legs, a
hunched, thrusting torso, and the barrel of a powerful gauss rifle replacing the entire right arm. Zane
almost gasped aloud at the 'Mech's paint scheme,
however. Garish colors had been slapped on haphaz-
ardly and rows of glyphs had been painted down
the sides of its legs. The thought of every 'Mech in
Xi Provisional Galaxy painted in this same manner
was revolting.

Nonetheless, the shock of that was nothing compared to the one that came next. Painted shining
white with scarlet accents, another 'Mech appeared
at the head of the ramp, then followed the *Shadow
Cat* down into the sunlight of Yamarovka. Zane had

heard reports, but this was the first time he had seen a *Bishamon* in the flesh.

It was a four-legged BattleMech only recently fielded by the DCMS. Though the Clans also made use of four-legged machines—Killian of his own Star piloted a *Snow Fox*—this one looked almost like a totem 'Mech. With its low-slung body and long, doubled-over legs, the *Bishamon* was shockingly reminiscent of a spider. Zane thought it must have a powerful load-out for its size and obvious speed, and he looked forward to meeting this 'Mech on the field.

Only after the 'Mech had taken its place next to the *Shadow Cat* did Zane recognize the apple-green katakana figure "2" on the *Bishamon*'s right torso. Zane knew that indicated that the 'Mech belonged to a *Chu-sa*, the Combine name for lieutenant colonel. The cockpit hatches on both 'Mechs opened almost simultaneously, and their pilots quickly descended retractable ladders to the ground, where the Nova Cat warriors awaited them.

On the left Zane recognized Star Colonel Jal Steiner. He was tall for a warrior and moved with the confidence of one accustomed to command. His dusty blond hair was long and tied back in a tail at the nape of his neck, though most Nova Cat warriors kept their hair very short.

The man with him was only a hair shorter, which irked Zane slightly because it made this enemy taller than he was. Except for his height, however, the officer had all the characteristics of pure Asian blood, including very straight, short black hair. He also radiated a proud arrogance that immediately set Zane's teeth on edge.

The two officers stopped just in front of the men lined up to greet them. Though Zane kept his eyes forward, he moved them just enough to observe the two men in whose hands would rest his and his comrades' fate. He noted that both had the same cool blue eyes that seemed to look into each warrior's soul and weigh what was there. Though a spurious thought, it still raised the hairs on the back of Zane's neck.

As the seconds stretched to minutes, he suddenly wondered why Galaxy Commander Tirant Higall was not here to greet these important personages. He normally had his fingers on everything the Galaxy did, so Zane assumed that Higall must have been ordered to stay away for some reason. Nothing else made sense.

More moments passed before the commander of Zane's Trinary stepped forward and spoke in a loud, firm voice. "I, Star Captain Kael Nostra, commander of Battle Trinary, 37th Garrison Cluster of Zeta Provisional Galaxy, welcome you to Yamarovka. May your visions always guide us down the path." Having completed the ritual greeting, he stepped back into line.

"Thank you, Star Captain," Jal Steiner said in a resonant voice that immediately commanded attention. He began to walk slowly down the line of Nova Cat warriors. "I know that many of you question why our Khan has ordered us to train with the Combine military. And many, if not all, of you may resent that I have been given command of you. Others are probably angry at how you have come to be in the Inner Sphere and posted to this world. In the coming weeks and months, I am sure many other grievances will also be brought before me."

Zane could not help thinking he was right about that.

"But," the Star Colonel continued, "none of that concerns me, nor will I let it affect my new Cluster."

Zane could not see the others around him while standing at attention, but he was sure the other Trinary members resented the remark as much as he did. It was as though Jal Steiner was trying to provoke them, testing them in some way.

Continuing down the line, Steiner continued speaking. "There are two reasons why. First and most important is that our Khan has commanded us, and so it must be. He has set our feet on this new path, and I will make sure that every one of us walks the line. And two"—he paused, again letting his gaze travel over the faces of his warriors—"I was given the opportunity to choose the Trinaries for my new Cluster, and I chose yours."

Zane flinched slightly in surprise. It was not the Nova Cat way for a commander to select his Trinaries. It was even more incredible that Steiner would have chosen his. He must know that the poor morale of Zeta Galaxy had given Galaxy Commander Higall no end of trouble, to the point that some warriors had openly questioned orders.

Fifteen warriors waited in silence for their commander to speak once more.

"Though you may eventually learn my reasons for selecting you, they are mine and I have no need to expose them. Suffice to say that I did choose you, and I expect you to meet, if not exceed, my requirements."

Turning slightly, he gestured toward the waiting DCMS officer. "This is *Chu-sa* Yoshio, commander of Third Battalion of the Eleventh Alshain Avengers. He is our permanent liaison officer and will aid us as we begin our exercises next month."

The Combine officer looked down the line of warriors with an air of superiority that galled Zane no end.

Jal Steiner began speaking again as a distant rumble heralded the approach of another DropShip. "The DropShip you hear is bringing Striker Trinary, First Garrison Cluster of Xi Provisional Galaxy, and Assault Supernova Binary, 246th Battle Cluster of Sigma Galaxy. Combined with your own Battle Trinary, our new Cluster will begin serious training immediately."

Steiner's voice rose in volume as the noise from the descending DropShip began competing in earnest. "The new Cluster will be known as the First Dragoncat Cluster, a name we will bear proudly. Tomorrow at 0600 hours, we will meet as a full Cluster on the training grounds. Until then, it is time the *Chu-sa* and I reported to Galaxy Commander Higall. Blessed path, warriors."

The Star Colonel and the Combine liaison walked quickly to a waiting hovercar.

The Trinary stood silent for some moments, without breaking ranks. "Blessed path" was a strange phrase, and it must mean the warriors were being dismissed. Zane wondered if that too was something from Steiner's Cloud Cobra traditions. On top of that, to be soiled with the name First Dragoncat Cluster!

With a deep breath, he closed his eyes and chanted silently to find his center, letting his angry thoughts settle until he could look at them one by one. Then he opened his eyes and saw the descending Drop-Ship just as it broke cloud-cover. He knew it would continue down until it touched the surface of Yamarovka, even if the captain were to change his mind and apply full thrust to his engines to brake the ship's descent. Gravity would overrule him.

As he watched, Zane was struck by the thought that even though the ship was falling inexorably from the sky, it would ascend once again. That was its nature. It made him realize that the same was true of the Nova Cats; it was only a matter of time. Whether it took weeks, months, or years, Zane knew he would find a way to lift above these dark days and the whole of his Clan would rise with him.

5

Peace Park, Newbury
Dieron
Al Na'ir Prefecture
Draconis Combine
9 July 3062

Lost in contemplation, the old man sat peacefully on one of many benches that dotted the park's tranquil walkways. He leaned forward slightly, studying the ivory tokens of *shogi* on the red and black checkerboard set into the ferrocrete table before him. Though no one else was visibly involved in the game, he gazed intently at the board, apparently trying to beat his unseen opponent. Every so often he would stroke his trimmed white beard or casually brush strands of shoulder-length white hair from his eyes.

Many people moved down the paths, lost in thought or talking softly with a companion. Stretching out in all directions, the trees, manicured lawns, and cultured gardens of Peace Park beckoned the soul to quiet introspection. Topiary bushes fashioned by loving hands into fantastical creatures also helped make this one of the Draconis Combine's most famed parks.

A shadow fell across the board. The old man raised his eyes, but he showed no surprise.

"*Ohayoo gozaimasu,*" the stranger said, his words courteous, his tone full of contempt. "*Shibaraku desu ne . . . O-genki desu ka.* I have not seen you for a long time."

"*Genki desu.* How are you?" The old man's strong, deep voice belied his ancient appearance. "I am fine and, yes, it has indeed been some time since last we met. Please join me."

"*Arigatoo gozaimasu.*" The stranger slowly sat down on the bench. Though his clothing was unremarkable, his bearing was undeniably military.

The old man knew that the man would sooner die than hide his rank and position, but he had somehow managed to show up without his uniform. The old man, too, had once worn the uniform of a commander, but even in the Draconis Combine, where the military was almost worshipped, he knew that the most important battles were fought far from any battlefield. He hoped that this officer was finally coming to see that immortal truth. Though he did not really expect to find unwanted observers, he glanced about quickly to be sure. Old habits died hard.

"You requested this meeting and in this place," the stranger said, looking around disdainfully. "Speak."

"What, no polite talk to pass the morning?" The

old man was amused. "Perhaps you would finish this game of *shogi* with me. My adversary appears to have gone astray."

The slight tightening of the officer's eyes betrayed him. Both men knew they were not here to while away the morning. Both also held exceedingly powerful positions in the Combine, and each word spoken would carry significance not readily apparent to the casual observer.

"I have always preferred *go*."

"Ah, the strategy game for the military-minded." The old man chuckled. "Though I do appreciate the infinite variety of tactics involved, I much prefer the cerebral play of *shogi*. I find it takes more patience. It is also so much more rewarding to trap your opponent in the inevitable than to capture him, thus making him your responsibility. *So ka*?"

The stranger glanced down at the board. Though every game began with the standard twenty pieces, far less than that remained. The old man had his *kaku*—which had been promoted to a dragon horse— and *kei* pieces almost in position to force his opponent's *gyoku* to admit defeat.

"I see that you are in position to force your opponent to move in your favor or capitulate," he said. "But you should never underestimate a worthy adversary, for the game is not over until checkmate has been declared. Contrary to your opinion, I will take the decisiveness of *go* over this slow maneuvering of assets."

Silence followed as they regarded each other with barely concealed animosity. Only the brief flicking of their eyes, scanning now and again for unwanted company, indicated that even these two, powerful beyond the common man's most ambitious dreams, knew fear.

The stranger glanced at the board once more. "Has your *kei* already been placed, *hanta akai?*"

A brief frown flashed across the old man's face. The barb had hit its mark. He had not been called *hanta akai*—the Red Hunter—for tens of years, and now this fool tossed it about for anyone to hear.

The old man's gaze moved past the bubbling fountains and swaying branches, searching out the towering peak of Tatsuyama Mountain just visible in the distance. Once, long ago, he had schemed under the nose of the dreaded ISF on the very doorstep of the forbidding Black Tower on Radstadt, but this glimpse of Tatsuyama Mountain sent a chill down his spine.

He knew that within its rock walls was the Dragon Roost, command center for the whole Dieron Military District. It was the headquarters of *Tai-shu* Isoroku Kurita, district warlord and cousin to the Coordinator himself. He could almost feel the waves of power emanating from it even as his plan was being hatched in its shadow.

Then he smiled to himself. He had essayed far more than this in the past, and though he had not succeeded, he had survived. Perhaps he was merely feeling his age this morning, but the moment had passed quickly. This was only the beginning of a very long road.

"*Hai*," he said, "the arrangements have been made. The mercenary Ramilie's Raiders have left the employ of the Magistracy of Canopus and find that life in the Inner Sphere can be very dangerous. Like all

such lucre-warriors, they believe that a sizable mone-
tary compensation is the answer to all problems.
They will carry out the task I have given them, and
in less then a month's time our most honorable *Gyoku*
will have no choice but to react."

Then, the old man loosed a barb of his own. "I
find it most amusing that the Fifteenth Dieron Regulars are now in disgrace because of their involvement
in the failed attack on the Davion world of Towne.
And yet, without knowing it, they will do more to
further the cause of the Society than they ever did of
their own free will. Is that not the perfect . . . place-
ment of assets and the essence of irony, *Tai-shu*?"

The officer's eyes flashed darkly, revealing his
barely concealed hatred. "I would be very careful
what you say. Though you have rescued the table
scraps of a Society bereft of leadership since the
demon Indrahar destroyed it, the achievement of our
mutual goal will put me far above you. And your
precious organization is not what it once was. The
spawn of Indrahar has carried out many bloody
purges in the last two years."

The old man reached out to the board and casually
picked up several pawn pieces. He held them in his
hand as though testing their weight. "You seem to
forget that there are always *fu* pieces to be found—
pawns unhappy with the direction our beloved Combine has chosen. What's more, it now appears that
almost every action of our *Gyoku* seems to generate
more such pawns."

Of all the Coordinator's decisions that had undermined the moral strength of the Combine, the Black
Dragon Society thought none so blatant as allowing

the Eridani Light Horse, a core unit of the new Star League, to occupy a newly renovated base on this very world. That single act had done more to generate discontent among the populace than any in recent memory.

"In an attempt to save the Combine, the *Gyoku* only sows the seeds of our beloved realm's destruction," the old man continued. "He must be stopped. To invite the enemy to sit at one's hearth is to invite destruction."

The *Tai-shu* stood up abruptly. "The bones have been cast, and we will see where they land. But never tempt my ire again." He turned and began to move quickly up a different path than the one that had brought him here, then was quickly lost from view.

Oh, I will not, the old man answered silently, watching him go. Not until it is far too late for you to see it coming.

6

Jarlton, Ko
Lyons Thumb, Freedom Theater
Lyran Alliance
1 August 3062

Sunlight streamed through the office window, re-
fracting on a dozen different reflective surfaces and
distracting the eye. With a sigh of frustration, *Tai-sa*
Michael Warner, commander of the Fifteenth Dieron
Regulars, gave up trying to read the pile of military
reports on his desk. He stood up and went over to
draw the blinds, but the view from the window only
inspired another heavy sigh.

The town spreading out from the building he had
seized for his command center was withering. From
a population of ten thousand when his forces first
arrived in the Lyons Thumb, less than half remained.
And every week more locals finally scraped together

enough money to bundle up their belongings and head out to make their homes on some other Lyran world.

It did not help his mood that the town of Jarlton was in a desert region with an annual rainfall of less than a centimeter and an average summer temperature hovering at around fifty degrees Celsius. Warner had been here for almost a year in this rotation but was still not used to the burning heat that seared the flesh, tortured the eye, and caused sunstroke in the unprepared—which most of his command had been at one time or another. He supposed it was a small price to pay for disobeying an order to withdraw in his previous posting.

The only good thing was that Jarlton's was a dry heat—the sweat simply evaporated from the skin. Of course, the ambient temperature and total lack of humidity literally pulled moisture from the body, requiring that one imbibe huge quantities of fluids. And piloting a 'Mech in that kind of heat was akin to submersing your body in liquid magma.

He closed the blinds and returned to his desk and the never-diminishing pile of administrative work. He sat down and leaned back with eyes closed, the oppressive heat leaving him in a state of profound lethargy.

Under the neutral auspices of ComStar, Draconis Combine troops had been stationed as a peacekeeping force on the several worlds of the Lyon's Thumb four years ago. To the local Lyran populations, however, they were the enemy—the reason so many were leaving Ko. Regardless of the stated neutrality of the

Kurita forces, some three hundred years of bitter wars could not be forgotten so easily.

Warner leaned forward, setting his elbows on the desktop and wearily letting his head drop into his hands. He rubbed his eyes slowly, reflecting on the sequence of events that had brought him to this point in his life. It had been more than five years since he'd been assigned command of the Fifteenth Dieron Regulars, but he had never stopped hating it. The unit had betrayed the Coordinator by attacking the Davion world of Towne, and Warner made sure that not a sun set without his subordinates suffering his ire at being assigned to such a disgraced unit. But not even he could sustain the bitterness, and a weary resignation had taken its place.

A sharp rap on the door startled him. *"Hairu,"* he said, lifting his head sharply. *Chu-sa* Robert Jimmu, his squat, ugly XO, entered.

"Sumimasen," Jimmu said in his gravelly voice, "but we have picked up an enemy DropShip burning fast for the planet. Troops could be dropping in less than twenty-four hours."

"What?" Warner exploded. "How is that possible? Why didn't we detect the arrival of their JumpShips days ago?"

"We would have, under normal circumstances, *Tai-sa*. But with so many merchant JumpShips passing through and the heavy traffic of civilian DropShips coming and going, the duty officer assumed it was another civilian craft."

Jimmu nervously averted his eyes. "It was not until he noticed that the ship was burning at a constant two gravities the entire time that he realized his error."

Warner stood up and walked around to the front of his desk. "First, that officer is to be demoted and you will assign him the most unsavory task you can think of to occupy him for the next month. He should be glad that I am not of the old school or even now he would be composing his death haiku."

He paused for a long moment, forcing Jimmu to look him in the eye. "I know this posting is eroding the unit's already low morale, but I can do nothing about that. Their previous commander led them to act in defiance of the Coordinator, and now the Fifteenth Dieron must reap the consequences of their actions. Being assigned to garrison Al Nai'ir for four years should have been punishment enough, but apparently *Tai-shu* Isoroko Kurita did not think so. Now he has sent us to this worthless piece of Lyran rock. Unlike the previous commander of this regiment, *I* follow orders."

"*Hai, Tai-sa,*" Jimmu said, which satisfied Warner enough to return to the pressing business at hand.

"Jimmu, if the Lyrans are planning to attack their own world, perhaps their hatred of us has finally overridden their better judgment. Though the locals hate us for being here, we serve under a flag of neutrality. The Lyrans know that attacking us will have grave consequences."

"I cannot explain why they risk so much," Jimmu said. "And though I do not esteem the Lyrans, even I had not thought them capable of such gross stupidity. With so many internal problems plaguing them now, they cannot really believe it is in their interest to provoke the Dragon."

"What you say is true, Jimmu-*san*. There is no denying it. Yet, we can take no chances. We may loathe this duty, but we are this planet's garrison and are honor-bound to defend it against any military force with hostile intent."

He gestured for Jimmu to follow him. "Come," he said, for once feeling some energy of purpose. "If these are invaders, then we shall show them that even a disgraced Combine regiment is more than a match for a gang of Lyran merchants attempting to act like warriors."

Michael Warner went quickly to the door. Jimmu had to move briskly to keep up with his commander, who seemed more animated in the past five minutes than in all his time on Ko.

At the controls of his ASW-8Q *Awesome*, Michael Warner strode his 'Mech forward into the strong winds that whipped the burnt sands into swells that completely swallowed up his BattleMech for long seconds at a time. The heat was particularly dangerous today, topping 55 degrees Celsius and threatening to shut down the 'Mechs of his battalion any moment now. With his *Awesome* at point, the other thirty-six 'Mechs spread out in arrowhead formation across a kilometer-long front, struggling through the shifting sands and stifling heat to meet the enemy units advancing toward their position.

There had actually been two hostile *Overlord* Class vessels. In a daring but almost suicidal move, the ships had traveled so closely together as to appear as one until they penetrated Ko's atmosphere. They had grounded several hundred kilometers from Jarlton.

Warner brought his First Battalion into position, hoping to punch through the disorganized enemy forces. It was risky to send a single battalion against two of the enemy's, but only an elite unit could form up this quickly to repulse an attack on its grounded DropShips. Warner was betting these enemy troops were not that good. Their DropShips had plenty of firepower, however, so he had no intention of closing too much. His command had the advantage of knowing the terrain and training in its hellish climate for almost a full year since starting their rotation. That counted for more than numbers in conditions like this.

While Warner's battalion went head-on, he had sent Second Battalion to flank the enemy, using the sandstorm for cover. He could have used the firepower of Third Battalion as well, but it had been impossible to recall the unit quickly enough from Ko's southern continent.

He broke the long minutes of radio silence. "Have the advance scouts reported any contact with the enemy, Jimmu?"

"*Iie, Tai-sa*. No reports as yet. But there is a good chance they may have already encountered the enemy's lead elements, and that this infernal storm is blocking the transmissions. Our technicians have done everything possible to boost the communications of our units, but these desert storms can still play havoc with them."

"*Hai*, this I know, but we must hold on to our

'Mechs. It is hard enough to pry even supply parts out of the Procurement Department.''

Sudden lightning strobed the twilight created by the sandstorm. At first Warner thought it was the manmade lightning of a particle projection cannon. Then he realized it was the real thing caused by the immense static electricity generated by storms of this kind.

A particularly savage updraft tossed up a fountain of sand, which spiraled into a dust devil in front of his *Awesome*. If visibility was poor before, Warner could not see a single thing now. Then the wind died down momentarily, and he was moving forward into relative calm. Just ahead, less then two hundred meters off, was a *Zeus*—the classic Lyran assault 'Mech. A strange blue-and-white checkered pattern covered its left side, and its left arm was already raised to fire its PPC. This time it was manmade lightning that flashed forward, the energy beams slagging more than a half-ton of armor off the *Awesome*'s right torso.

Warner squared off with the *Zeus*, ignoring the armor melting off his 'Mech's torso in rivulets. He locked on to the target and unleashed his own PPC. Three azure beams leapt toward the *Zeus*.

Heat washed over Warner's cockpit, amplified by the intense temperatures outside. Gasping for breath inside his neurohelmet, he watched the *Zeus* take the terrible energy of his hits. Two of the beams struck it squarely in the chest, while the third slashed across the ground, turning a long stretch of sand into polished glass. Warner was proud of those hits; targeting energy weapons through a sandstorm was no easy feat.

He maneuvered his *Awesome* to the right, checking his secondary tactical monitor for how many enemy units he could see. Over a dozen 'Mechs had already begun trading fire with his own emerging units.

The commline crackled. *"Tai-sa,* we have contact across almost our entire front." Jimmu wasn't telling him anything he didn't know.

"Do we have a sitrep from *Chu-sa* Sharon Carrols and her Second Battalion?" Warner asked.

"Not at this time. The storm is still interfering with our communications. But given the amount of time that has passed, she will know by now that we've made contact with the enemy. She will begin to turn soon."

"If she doesn't get completely lost in this cursed storm and end up moving in the opposite direction," Warner muttered. He swiveled the *Awesome*'s torso left and again opened fire. Trying to keep his heat within manageable limits, he fired only two of his PPCs at the enemy 'Mech.

At the same moment, the *Zeus* again lifted both its arms and fired all its long-range weapons at once. The PPC and large laser flashed across the intervening space, vaporizing armor on the *Awesome*'s left torso and arm. From the *Zeus*'s right-arm LRM came a wall of missiles. But a sudden surge of wind and the speed of Warner's 'Mech threw the missiles off course, and they exploded harmlessly against the ever-shifting dunes.

The *Zeus* did not escape Warner's fire so easily, and a gaping tear had been slashed across its center torso. Warner was glad to see how accurate he had been, but mostly he was elated to be sitting at the controls of a 'Mech once more.

As the *Zeus* began to move backward, trying to put distance and the sandstorm between itself and the *Awesome*, Warner realized he still hadn't even tried to identify the enemy forces, only to vanquish them. That was how excited he was to be in combat again. He toggled the amplification on his monitor, hunting for the insignia that would put a name to these faceless invaders.

The emblem he saw was a blue mailed fist against a white pentagon, the very recognizable symbol of the Lyran Alliance. That was no surprise. He didn't recognize the emblem below it, however; it looked like an archer's bow set against a yellow moon. Until this moment, Michael Warner would have said that he knew the insignia of every unit in the Lyran Alliance Armed Forces.

"Jimmu, that emblem below the Alliance symbol—do you recognize it?"

A few moments of static passed before he heard Jimmu reply, "*Iie, Tai-sa*. I do not."

"*Tai-sa*," interrupted another voice. "This is *Tai-i* Akura. I recognize the insignia from a Lyran news holocast I saw a few months back. It's the symbol of the First Skye Jaegers."

"What! Are you certain?"

"Absolutely, *Tai-sa*."

Warner could not believe it. He was unprepared for the implications of this particular unit's involvement. As the 'Mechs of his battalion took the offensive and began pushing the Lyrans back, Warner let them move past him. He needed a few moments to think this through, and he slowed the *Awesome*'s pace.

He knew who the Skye Jaegers were even if he had not recognized their emblem. First formed three years ago, the Jaegers consisted of five strong regiments. Each was based on the capital world of one of the five Lyran provinces, and each regiment recruited exclusively from its particular province. When Warner had first heard of their formation, he'd guessed that the purpose was to foster Lyran pride and patriotism. He had also heard that the Jaegers were fanatically loyal to Katherine Steiner-Davion. That one of them was attacking the Combine peacekeeping forces on Ko was more than disturbing. It meant that the Lyrans were not simply probing the Combine's defenses, but had launched a full offensive, possibly attacking other worlds of the Lyons Thumb at this very moment.

With the *Awesome* slowed almost to a standstill, it felt again like it had been swallowed up in the sandstorm. Warner knew it was urgent that he report this new development to his superiors immediately. He was confident of the outcome of this battle, but it looked like something even bigger was in the wind.

7

Zeta Command Compound
New Circe, Yamarovka
Irece Prefecture, Draconis Combine
1 August 3062

The blow snapped Zane's head up and back, and sparks of pain exploded in his brain. Another stab of pain shot up his spine as he hit the ground hard. He lay there for an instant, still seeing stars.

Then he rolled quickly to his left. It was all he had time for even if it took him outside the Circle of Equals. Several blows to the head, the last of which had been devastating, had left him momentarily blinded. He pulled himself into a crouch and spread his arms to keep his opponent from pinning them to his side. With eyes shut, he concentrated only on his hearing.

At first he could not make out one sound from

another, but he forced his mind to distinguish between them—noises from the spaceport in the distance, vehicles and 'Mechs moving much nearer, the shuffling feet and low voices of his fellow Trinary members gathered around the Circle of Equals. He identified and then discarded each one as he tried to pick out the sounds made by his opponent.

Some sixth sense warned him of an impending attack. Diving left, he felt rather than saw the roundhouse kick meant for his head. Had the kick connected, he would now be unconscious.

Zane opened his eyes, but still saw the same pinpoints of light. Sensing rather than seeing, he uncoiled himself like a slug from a gauss rifle. With all the power of his muscular legs and his training, he shot forward, intending to knock his opponent to the ground.

Instead, he flew through the boundary of the Circle and stumbled into the surprised arms of several fellow members of his Trinary. They pushed him roughly aside, and Zane collapsed to the ground. He lay there, gasping for breath.

General laughter broke out among the dozen gathered warriors, some of it good-natured and some not. Within minutes the group had dispersed. The Trial was over. Bruised in body and soul, Zane lay face down where they had dumped him, too ashamed to face his fellow warriors right now. He was just glad Yoshio had not been present. Ever since the Dragoncat Cluster had begun training with the Alshain Avengers, Zane had been grudgingly forced to recognize the Combine warrior's superior skill in a 'Mech. He piloted his *Bishamon* like an extension of his own body, with a fluidity and grace that Zane had come to envy.

"Must it always end like this, Zane?" Jal Steiner said, standing over Zane, who still lay in a heap from the beating his commander had just given him. "I am a Clansman and will fight to defend what is right, but combat is not always the answer. The other warriors of the Cluster at least try to coexist with the Combine warriors, despite what some of them feel. Must you make it so difficult? This is your third challenge and the third time I have beaten you in a Circle of Equals. I could refuse further challenges, but I will not invoke the right. You would only use it against me, calling me a coward and challenging me to yet another Trial of Grievance."

Still lying face down in the grass, Zane did not even bother to lift his head.

"I hope you will cease this fruitless hostility, Zane. As one Nova Cat to another, I again ask you to seek the Rite of the Vision. With a vision, you might gain a truer understanding of our path and join us willingly."

Zane still did not move.

"Blessed Path, Zane," Jal said finally, and then Zane was alone with his humiliation.

Stravag, he cursed silently, digging his fingers into the dirt, furious with himself. To be beaten because of a mistake was the ultimate dishonor. And he took no consolation in the fact that only members of his Trinary had witnessed this Trial. They would talk and soon the entire Dragoncat Cluster would know of his disgrace . . . again!

He heaved himself upright, staying crouched lest

he pass out from his head wounds and shame himself further.

"Why do you fight everything we do here, Zane?" This time it was the gruff voice of Samuel speaking to him. "Tenacity is an admirable virtue, but many see you as obstinate, unwilling to change. We Nova Cats have learned to embrace change when necessary, regardless of the price. If, as you say, you wish to show our Clan a truer path, you have failed to impress those you would lead."

Zane felt a flash of anger, but he also admired Samuel for always being direct and truthful. He did not wish to lash out at the only person in the entire Cluster he might call friend. He cleared his throat to speak even though it felt like he had swallowed a bucket of sand. Maybe this time he would make his friend understand what drove him.

"What we do is wrong, Samuel. Everywhere I look, I see our way of life, our culture, our heritage, our birthright as descendants of the blessed Founder being trampled while we gaze in awe at the lush worlds of the Inner Sphere that have been given to us. Given!"

He did not try to suppress his anger; he rarely did anymore. "When have we ever accepted gifts instead of taking what we need, as warriors should? By now we have all heard the tapes of the Grand Council after the Great Refusal. I have no use for Wolf warriors, but I respect what the Wolf Khan said that day. He tried to warn the others that by accepting defeat at the hands of the Inner Sphere, our technology would be sold to the highest bidder and our culture become mere rootstock for trends. This will be the greatest shame any of us have ever suffered. Khan Ward understands what will happen—what is happening right now with our own beloved Clan."

The unexpected warmth on the back of his neck announced that the sun had momentarily breached the ubiquitous cloud cover over New Circe. The flashes of light no longer blinded him, and he could see the orange ball of sun beginning to set behind the jagged Lasden Mountains in the distance. Zane wondered if the ray of sun had conferred some healing properties or if it was mere coincidence that his vision had begun to clear at that precise moment. He snorted to himself. Such a fanciful thought made him think he had surely suffered a concussion.

Samuel was shaking his head sadly. "Zane, our Remembrance, all the Remembrances of all the Clans, tell us that the Founder created us to one day return to the Inner Sphere to build a new Star League. Has not a new Star League been formed? Did we not aid and fortify it in its infancy, so that it will continue to grow in strength for generations to come? Is that not why our Khans chose this path for us?"

Zane looked at Samuel, once again struck by his friend's simple, honest nature. The earnest look in Samuel's eyes bespoke a real desire to understand.

"But *we* did not form this Star League," Zane said. "It was not created to bring a golden age to humanity, but to make war. The so-called Star League has exterminated one whole Clan. It has led us astray and lulled the rest of the Clans into inaction. Look at how First Lord Liao immediately used his power to make war on another member-state of the

League—a war that is still going on! That is not the spirit of the original Star League."

Samuel squatted down beside Zane. "You speak true, Zane, but your words do not tell the whole truth. That member-state was a renegade nation that had illegally gained its freedom from the Capellan Confederation during one of the many wars of the Inner Sphere. Does the original ruler not have the right to fight for territory that is his? Do the Clans not fight in continual Trials of Possession for worlds, even though some of those worlds have been held by one Clan or another for almost three centuries? Besides, the old Star League also made war soon after its formation."

Zane, now confident that he could stand without swaying, got slowly to his feet. "That is not the same thing, Samuel. The war you speak of was waged by decision of the whole Star League High Council. The Council Lords wished to include the Periphery states in the golden age of humanity, but the Periphery refused to listen. The Star League went to war to lead them to a better life. *This* First Lord was not carrying out the will of the High Council, but abused the power of his position to further his own ambitions."

Zane touched his head, exploring the bruises and cuts he knew to be there. Most seemed minor, but one particularly large knot, just behind his eye and above his right temple, was very tender to the touch. He had been trained in enough basic first aid to know that a concussion was a real possibility. No warrior wanted to be branded weak, but it would be far worse if he passed out in the cockpit. He would see a doctor immediately.

Samuel stood up, too. "Before you go and see whether or not your brains have been scrambled, I want to ask you to think about something. It is true that the new Star League was founded to help end the Clan invasion of the Inner Sphere, but why should that invalidate its existence? Regardless of the reason, it *is* here, even though some Clans choose to ignore what is before their eyes.

"Perhaps you are correct in claiming that First Lord Liao abused his powers, while the Council did nothing to stop him. But now Theodore Kurita serves as First Lord, and he has not used the position to increase his power. Even you have to admit that he has behaved honorably by awarding us worlds and the chance to integrate with his military.

"Finally, Zane, is it not our obligation, as the true descendants of the Star League Defense Force, to act as protectors and guardians of mankind's best hope? Think about it, Zane. That is all I ask."

Samuel waited a long time for Zane to reply. When Zane did not, he turned and walked away into the darkness already falling.

Zane watched him for a moment and shrugged. Then he turned toward the compound, angling off in the direction of the medic station. He would never admit it, but Samuel had indeed given him much to think about. Zane wished that Samuel was the Nova Cat Oathmaster instead of the imposter who now held the post. He had a way of seeing that Zane admired, despite their disagreements. Where Zane found only contradictions, Samuel was able to see them as part of a larger pattern.

Reaching the steps up to the compound, he slowly began to ascend the hill. At the top, he looked around one final time before going in. Night had descended, and he could no longer see the field where he had just lost another Trial of Refusal and then spoken with Samuel. He knew it was there. He just could not see it.

8

On the day following Zane's fight with Jal Steiner, the Dragoncat Cluster moved its base of operations to the outskirts of Yama, a city built on a small rise about twenty kilometers from the spaceport. Some of the Dragoncat warriors had taken to sleeping in quickly erected field tents. Though Zane was not sure why, he surmised that Jal Steiner wanted to keep his Cluster from being infected by the increasingly low morale of the rest of Zeta Galaxy.

The Star Colonel had commandeered a theatre building for use as a command center the day of the move, and he used its cavernous auditorium whenever he wished to debrief the entire Dragoncat Cluster. The arced ceiling was carved with fantastical beasts, and dozens of fluted buttresses supported walls blazing with brilliant murals depicting Oriental mythological figures. The hall could seat a Galaxy of warriors, and even Zane experienced awe at the vastness and alien décor. He wondered if Jal Steiner had chosen it because it echoed the Cloud Cobras and the mystical Cloisters they created.

The immense circular room was some forty-five meters across, with tiered seats surrounding a large open area. At the moment the area contained a holo-tank replaying a 'Mech engagement. Even from his seat high in the tiers, Zane could see and hear perfectly. The room's design gave a clear view of the platform from any given point, and its phenomenal acoustics eliminated the need for electronic voice-amplification.

"I am sure I need not belabor the fact that yesterday's exercise was seriously lacking," Jal Steiner was saying, his strong voice echoing across the resonant space.

Zane was only half listening. He didn't need to be reminded of what had happened the day before. His own unit, Striker Trinary, had faced off against the Alshain Avengers and been beaten. Now he and the rest of the Trinary had to suffer an even worse humiliation. Jal Steiner had requested that the Avengers who had participated in the exercise be present at today's debriefing, though Zane was sure they had only come to gloat over their lucky win.

The twelve members of the Eleventh Alshain Avengers First Company, Third Battalion, plus *Chu-sa* Palmer Yoshio's command lance, stood out among the Nova Cats. All wore dark gray jerseys, striped in red diagonally across the chest, and dark gray trousers, red-striped along each leg. The trousers were tucked into calf-length black boots.

Zane had almost become accustomed to the sight of them moving routinely among his Clan, which only proved you could get used to anything. But to have the same filthy freebirths who'd defeated his unit listening in while Jal Steiner berated them was too much to take.

The Zeta Galaxy warriors were familiar with the dishonorable tactics of Inner Sphere MechWarriors—running, hiding, concentrating fire on a single unit, attacking JumpShips and supply depots. They had been prepared for that, not to face opponents who stood their ground, risking complete shutdown of their 'Mechs as they brought as much weaponry as possible to bear in one-on-one battles.

It was just another Inner Sphere trick and not the first time the Inner Sphere had twisted Clan traditions to win a battle. This time they had used *zellbrigen*, the Clan's honor code of battle, to achieve victory by taking his Trinary by surprise. It had worked.

Yet Zane had experienced something inexplicable in the midst of yesterday's battle. At one point he had faced off with Yoshio's *Bishamon* for almost a full minute. When he realized it was Yoshio's 'Mech, he had felt his old, familiar anger rising as he prepared to open fire. He imagined he saw the Combine warrior's cool blue eyes finding him even through the smoke and laughing at him. Then something happened. His anger abruptly blossomed into a wave of euphoria, a sensation unlike anything he had ever known. He suddenly fought with a skill far beyond anything he had ever achieved, piloting his machine in ways he would have, moments before, thought impossible. The exchange of weapons fire was brief, but he managed to inflict considerable damage to the *Bishamon*, while denying Yoshio the opportunity to give as good as he got.

Then the ebb and flow of battle had pulled them apart, and Zane was eventually downed when a Combine *No-Dachi* surprised him with a physical attack from behind. It was exactly the kind of treacherous tactic for which the Inner Sphere was infamous, and it denied Zane the opportunity to vanquish his enemy in honorable combat.

He did not dwell so much on that, however, more obsessed with wondering what had lit such a fire under him on the field yesterday and if he would be able to recapture that superior ability. As he pondered the mystery, he instinctively touched the leather pouch of vineers fastened at his belt.

Every Nova Cat warrior carried a vineer pouch on his or her uniform, a dignified way to proclaim one's exploits as a warrior. Each vineer was a memento from a past battle, be it a shred of armor, a captured enemy patch, or a torn piece of clothing. The important thing was that it encapsulated a momentous event in that warrior's life. The item served as a focus for recalling the feelings, impressions, thoughts, sensations, and reactions of a combat experience— flashpoints of memory that defined who and what a warrior was and would become.

For Zane, who until yesterday had experienced

only two events he'd deemed worthy of a vineer, the act of acquiring one held a sacredness all its own. He'd returned to the ground where he had fought Yoshio, then searched for hours until he found a palm-sized piece of armor that, though scorched, still showed traces of gleaming white with scarlet accents. The unique grid lines across one side of the metal assured Zane that this piece had indeed come from the leg he had almost severed from the *Bishamon*.

Holding the piece in his hand as the sun began to set on the battlefield, it was like a sign that it was time to enact the Rite of the Vision. The Khan had advised it more than a year ago and Star Colonel Steiner had been doing the same for the last few months. Zane had resisted, uneasy for reasons he could not articulate. He closed his fingers around the jagged-edged metal and felt it pierce the skin of his palm. He would petition Galaxy Commander Higall tomorrow for permission to travel to Irece to undertake the Rite of the Vision with the Oathmaster at hand.

"It is obvious that they took you by surprise," Jal Steiner was saying, "using tactics more akin to the way of the Clans than the Inner Sphere. In all fairness to our respected opponents, the Combine also has a long tradition of one-on-one battles. But is not surprise the essence of battle? To do that which the enemy does not expect and thus end the engagement quickly, decisively? That is what occurred yesterday, and it will not happen again. Always expect the unexpected and you will never be taken by surprise."

With a sweep of his arm that took in the entire Cluster, he brought the meeting to his usual abrupt ending. "The Assault Supernova Binary will contest the Avengers Third Company tomorrow. The rest of you will observe the battle and learn, just as those warriors learned from you in yesterday's combat."

As the meeting broke up and the warriors began to move toward the various exit doors, Zane became aware that *Chu-sa* Yoshio had fallen into step beside him. Zane sensed that Yoshio might speak, probably eager to rub in the Nova Cat defeat. Hoping to lose him, Zane turned and headed quickly toward another exit.

"*Sumimasen*, MechWarrior Zane . . . please, MechWarrior Zane, excuse me, but I would have a word with you." Yoshio's heavily accented voice was perfectly audible as Zane reached the top of the stairs. Thanks to the acoustics, his words carried all the way across the auditorium. Zane noticed at least a dozen Nova Cat warriors turn to look at him. He sighed and turned to see Yoshio coming up the stairs behind him. Zane did not try to hide his irritation.

"I am sorry to hail you in such a rude manner," Yoshio said, "but I would speak with you. Are you on the way somewhere? I do not wish to detain you any more than necessary. We can walk while we talk, no?"

Zane could not help but notice that Yoshio's even tone matched his expressionless face. From what he had seen of these Combine warriors so far, the deadpan facade was always in place, rarely wavering. Unexpectedly, he wondered if they returned the hatred the Nova Cats felt toward them. The Clans had first come to the Inner Sphere to conquer it, and many Spheroid warriors had died fighting them. Zane hated Yoshio as a barbarian who had defiled all that was sacred to the Nova Cats. Perhaps Yoshio also hated Zane for being an invader who had come to despoil his homeland.

This new thought startled him so much that he answered without meaning to. "I am on my way back to the Zeta command compound to speak with Galaxy Commander Higall."

"Then, if you do not mind, I would walk with you."

Zane nodded, but said nothing more. He continued toward the exit, his unwelcome companion at his side. As they left the building, the sky was the standard gloomy and overcast. The bad weather had only arrived in the last few days, but was so oppressive it felt more like weeks, even months. Several minutes passed in silence as they walked, and Zane began to wonder if the *Chu-sa* had changed his mind.

"I was most impressed with your skills in yesterday's exercise," Yoshio began abruptly. "Forgive me if I sound boastful, but I had not thought anyone but your Star Colonel to be my equal on the field. And yet, you outmaneuvered me and managed to inflict superior damage. It is true that your 'Mech has more inherent speed than my own, but that has never been so much of a disadvantage before."

Zane turned to stare at Yoshio, but said nothing. He could hardly believe what he was hearing.

Yoshio gave a small bow of his head. "Please excuse me if I am too forward in my question, but my curiosity has gotten the better of me. How can one of your skill be only a MechWarrior? Though you are young by Combine standards, with your ability you would have risen to at least a *Chu-i*, if not a *Tai-i* by now. I am still learning the ways of your Clan, but is it possible the Nova Cats have so many skilled warriors that one is allowed to languish without command? Are all the Nova Cats then as skillful as you?"

The question caught Zane so totally off guard that he continued to stare blankly at Yoshio. He was speechless.

"I have offended," Yoshio said. "I apologize. That was not my intention."

"Neg, you have not. We Nova Cats are known for our mysticism, but we also prefer plain words. Your question is unexpected. That is all." Zane paused. This warrior, this enemy, had come to praise his ability. The problem was that Zane could not explain even to himself what had happened on the field yesterday. And he did not intend to respond by saying that he was less skilled than Yoshio believed.

"I do not know why you are surprised," Zane said roughly. "I am a Clan warrior, genetically bred to be superior in battle."

Yoshio was quiet for a moment, then nodded his head slightly. "*Hai*, MechWarrior Zane. *Sumimasen*." As they came up to the Indra transport that would take Zane back to the Zeta command compound, Yoshio gave another slight bow of his head. "Again, I apologize. We will speak no more of this, and I beg your pardon for intruding," he said.

"No need," Zane said roughly. "We are all allowed to question, even if some questions have no answers."

Zane was about to board the transport, then turned

back at the last minute. Thinking of his Rite of the Vision, he said, "I will not see you for some weeks. Perhaps then I will have an answer that will satisfy us both."

Yoshio looked at him with those cool blue eyes. Then he nodded. "Until then, MechWarrior Zane."

Zane turned away again and climbed into the Indra. The exchange had disturbed him somehow, but he could not afford to dwell on it right now. He had to prepare himself for his meeting with Galaxy Commander Higall.

A cold rain began to fall as Palmer Yoshio watched the long, squat frame of the Indra speed away. The rain began to fall harder, and he hunched his shoulders and turned up his collar as he hurried down the street to find his own transport. He tried to stay in the lee of the buildings to keep from getting drenched, but the shifting wind whipped the rain in different directions.

He thought about his conversation with Zane, thinking that the young man did not really fit the barbarian stereotype. Even in a society of warriors, where combat was the constant that shaped their lives from day to day, there were always exceptions.

As he turned the corner, the wind howled, driving the pelting rain almost horizontal. It nearly knocked Yoshio off his feet, but he grabbed onto the pole of a streetlight to stay upright. Giving up all hope of remaining dry, he forged on, mulling over a debate he had been having with himself for months, perhaps years.

How could he hate the Nova Cats when, like him,

they were warriors, honorable in their dealings and respectful of the powers of the unseen? He had posed that question to himself dozens of times and always come up with the same brutal answer. He hated them because they had savaged Combine worlds—savaged Alshain worlds! Worlds Yoshio was sworn to protect. Worlds that were still under Clan rule.

Retaking the Alshain District worlds occupied by the Clans was so important that the Alshain Regulars had changed their unit designation to the Alshain Avengers to express their intention of doing that. Hatred of the Clans had been drilled into them. Yoshio knew that Theodore Kurita, the lord to whom he owed complete obedience, had actually awarded some of those worlds to the Nova Cats. Yet he could never understand how the Coordinator could give away Combine territory to the barbarian Clans, how the Dragon himself could give his own people into the hands of an enemy.

As time passed, Yoshio had discovered others who shared these doubts and questions. They called themselves the Black Dragon Society, a secret group rumored to have plotted the recent assassination attempt against the Coordinator. At first, they had asked nothing of Yoshio, and he had been able to vent his frustration and concern in their company. Eventually, they began to ask his help, though at first the requests had seemed harmless enough. Now, Yoshio was deeply bound to the Society. The true test of his loyalty still lay ahead.

Yet here he was, training alongside hated Clansmen, wondering what his fellow Black Dragons would think if they knew he felt a budding respect for the enemy.

Just then a truck sped past, splashing through the water that had pooled in the street. Yoshio didn't see it till too late and could not get out of the way in time. He was instantly soaked from the waist down, and the water ran into his boots.

As the hard rain continued to fall, Yoshio realized that he was as helpless to stop these conflicting feelings as he was to protect himself from this cloudburst. He acknowledged the feelings, but in the end only his actions mattered. *Ninjo* and *giri*—compassion and duty—were a warrior's two touchstones. No more and no less. His duty was clear, no matter what his feelings. As for compassion, samurai had been asking themselves the same question for millennia: who was worthy of it? When all was said and done, Yoshio knew what was demanded of him. His path was clear and he would not stray from it.

9

Unity Palace
Imperial City, Luthien
Kagoshima Prefecture, Draconis Combine
11 August 3062

Sitting in the Black Room deep inside Unity Palace in Luthien's Imperial City, the most secure chamber in the entire Draconis Combine, shielded from every eavesdropping device known to man and protected by five crack regiments of fanatically elite troops, Theodore Kurita, Coordinator of the Draconis Combine, First Lord of the Star League, Duke of Luthien, Unifier of Worlds, unquestioned ruler of three hundred-fourteen inhabited star systems and numerous uninhabited systems that spanned almost five hundred light years, felt helpless.

Staring at the data terminal before him, he scrolled through the relevant information, aware that it was completely accurate even if he wished it otherwise. The report described attacks by several Lyran regiments against the worlds of Ko, Imbros III, and Yorii in the Lyons Thumb. All three were garrisoned by Draconis Combine peacekeeping troops, under the neutral auspices of ComStar. Duty-bound to defend their garrisons, the Combine units had fought back. They succeeded in driving off the invaders, but they had been bloodied, especially on the world of Ko.

This wasn't the first attack on the Lyons Thumb worlds in the four years Combine units had been stationed there. Other small, punitive raids had occurred, though actual reports of those incidents had never crossed his desk. There were many matters his subordinates thought the Dragon need not be bothered with—and those were exactly the ones he made sure to keep abreast of.

This attack was different. It was a full-scale assault. Considering the centuries of animosity between his realm and the Lyrans, especially the Lyrans of the Skye region, the aggression wasn't what surprised him; it was the boldness and strength of the attack. Theodore disliked being caught off guard, and it did not occur often.

He wanted to know who was responsible. Katherine Steiner-Davion was a politician not a warrior. She had proved herself the true inheritor of her father's craftiness, too masterful at maneuvering the shoals of Inner Sphere politics for a blunder like this. More than anyone, she knew that her realm hung on the brink of civil war. A war against the Draconis Combine at this time would not serve her interests in any way.

He turned to the room's only other occupant, a red-haired man clad all in black. Ninyu Kerai-Indrahar, Director of the Internal Security Force, had been with him since his earliest days as a warrior. If Theodore Kurita was the most powerful man in the Draconis Combine, Ninyu was the most feared. It was his disturbing report Theodore was perusing.

Raising an eyebrow, Theodore looked squarely at Ninyu and waited.

"No, *Tomo*, Katherine would not have made this mistake," Ninyu said softly, reading Theodore's thoughts. The two had known each other for more than thirty years. They had fought together and been Sons of the Dragon together. Few people knew Theodore so well. It was no surprise that Ninyu could intuit a question Theodore had not even spoken aloud.

"She might have attacked back when the Combine troops were first sent in, though even that is doubtful. But now? No, she is much too clever for that. The way she stole the throne from her brother Victor without even firing a shot is proof of where her talents lie. As I summarized in my report, there are only two possible explanations."

"The Isle of Skye or the Black Dragon Society," Theodore said.

Ninyu nodded. "The Lyons Thumb worlds belong to the Skye Province, and the Skye radicals are desperate to see our troops off their soil. Young Duke Robert Steiner is young, hot-blooded, and eager to advance the cause begun by his father. Like Katherine, he too has inherited his father's skill in political maneuvering, but he is still new enough to make just this sort of blunder."

Ninyu gestured to the data display in front of Theodore. "We have verified the First Skye Jaegers as the unit that attacked Ko. How hard would it be to convince a troop of Skye patriots that it was time to fight for their homeland? And what better time to act than when the Queen is away tending to her other throne? We also have compelling evidence that General Richard Steiner, commander of the Cavanaugh II Theater, might be supporting young Robert. With that kind of muscle and the prestige of another Steiner name backing him, Robert might have decided he was strong enough to make his move."

"You make a convincing case," Theodore said. "But young as he is, Robert must know how volatile the Federated Commonwealth is now. His actions could be the spark that sets off the conflagration."

A slight smile twisted the corners of Ninyu's mouth, but did not reach his eyes. "When have men in power ever cared about the consequences of starting a war? Especially if the man believes he can benefit from that war?"

Theodore nodded once, acknowledging a truth as old as the dawn of man's existence. "And the *Kokurya-Kai*?"

The slightest narrowing of Ninyu's eyes was the only sign that this topic was of great personal interest. "My father sacrificed his life to destroy the Black Dragon leadership, and the purges I ordered have rooted out most of them."

Theodore nodded. "But can they ever be eradicated while I continue to push for reforms that my own nobles object to? Your earlier report was adamant that we not underestimate the Society's ability to survive even our severest measures. Giving the Nova Cats the Irece Prefecture would only have fueled the flames of their opposition."

"*Hai*, my lord, that is so. My instincts tell me that they are still out there, just waiting for their chance."

In a break with custom that threatened to disrupt the harmony of the meeting, Theodore stood slowly and began pace up and down the room. He knew it allowed Ninyu to see how agitated he was, but the head of the merciless Internal Security Force already knew that.

"You have purged every known and suspected cell, and the Voice of the Dragon has ramped up our propaganda machine, working it nonstop to educate my people. They must understand that the Nova Cats help defend our border from Clan Ghost Bear and that the Combine needs to rebuild its strength, not to start another war. I am confident that you and all others loyal to the Dragon have done everything within your power. Why should we continue to speculate about what the *Kokurya-kai* might do next? If we are doing everything we can to stop them, we need not torment ourselves for the lack of success."

Ninyu shook his head. "Think, *Tomo*. How many sacrifices have you made in this life for the good of the Combine? Losing friends and comrades in battle, hiding your own children and wife for many years, attacks on your life, alliances with filth and hated enemies, the death of your father. Vigilance is our best defense against the Black Dragons."

Theodore stopped pacing. Was he getting too old?

Losing his nerve after all this time? Surely he would not have reacted this way a few years ago.

"You have accomplished much for the Combine, *Tomo*, and you now stand as First Lord of the Star League, trying to keep the Inner Sphere from cutting itself into pieces. You have sacrificed everything for this moment, and the Black Dragons are set upon destroying all you have forged. Do not be surprised if you are weary."

Ninyu paused and his tone softened. "Only do not show such weakness to the common people. I do not believe they would survive the ordeal of seeing the Dragon brought low by the Yellow Bird."

Theodore tensed, instinctively bridling at the reference to the only creature that could harm the Dragon and the insinuation that the Coordinator had been weakened. He calmed himself, knowing there was no hiding his feelings from his old friend. He had given that up decades ago.

"So, you believe that the *Kokurya-kai* are responsible for this action?"

Ninyu did not answer for a few moments, then with great deliberation said, "No."

"Then we are in agreement that the attack is the work of either Duke Robert or other radical elements in the Isle of Skye?"

"Yes."

"The Combine troops on those worlds are there under the flag of neutrality. This act of aggression is a declaration of war."

"*Hai*, my lord."

"Our *giri* is clear."

Theodore went back to the table and tapped a stud

that brought up a three-dimensional holoprojection of the Lyons Thumb: Ko, Imbros III, Yorii, Lambrecht, Dyev, Moore, Sabik, and Atria floated in the air above the display. This blatant attack on the Lyons Thumb had forced his hand. Those worlds would soon be flying the flag of the Draconis Combine.

"I will issue the orders this day and will personally draft an announcement to the Star League Council. My duty is clear. To protect the interests of my realm and my people, the Draconis Combine will officially annex the planets of the Lyons Thumb."

"*Hai, Tomo,*" Ninyu said, his face expressionless as ever.

After several moments, Theodore punched the control stud on the holoprojector once more, and the three-dimensional projection morphed and zoomed out to show the entire border between the Draconis Combine and the Federated Commonwealth. A soft grunt from behind confirmed that Ninyu's thoughts were directed along the same line.

"What is the disposition of our troops along the Dieron, Benjamin, and Galedon Military District borders with the Federated Commonwealth?" Theodore asked. He already knew the answer, having personally ordered the troop assignments. But he wanted to hear the thoughts of his shrewd advisor.

"We are stretched thin," Ninyu said. "The nonaggression agreement between you and the Davions allowed us to scale back to a skeleton defense along our FedCom border. We have also freed up other units since regaining the worlds occupied by the Smoke Jaguars. With the Nova Cats safeguarding a portion of our Clan border and the relative non-aggression of the Ghost Bears, we have redeployed several units from along that border. Those redeployments have been necessary ever since Katherine seized the throne of the Federated Commonwealth. However, even with these additional troops, the FedCom border is still dangerously weak."

"*Hai*, Ninyu-*san*. I concur. My warlords have all informed me of their opinions on this matter, as have my other close advisors, yet you have refrained until now. I appreciate your reticence to speak hastily on an important matter like the civil war that is brewing next door. However, the time has come for your counsel. When do you think the war will begin?"

Seconds of silence turned into minutes, and Theodore returned to contemplating a border that stretched almost five hundred light years. A border that could be penetrated with ease in the FedCom civil war that looked all but inevitable. In the chaos of war, some radical groups might take it under their own authority to strike out at the hated Draconis Combine.

"Soon," Ninyu said.

Theodore waited patiently for more. When Ninyu was in this mood, a company of BattleMechs could not drag words out of him. He would reveal himself in his own due time.

"Though I dislike Victor Davion for the position he holds, I believe he is a man of honor. He has said that he will not drag his people into a war with us, and I believe him. However, we do not know what will happen if Katherine forces Victor's hand. You have read all of the reports. The Federated Commonwealth is in disarray, with demonstrations in support of the removal of the Archon-Princess already erupting on many worlds. Only the ruthless efficiency of her propaganda machine has kept events at a low simmer for this long."

Stepping forward, Ninyu came alongside Theodore, and the two of them stood gazing at the map hovering above the display.

"The recent mobilization of the Capellan March Militias and Hasek-Davion's secret raids into the Confederation show how tenuous Katherine's hold is becoming. Her ability to control all aspects of the situation is wavering. I believe she will find a way to force Victor to arms before the year is out, thus triggering a war she believes she will win."

"That she cannot be allowed to do," Theodore said softly, but with the authority gained over a lifetime. "If she is able to vanquish Victor and erase him from the mind of the common man, that will cement her rule of the Federated Commonwealth and perhaps allow her to reunite the two halves. I need not tell you what an immense threat that would represent to the Combine. It would be as devastating for us as for the rest of the Inner Sphere."

Ninyu did not comment, and Theodore did not expect him to. If anything, his words were an understatement of the threat.

"Yet, as the First Lord of the Star League, I cannot directly intervene to aid Victor."

"The Ghost Regiments?" Ninyu asked, then paused as if awaiting permission.

Theodore nodded for him to continue.

"We cannot turn our backs on a powerful enemy

like the Ghost Bears, but they seem content to look after their borders and solidify their position in the Inner Sphere. We also have reports that they are fighting with a new Clan, the Hell's Horses, on their far border. I believe we could pull all of our Ghost Regiments away from the Ghost Bear border and redeploy them to our FedCom border. The anonymity of the Ghost Regiments is part of their strength, and we have continued to mask their movements. This deployment would be no different than many others they have made and would arouse no suspicion if discovered.

"They can be used in defense of the Benjamin, Galedon, and Dieron Military Districts should any Draconis March units decide that the civil war is the perfect opportunity to right the wrongs of centuries by attacking our border. They would also be on hand to provide you with a cadre for attacking targets of opportunity. Surprise strikes—which can be denied—across the border at units loyal to Katherine would create havoc. It would also provide Victor with the toe-hold he will need to take back his throne."

Theodore smiled at Ninyu, thinking that he was a true son of Indrahar Kerai, even if not by blood. "As always, more than any of my other advisors, you prove your worth to the Combine and honor your father."

"*Doomo arigatoo gozaimasu kunshu.*"

"*Doo itashimashite*, Ninyu-*san*. Then again, you have had my thanks for many years, and I doubt that will change any time soon. Along with the decree to annex the Lyons Thumb, I will issue orders for the immediate redeployment of the Ghost Regiments. See that every effort is made to keep their movements secret. As you say, they will be needed before year's end."

Theodore gave a small sigh as he turned back to the map of his realm. He knew that his *giri* demanded that he protect his people and his state, yet his heart was saddened by man's eternal need for war.

10

Ways of Seeing Park
New Barcella, Irece
Irece Prefecture, Draconis Combine
21 August 3062

"Seyla!"

The sound of the solemn oath swelled as hundreds of voices sent it soaring into the crystal-clear cobalt sky, hailing Khan West as he finished opening the Oathmaster Grand Melee. The rite, one of the Clan's most important, was performed annually on the longest day of the year. On Irece, the new Nova Cat homeworld, that was today, August twenty-first.

Standing among the throng of warriors gathered around the Circle of Equals, where the first test would take place, Zane felt a profound awe that he was about to witness a rite he had only heard about all his life. Today's Trial was the first of two that would decide the Clan's next Oathmaster. Any Nova Cat could enter the Circle of Equals and fight hand to hand and unaugmented, the combat as no holds barred as any brawl. Only someone of superior martial skills could hope to emerge victorious from the fray, which was why only members of the warrior caste ever had.

But the position required much more than physical prowess. The Oathmaster, whose wisdom was unquestioned, was the Khan's—and by extension, the entire Clan's—most important counselor in guiding the Nova Cats on their proper path. To test this ability, the victor of the melee would then undertake the Forum of Law. There, he would have to prove to the satisfaction of the Khans and all opponents from the Circle of Equals that his knowledge of the Nova Cat Remembrance, Clan law, Nova Cat tradition, and the many exceptions to the law and traditions was unquestioned. In so doing, he or she proved their worthiness to become Oathmaster of the Nova Cats.

If the candidate failed this Trial, then the last opponent defeated in the Circle of Equals became eligible to test in the Forum of Law. If that individual also failed, the standing Oathmaster remained in place. Biccon Winters had held the office for as long as Zane had been aware of its importance in the Nova Cat way of life. Then, she had shocked the whole Clan and outraged Zane by announcing that she would retire as Oathmaster. If Zane still needed proof that the Nova Cats were crumbling from within, surely this was it. Khan West, in what Zane thought particularly fit punishment, had assigned her the task of babysitting the new Star League Defense Force. She was now a member of the Commanding General's personal staff, giving them a real warrior to look after their precious Star League.

Zane had postponed his Rite of the Vision until after the selection of a new Oathmaster. Then, in another stunning announcement, Biccon Winters had proclaimed that regardless of how many candidates might fail the Forum of Law, a new Oathmaster would be selected. For Zane, this was an even greater affront to Nova Cat traditions than her retirement.

Located just north of the Rosse Spaceport, Ways of Seeing was a stretch of ground that had been consecrated as the most holy of Nova Cat sites. It was surrounded by a high wall and held all the Nova Cats held sacred. As he stood with the many other Nova Cats waiting for the Grand Melee to begin, he thought about all he had seen since coming to Irece. When the Nova Cats conquered the planet in 3051, they took over an insignificant Draconis Combine town with a modest spaceport and renamed it New Barcella. Since then, the population had swelled to five million—most of it Nova Cat lower castemen. The city now boasted an ultra-modern spaceport covering a hundred square kilometers, a mammoth 'Mech production facility, two primary training facilities, and military installations that housed the entire Alpha Galaxy.

The crowning glory of all this was the primary genetic repository built to replace the one left behind in the Clan homeworlds. Zane knew of its existence before arriving on Irece, and he understood it was the only way the Nova Cats could continue their genetic breeding and sibko programs. But when he saw what had been done here, it was just one more proof of how far his Clan had gone astray.

To Zane's left, some five hundred meters distant, rose the imposing structure of the Nova Cat's new genetic repository. The circular, Neo-Gothic building clawed at the sky with its flying buttresses, freestanding out-rider piers, triforium, and vaulted roof. Rising almost three hundred meters, the structure incorporated advanced molecular materials combined with native stone, and it shone glossy black in the morning sunshine. It stood as a silent sentinel of tradition wedded to forward thinking—the hallmark of the Nova Cats.

The impressive genetic repository was surrounded by house-sized chapels, eleven in all. Built of limestone quarried from mountains on Irece's southern continent, their smooth, gleaming walls spoke of how recent was their construction.

Zane shook his head at the audacity of his Clan, for the chapels were replicas of the Bloodname Chapels on Strana Mechty, which surrounded the Hall of the Khans and were also constructed of limestone. Each was carved with ornate friezes depicting the exploits of the founder of each Bloodname and any notable descendants. The chapels were works of art in progress, with new friezes added whenever a worthy subject presented itself. Each chapel represented a Bloodname House and held the DNA of every member of that House, living or dead. Without exception, there was nothing more holy or sacred to all the Clans than those chapels.

That the Nova Cats had constructed new Bloodname Chapels for the eleven Nova Cat Bloodnames was an affront to all that the Clans held dear. Though Zane knew why it had been done, he was sure the consequences would be devastating if the other Clans should ever learn of it.

Beyond the repository stretched a majestic forest that had been allowed to run wild. It was home to a small population of nova cats brought all the way from Dagda in the Pentagon worlds. Zane had heard that they had adapted so well to Irece that most would be released from captivity within another two years. The rest would stay to maintain the sacredness of this site.

The crowd was becoming more agitated, and Zane turned back to the large field with its waist-high hedge that formed a perfect circle some two hundred meters across. This was the location of the Oathmaster Grand Melee, as well as any rites the Oathmaster deemed worthy.

Jostled from behind, Zane turned to look, and instantly all thoughts of the past, this park, and the momentous events about to occur were swept from his mind.

"*Sumimasen*, MechWarrior Zane," *Chu-sa* Yoshio said. "There are so many people here." His heavy accent attracted even more attention than his DCMS uniform. Immediately, Yoshio had ample room to move, as Nova Cat warriors drew away from him.

Zane felt the same rage that always started his blood thrumming. He had known for the last twenty-four hours that Khan West had granted Yoshio permission to attend this ceremony in order to further educate himself on the ways of the Nova Cats, but he had done everything in his power to avoid the Combine officer.

When Zane arrived at the Yamarovka spaceport on his way to Irece, he had found Yoshio waiting for him with signed permission from Galaxy Commander Higall to accompany Zane to Irece. His position as liaison had apparently gained him entry to Nova Cat rituals that he would otherwise never have been able to attend. The journey had required the JumpShip to use its lithium-fusion battery to make a double jump through an uncharted system, where another JumpShip waited to take them on the final jump to Irece. Zane had done his best to avoid Yoshio during the two-week trip but didn't always succeed.

"You are angry, this I can see. Please, forgive this interruption," Yoshio said again, bowing low in apology. "If you wish me to leave, I will not be offended. However, as you are the only one I know on this entire planet, I would very much like to stay at your side. After all, I am very interested in your traditions, and your explanations would help my understanding immeasurably."

Zane closed his eyes, blotting out the sight of the Combine officer and gaining control of his anger. Aware that he would gain nothing by challenging Yoshio to a Trial of Grievance for trespassing on Nova Cat rites, he calmed himself enough to open his eyes again.

"I know that you have read everything available to you on Irece about our traditions. I doubt you need any questions answered by me." Then, affecting nonchalance, he added, "Perhaps it is that you have heard rumors about today."

Yoshio seemed to consider for a moment. "Yes, I have. From what I understand, this is to be a special Oathmaster Grand Melee. Biccon Winters, I believe, has retired from the post—something that has never occurred in Nova Cat history. *Hontoo desu ka?*"

"Yes, that is correct. However, there are rumors that something else more significant might also occur on this day. Tell me, have you ever seen a noble of your House?"

A slow blink was the only sign that Yoshio had heard Zane at all.

Zane wondered if all Kuritans were so withdrawn. Questioning Yoshio always seemed like talking to a wall.

"No, it has not been my pleasure to speak with someone of such high birth."

Zane could tell that Yoshio had chosen his words carefully. "See" and "speak with" were two very different things.

"Why would you ask such a thing?" Yoshio asked bluntly.

"You seem to have such curiosity about our Clan that I thought I would indulge a small bit of my own. After all, we do share worlds now, quiaff?"

Before more words were exchanged, the soft hubbub of the crowd suddenly became a loud murmuring, and shouts rang out from those warriors lining the pathway through the throng to the Circle of Equals.

Both men turned their attention to the cause of the commotion and began to push their way through the crowd. Zane would never had made it through the tightly packed throng, but many warriors moved aside at the sound of a Combine officer's voice begging the pardon of everyone in his way.

When he reached the front of the crowd, Zane saw a troop of people making their way toward the Circle of Equals. They were mostly warriors, some of them obviously freebirths, bracketed on both sides by a crowd of ceremonially clad warriors who had begun to jeer and taunt. Zane scanned to find the source of the agitation and caught Yoshio with the closest he'd ever seen to an expression on his face. He followed Yoshio's gaze, then saw it. The ultimate death of his Clan. The beginning of the end of everything he believed in. An avatar of doom moving confidently toward a destiny Zane had no power to change.

Striding alone, for none of the other warriors would have anything to do with him, walked a lithe Asian man of thirty-odd years. Clad in the ceremonial leathers of the Nova Cats, wearing a bandanna that displayed the red dragon of his origins, Minoru Nova Cat, youngest son of the Coordinator of the Draconis Combine, strode toward the Oathmaster Grand Melee, with the obvious intent of competing to become Oathmaster of Clan Nova Cat.

11

Ways of Seeing Park
New Barcella, Irece
Irece Prefecture, Draconis Combine
21 August 3062

A slight breeze ruffled the trees as the lone Elemental strode from the Circle of Equals, having vanquished his final opponent and won the first stage of the Oathmaster Grand Melee. Such a feat was praiseworthy—enough to earn him a line or two in the Nova Cat Remembrance—and those present should have watched with pride as a warrior of such skill walked past. Instead, all eyes were locked onto the Elemental's final opponent, Minoru Nova Cat, just getting to his feet. If the Elemental failed the Forum of Law, the battered but still conscious Minoru, newly adopted as a Clan warrior, would be next in line to attempt it. Beyond Minoru lay the other defeated warriors, most of them still unconscious.

The crowd was utterly silent, the only sound the heavy breathing of the two bloodied warriors.

Disgusted by the spectacle, Zane had only one thought—to get away from here as fast as his feet would take him. He did not care that Minoru had proved himself a superb warrior in the Oathmaster Grand Melee. All Zane saw was a filthy spheroid freebirth who was now a giant step closer to becoming his Oathmaster.

Minoru had dominated everyone but the last Elemental, at times fighting off numerous attackers simultaneously with a speed and force that seemed beyond human. All Clan warriors trained in the martial arts, but Zane had never seen the flying kicks, devastating strikes, and exploding blocks executed in such a manner. He could not help a grudging respect, but it was quickly subsumed by his outrage.

Only Clan Wolf had ever allowed an Inner Sphere warrior to attain high rank—and look what had happened to them. They had taken Phelan Kell bondsman early in the invasion, later permitting him to become a warrior and even saKhan of the Clan. Not long after, the Wolves split from within, one side going off to join the Inner Sphere while the other was forced to ally with hated enemies to survive.

It enraged Zane that the Nova Cats seemed to be traveling the same road. As he pushed his way through the crowd, he saw others who looked equally angry, but many more did not. Hundreds had attended today, and yet so few had lifted their voices in protest. How could his Clan kin be so blind?

Zane headed toward a gate in the wall that surrounded Ways of Seeing Park. All he wanted was to escape this travesty of Clan tradition. Several minutes later, he had left the park behind and reached the tarmac of Rosse Spaceport.

Zane knew one thing at this moment. If he thought the Oathmaster waiting to help interpret his Rite of Vision at the end would be Minoru, he would never have the heart to undertake it. He had to go now or never go at all. And he needed a vision. With everything that had once defined the Nova Cats collapsing around him, Zane believed that only a vision would fortify him enough to go on. Without inner guidance, he too might stray from the path.

He would catch a ride back to Alpha Galaxy's headquarters, where his gear was stowed, and then be off. The most important thing right now was to prepare himself mentally and spiritually for the ordeal to come.

Exhausted beyond all reason, his muscles cramping uncontrollably, Zane clung to the mountainside, his right foot balanced precariously on a miniscule outcropping. The cold wind howled and bit the skin of his face raw as he shifted slightly, trying to relieve the pressure on his foot. He rested his head against the rock face and felt his mind begin to drift again—a sure sign that fifty-six straight hours without sleep was affecting him. Just as he had done so many times over the last four hours, Zane looked down, knowing that the sight would shoot enough adrenaline through his body to clear his mind.

Dropping away was nearly a kilometer of rock, a sheer fall as smooth as the surface of a reflecting pond. And further down, below that glassy surface, the mountain plunged at another eighty-degree incline, with shattered rocks and ancient gullies waiting at the bottom.

From his current height, Zane had an unparalleled view of the world below him. No clouds obstructed the vista of the mountainside, the foothills, and the endless series of rolling hills he had crossed two days ago; he could see even as far as New Barcella and the Rosse Spaceport more than a hundred kilometers in the distance.

After hastily gathering his gear and leaving word of his departure, it had taken him almost two full days to travel to the base of the mountain known to the locals as Tengoku. Zane had heard that the word meant heaven, and he could understand why. Its peak rose a mind-numbing 9.7 kilometers into the sky, breaking into the stratosphere. Though he had only conquered a small portion of its dizzying height, he was proud of the accomplishment. That is, if he made it the rest of the way. He looked up, gauging that he had only a few meters to go until he reached the slim plateau of this particular face.

He had been climbing Tengoku for two solid days, stopping to rest—but not to sleep—only a few hours each night. He was fasting, too, though halfway into the climb he realized he had to drink fluids or he would never make it. Dying was not part of the plan.

He studied the rock face, searching out the best

place to secure the next section of his safety line. With one hand he positioned a piton through the hole in a bolt hanger. With the other hand he used his piston drill to hammer in the piton. Zane had not used the power tool at first, preferring the solid feel of a rock hammer driving the shank bolt into the rock. He waited until it was absolutely necessary, which was about halfway into his climb.

He reattached the tool to a loop in his climbing harness, then fumbled for another loop, which held the carabiners. He pulled the oblong piece of metal free and pushed his rope through the breakaway lever built into one side of it. He snapped it into the bolt hanger and screwed shut the locking mechanism that would hold the lever. Several strong, quick tugs assured him that the safety line was securely in place.

Equipment failure was not a concern. Only misjudgment about where he drove his pitons into the rock could lead to catastrophe. The carabiners and bolt hangers were forged of endo-aluminum, the same material used to construct the frames of Clan OmniFighters. Extremely light and designed to withstand the force of several gees on an aerospace fighter in the depths of space, Zane was confident they could sustain his light weight. Using such expensive material for his equipment would have been anathema to most Clansmen, a waste of precious resources. However, Zane had known for years that he would turn to his love of mountain climbing when he finally sought his Rite of the Vision.

As for the rope, Zane had never heard of this type breaking because of strain. Though only a few millimeters thick, its core was composed of several thousand strands of ferro-aluminum wire, each less than a fraction of the width of a human hair. Around this was the mantle of myonylon, a polymer with microfilaments of myomer introduced into the nylon during the polymerization process. Clan Goliath Scorpion had originally developed the rope to tap the huge mineral resources of the formidable mountains of Dagda. Those expeditions had required material that was practically unbreakable, and the Scorpion scientist caste had delivered.

Having rested enough to get some control over his twitching muscles, Zane ignored the screaming wind that sought his death and began looking for the next handhold, then foothold, then handhold, and the next and the next. Like combat, rock climbing required continually thinking a step ahead even as he focused intensely on the present. What appeared to be a good series of handholds could lead to a deadend a short time later, or a stretch that could be ascended, but could not be descended, trapping the climber.

Zane concentrated on releasing his exhaustion through deep breathing and soon lost himself in the sheer exhilaration of the climb, becoming one with his body. An hour later he pulled himself past the lip of the precipice and onto the plateau he had located on satellite-imaging maps. Several hundred meters to a side, the ground sloped gently upward before meeting the steep incline that led the rest of the way up the mountain as it stabbed into the sky. Local scrub trees dotted the landscape, enough to provide wood for the fire he needed to build against the rapidly approaching night. He was also pleased to see some growth on the far side of the plateau, signaling the presence of a spring.

Zane turned back toward the cliff edge and lifted his arms to the sky. He breathed deeply, the sense of accomplishment almost as sweet as the one he got while piloting a 'Mech. The euphoria made him feel like falling to his knees, and he felt tears well up. This had been the greatest climb of his life, one that had purified and readied him to receive a vision that would guide him into the future. The exhilaration was so heady that he kept back from the cliff edge to keep from getting dizzy. The irony of coming so far only to pass out at the top and tumble down the mountainside made Zane laugh softly. Still smiling, he turned and approached the spring.

He bathed in the freezing water, trying not to rush. When he was done, he went back to his satchel bags. With slow, deliberate movements, he took out each piece of his ceremonial clothing. With the same solemnity, he dressed himself, using the familiar actions to open his mind even further. He began reciting his favorite passages of the Remembrance as he walked over to the pile of deadwood he had gathered. Though he had several modern ways to ignite the wood, this, his first Rite of the Vision, called to him for a more primitive approach. He crouched down where he had set out several implements he had fashioned himself.

Kneeling on one leg, he flattened a large branch, then dug a small depression into the wood, leaving the wood shavings in the depression. He set the branch down and picked up a long, straight stick he had sharpened on one end. In his other hand, he held a bow fashioned from a live bough he had cut from a tree and a piece of wire from his pack—his only use of modern materials. Looping the wire around the stick, he placed the point into the depression of the first branch, then laid another piece of wood he'd cut on top of the other end. Pushing down with his weight on the top piece, he moved the bow quickly, which spun the stick in place. In less than a minute, the friction heated the moving stick enough to ignite the wood chips. Zane blew softly on the chips, shielding them from the wind and fanning the fledgling flames. Then he carefully pushed the bottom branch under the pile of wood and continued to softly blow. Minutes later, a bonfire was snapping and crackling with evaporating sap, sending sparks soaring toward the black sky.

He placed a leather mat near the bonfire and kneeled on it as he removed the vineers from his pack. How many times had he imagined this moment? How many times had he wondered what might occur? Already, the experience was beyond his greatest expectations.

Chanting passages from the Remembrance, he stared into the flames, letting the heat wash over him, leeching out the last of his cold. Then he let his focus go soft so his eyes could see what they would. The wind whipped at the fire. The spiraling smoke whirled out in every direction, stinging his eyes and sending tears down his cheeks. But he would not close his eyes.

Minutes passed, the only sounds coming from the crackling fire and the whipping wind. Without conscious thought, Zane picked up the piece of metal he had claimed from Yoshio's *Bishamon*. He held it in his hand, letting it carry him back to those exhilarating moments when he had outmaneuvered and out-shot the man he thought of as a bitter enemy. He held the vineer over the fire, all the way to the edge of the flames, then let it drop onto the coals that had begun to form. It burned his hand, perhaps seriously, but Zane barely noticed. He was far removed from such physical sensations.

Time passed. Whether they were minutes or hours Zane could never say. He was now holding another vineer, a shoulder patch bearing the yellow and red sunburst insignia of a Nova Cat Galaxy Commander. Zane had taken it from the uniform of Tol Lossey, commander of Rho Galaxy, after watching him die on Bearclaw. Vowing that such a thing would never occur again, Zane had kept the patch as a vineer. Once more, he extended his hand into the flames and dropped the patch on top of the armor plate.

Unlike the armor plate, which had yet to react to the heat, the patch immediately burst into flames. Zane did not feel the skin along his palm begin to blister or the hair flash-flame off his hand and lower arm.

Chanting softly, he spoke some lines by Sandra Rosse from the *Ways of Seeing*:

> *Flames grant sight*
> *To eyes wide shut*
> *Visions unfold*
> *Purified in soul*

As he sang softly to himself, an image began to

form in the leaping flames. He did not force the shape, which might have driven it away. He simply waited, open to what would come. Writhing in the heat eddies, a garnet dragon gradually appeared in the blaze. Beyond it, Zane could make out what looked like a nova cat.

For several seconds, nothing changed. Then another dragon formed, identical to the first except that it was ebony. The garnet dragon began to shift from side to side in the blaze, as though aware of the ebony's existence but unable to locate it. For several more long seconds, the ebony dragon did not move. Then, with terrifying speed, it launched itself. But not at the garnet dragon! Instead, it leaped out of Zane's field of vision. An instant later a blurred white shape bearing a standard with the emblem of a canine head came hurtling back into the fire, seizing both the garnet dragon and the nova cat. Blood exploded everywhere.

The vision broke in an explosion of sparks as the deadwood in the fire settled. Zane lurched forward and fell on his hands as physical sensations returned in a torrent: hunger, sleep deprivation, exhaustion, the pain of his burned hand. He gasped for breath, suddenly aware that he had not breathed for the last dozen seconds. Cutting through it all was the question, *What was that?* It was not what he had expected at all. Had that been a wolf's head on the banner? What did the Wolves have to do with anything?

He heard the soft sound of footsteps behind him, and was angry that someone was about intrude on the most sacred moment of his life.

Then he realized he had heard the thump-thump

of a VTOL's whirling blades some time earlier, but it did not register in his conscious mind until now. Zane prepared himself for another vision, one he did not want to see. He slowly raised his head.

Standing on the other side of the bonfire, sheathed in leathers and wearing the sacred mask whose lacquered finish portrayed the head of a nova cat roaring in defiance was Minoru.

During the long climb up the mountain, Zane had known he must be ready for this to happen, but did not let himself think about it. He was aware that the Oathmaster would seek him out to assist in interpreting any vision that came and that the new Oathmaster might not be a true Nova Cat. Zane had seen Minoru prove himself a warrior, and he was sure Biccon Winters would never support someone who had not mastered Nova Cat lore and traditions. Still, in his weakened state, the sight of Minoru wearing the ceremonial mask brought tears to Zane's eyes.

He quickly lowered his head, not wishing to show his weakness to an enemy.

"You have been given a vision," Minoru said. Zane was surprised that his soft voice carried only the hint of an accent. Probably just another filthy trick to disguise himself as he furthered his father's ambitions.

Zane would not remain on his knees in front of him. He overcame the numbness of his legs and stood up, his back to the fire. He started to speak but choked. He tried again, squeezing out a "perhaps." Zane would not violate the sanctity of this place by being actively hostile, but that did not mean he had to reveal anything.

"You have seen a vision," Minoru repeated.

"Many warriors attempt a vision of the future. A vision that will purify them and give them knowledge to aid the Clan. But very few attain a true vision."

Minoru moved slowly around the fire, the fluidity of his form and the dancing shadows transforming him from a man into the avatar of the nova cat made flesh. A part of Zane wanted to retreat from the force of Minoru's gaze, but he would not.

"I can see it in you . . . feel it around you. You have been touched—as has Khan West, Biccon Winter, others . . . myself." The last was spoken in a whisper almost lost to the sound of the crackling fire.

"You despise me, Warrior Zane, as do many others of this Clan. It is plain for all to see, though you do well in trying to mask it. My words will mean nothing to you, yet I speak them now, in this place, in the hope that you might one day confirm their truth.

"I am not who I once was. Though I was born to the Kurita clan of the Draconis Combine and followed all its traditional paths, I have passed from that life and become a warrior of Clan Nova Cat. The path I now seek is wide enough for both the Nova Cats and the Combine to walk abreast in a universe of turmoil, where every hand is raised in menace. There can be brotherhood in unexpected places. You have seen a vision, but I do not ask that you recount it to me."

Minoru came face to face with Zane. Backlit by the flames, his face hidden, he became the shadowy outline of a Nova Cat warrior.

"Ponder the vision you have witnessed," Minoru said. "Seek its meaning, and know that I, warden of this Rite and keeper of the Clan rede, will aid you if you but ask."

Zane turned away, his hands beginning to shake from the entire experience. He began to run toward the waiting VTOL, but Minoru's words followed him.

"Ponder my words and as the future unfolds," Minoru said, "ask if they are not true."

12

Tai-shu Toshimichi Uchida, Warlord of the Alshain Military District in absentia, opened the door to his private office and froze at the sight of the tall, white-haired man seated there. The shock was followed by a flash of hatred he could not conceal. Quickly composing himself, Uchida closed the door behind him and entered the room.

His visitor showed no sign that he had noticed Uchida's lapse. He merely continued looking around the room, nodding his appreciation for the numerous paintings, all of them war scenes executed in the traditional Japanese style.

"You have such a serene office, *Tai-shu*. Not what

I would have expected of you," the white-haired man said quietly, absently pulling at his beard.

"Why not?" Uchida said, taking a seat. This was his office and his desk, and from this place, he was master of everything around him. The unexpected appearance of the old man was unnerving enough that Uchida needed the strength of his office to face him at this moment.

"Again, I see that we have dispensed with the traditional polite conversation," the man said.

"Polite conversation is for those who wish to be polite with one another, regardless of their personal feelings. We have neither the need nor the desire. Therefore, we can leave such traditions at the door."

Laughing softly, the white-haired man leaned back in his chair. "Ah, such honesty is refreshing, Ushida-*san*. I am as fiercely proud of my ancestry as any, but I find forced prattle annoying. Perhaps it is that I grow old and no longer have time for matters of no importance. What say you?"

"*Hai.*"

"Ah, direct and short. You have brightened my entire day, and I have spoken to you for less than a minute. Perhaps I should come see you more often." The implied threat was not hidden by the sham civility.

"You should not be here now, old man," Uchida snapped, again failing to conceal his anger. He took a deep breath, calming himself. His position was higher than his visitor's, but the old man could still make his life difficult if he so chose. And who knew how many contacts the man had among other dukes of the districts? The thought was instantly sobering.

"Ah, such hostility toward an old man. What has happened to the younger generation?"

"Our generation, old man, was led astray by yours," Uchida said. "How can we be anything other than what you made us?"

"Such wisdom—it does you credit," came the slightly mocking response.

"Why are you here, old man? Our last meeting was dangerous enough. Why risk one here?" Uchida, as always, tired quickly of the word games. They hated each other, so why should they conceal it? Of course, they could not speak too plainly—the walls always had ears.

The old man made a languid gesture with one hand. "I was merely passing through this system and decided to visit an old friend to catch up on old times. Have you heard that my . . . investments have proven to be more than worth the expenditures?"

The old man could not help a note of pride, and Uchida hated him all the more for it. "There is no way any DCMS officer, much less a *Tai-shu*, could not have heard about the attack on the Lyons Thumb. By now, the entire area has been annexed by the Draconis Combine. You did not simply 'pass through' to ask me that, however."

"Most perceptive, Uchida-*san*. You prove more and more why our beloved Coordinator made you War-lord of the Alshain Military District—*in absentia*."

The sarcastic tone made Uchida see red, but he would not lose face in front of this ancient figure again.

"Do you have songbirds on this planet?"

Uchida understood the question—was this room "clean" of eavesdropping devices?

"*Hai,* of course we do. Does not every world have songbirds? But I have tried to keep them away from the command compound, as they are noisy and tend to pollute the area. I have not seen any excrement in months."

The old man nodded. "I have heard that the unseen regiments are being redeployed." This change of subject came without any change in his tone.

Uchida sat back, slightly shocked. The old man's sources had always been accurate, though sorely tested to prove their worth. He did not doubt the accuracy of their information, but was only surprised he had not already heard it himself. "They are on the move—away from the Ghost Bear Dominion border?"

"*Hai.* My sources could not provide me with their destination, though I have my guesses. This will make our plans all the easier, and we should move up the timetable."

Uchida kept his face impassive, though he could hardly believe his ears. "You want to change the timetable? Why?"

"Because we have had success," the old man said forcefully, suddenly leaning forward. The easy manner had evaporated, and the energy of a young man now shone through his clear eyes as he gazed directly at Uchida.

"We have a success perhaps greater than any in the Society's history, and that creates a momentum we should not squander. With the unseen units on the move, it will help shield the secret movements of our own forces. And the Eleventh Alshain Avengers fighting wargames against the damnable Nova Cats on Irece will actually be in the best position to move when the time comes, and I am sure they will not let us down."

"I know that," Uchida snapped, irritated that the old man would even hint at the possibility that one of his units would not instantly obey his command. He had spent the last few years working with his regiments. They would never let him down.

"The timetable only needs to move up by five months. The necessary logistics are already in place, as our contingency plan called for our troops to be ready to move any time during the past six months. In fact, it would not be so difficult to request a redeployment of the Eighth to Kiamba, which is only garrisoned by planetary militia. Perhaps the other Alshain units can also redeploy under the guise of reinforcing the border now that the Ghost Regiments are gone."

Uchida looked away from the old man, his gaze wandering to the holos of himself and the command staffs of his four Alshain regiments that hung on one wall. Though not a sentimental man, he could not help the pride he felt in those warriors, whose devotion to protecting the Combine was unwavering. A devotion too many others had forgotten, he thought angrily.

"*Hai*, I concur. We should use the momentum you have created to bolster the morale of our troops. I will send out the necessary commands in the next week. Though no songbirds are in the immediate vicinity, such large-scale use of the hyperpulse generator could raise suspicions. Regardless, Operation Batsu will commence in seventy days."

Uchida was surprised and strangely moved when the old man stood slowly and bowed formally to him.

"*Doomo arigatoo gozaimasu,*" the old man said.

Though Uchida still hated the man, to have the Red Hunter show him such respect made him rise and return the gesture in kind.

"*Doo itashimashite,*" he said. *You are most welcome, Duke Hassid Alexander Ricol.*

$\equiv$ 13 $\equiv$

JumpShip **Far Star**
Nadir Jump Point, Caripare
Irece Prefecture, Draconis Combine
1 September 3062

"If Minoru won the title honestly, should it matter that he was not born to the Clans?" Yoshio asked for what seemed the hundredth time.

"Of course it should," Zane said in exasperation. "Why can you not see what is before your eyes? Perhaps because you take pleasure in knowing that your prince is now the Oathmaster of the Nova Cats, practically giving your Coordinator control of our Clan." He could not help the anger in his voice. Why was he speaking with Yoshio at all?

Turning away, Zane moved toward the viewport of the ship's officers' lounge. He stepped carefully to keep from dislodging his magnetic boots, which would set him afloat in the micro-gravity of the *Mystic Spheres*. At the moment, the DropShip was docked to *Far Star*, a *Star Lord* Class JumpShip, which was recharging its jump drive at the nadir point of the Caripare system. By his own calculations, the klaxon warning of imminent jump would be sounding in minutes.

Zane gazed out into the brilliance of space. He appreciated the unimaginable distances involved in what he saw, suspended as the ships were above the elliptical plane of this entire solar system. He needed a respite from this wearisome conversation with Yoshio. It had been hard for him to think about anything except his Rite of the Vision, now a week past.

"I do not believe that is a fair estimate of what I feel," Yoshio said after several minutes of silence. "You have no real way of knowing my personal sentiments about that situation."

"That is true," Zane said, turning back toward Yoshio. "I do not really know. I simply assumed that any Spheroid, especially one of the same Clan, or House as Minoru, would be ecstatic that the Coordinator's son has reached such high position within the Nova Cats. One more yoke to control a barbarian Clan."

"You are observant enough of us Spheroids"—Yoshio seemed to find humor in the term—"to know that what you say is true. Most of the Combine, most of the Inner Sphere, sees Minoru's rise as a glorious event, placing another brake on a Clan, even if that Clan has espoused the Star League and actually fought with us against the other Clans. Most will see it as similar to what occurred with Phelan and the Clan of Wolf."

Zane nodded, surprised to hear Yoshio express almost exactly his own thought from the day of the Oathmaster Grand Melee.

"There is always a price to pay for such . . . protection," Yoshio went on. "What has the Combine had to do to achieve such 'success'?"

The slightest shift in Yoshio's tone caught Zane's attention. He did not understand it, but saw that a strange look had come over the other man's face.

"I do not know where this conversation is going, Yoshio. We Nova Cats appreciate plain words, even if that is not the Kurita custom. Just as I have observed your people, you have observed mine enough to understand that."

"I apologize if I have offended you," Yoshio said with one of those polite bows Zane found so irritating. He'd asked him at least a dozen times not to do it, but the gesture was so habitual as to seem almost automatic.

"What I meant is that in safeguarding the Combine, in tying the Nova Cats to us, we have tied ourselves to the Nova Cats. Minoru Kurita is no more, and in his place stands Minoru Nova Cat. I was granted permission to attend the Forum of Law after you left Yamarovka, and I witnessed his recitations and commentaries. It was clear to me that he is no longer the son of our Coordinator. The Combine has won the aid of the Nova Cats, but in doing so we have allowed the offspring of the Dragon himself to be perverted beyond recognition. How can I be happy about such as that?" The sorrow in his eyes was evident.

Zane stared at Yoshio in astonishment. The words were different, but once again the sentiments were the mirror image of his own. Like Zane, Yoshio was witnessing the desecration of all he knew. The two of them walked in each other's shoes, railing against the same fate, if not the exact circumstances. The thought was unsettling. He realized that at this moment, floating in space some ninety million kilometers above a burning ball of gas, he actually felt empathy for the man he had considered an enemy for long weeks.

"I must apologize then, too," Zane said, hardly believing he was saying it. "Perhaps we are more alike than I could ever have imagined. I have fought since the Great Refusal to see our Clan preserved, untainted by the Inner Sphere. What use is a path of survival if we corrupt ourselves in taking it? Though the Smoke Jaguars were fools, they understood that maintaining purity, even if it meant their own destruction, was preferable to the alternative."

He and Yoshio stood staring at one another as the silence drew out between them.

The vision Zane had seen on the mountain floated through his mind. Garnet Dragon, Ebony Dragon, nova cat, white blur, dog's head. Zane knew that the Garnet Dragon must be an image of the Draconis Combine and that the nova cat, of course, represented his Clan. Though he was not sure, the white blur might refer to ComStar, the semi-religious order that handled interstellar communications. During the Clan invasion, Oathmaster Biccon Winters had had a vision in which ComStar was represented by a trail of white. It was possible the organization was involved in some treachery against the Combine, but that did not seem likely with Victor Davion commander of the ComStar military. The former Prince of the Federated Commonwealth had drawn too close to the ruling Kuritas. As for the Ebony Dragon, Zane had no idea who or what it might represent. Worse, he sensed that even if he did know, he still might not understand the vision.

The words tumbled out. "Yoshio, what is an Ebony Dragon?"

Yoshio paled visibly, a severe breach of his usual façade.

"What did you say?" Yoshio asked in a strange voice.

"What is an Ebony Dragon?" Zane repeated, wondering why Yoshio seemed so stunned by the question. He knew that the people of the Combine seemed to worship dragons.

Yoshio had regained his unreadable expression, but Zane knew him enough by now to see the confusion in his eyes.

"I do not understand what you are asking," Yoshio said.

"It is nothing. Simply a phrase I heard once on Irece, and I thought you might know its meaning. After all, the Dragon is sacred to your people, quiaff?"

"*Hai*, Zane, we do honor the Dragon. The Coordinator himself is the Dragon of the Kurita Clan and the whole Draconis Combine. Yet I must admit that I have never heard the term Ebony Dragon."

Zane was not sure what it was made him think that Yoshio was hedging, telling the truth and a lie at the same time.

"Jump commencing in five minutes," came the loud mechanical voice from the speaker mounted in the bulkhead, startling both men.

"Perhaps we should retire to our quarters for the jump," Yoshio said, inclining his head toward the hatch.

Zane nodded. He knew Yoshio was covering something, but was not sure what or why. Besides, he also felt better lying down during the transition through hyperspace. Some people were not affected by the experience, but Zane was not one of them. "Perhaps you will remember something along the rest of our journey," he said.

The minute hunching of Yoshio's shoulders seemed to say he would not. But if the man was telling the truth, why did he react so strongly to the whole issue? It was just one more question to add to the long list that had been generated by Zane's trip to Irece.

Lost in thought, Zane took the corridor that led to his quarters, still pondering this strange conversation with Yoshio.

14

Plain of Horses
New Circe, Yamarovka
Irece Prefecture, Draconis Combine
14 September 3062

Zane used his left hand to move the throttle forward, cranking up the speed on his 'Mech while he peered at his secondary screens, trying to locate his elusive enemy. Moving forward with long strides, his *Jenner* 2 sped across the seemingly peaceful prairie. He knew that was an illusion, however. They had fought here before, and he knew that this prairie was anything but flat. Gently rolling hills created troughs easily large enough to hide a crouching BattleMech, so he had to be careful. Cycling through his *Jenner*'s sensors produced nothing suspicious. His 'Mech appeared to be the only moving object for a klick in any direction. That had him worried. Very worried.

Upon returning to Yamarovka several days before, Zane was astonished to find the entire Eleventh Alshain Avengers regiment on planet. Apparently, the war games were deemed so successful that the process was being accelerated. Now the First Dragoncat Cluster was to fight a mock battle against the Avengers' First and Second Battalions. Perhaps even more disturbing was that a Second Dragoncat Cluster was being formed.

Zane still resented having to participate in these exercises against Kuritans, especially the Alshain Avengers. He had only recently come to terms with the necessity of dealing with *Chu-sa* Yoshio and the Avengers' Third Battalion. It galled him, but Zane reminded himself that this was a long-distance race. It could take years for him to advance to a position where he could truly influence the path of the Nova Cats. And until then, he could not afford to waste his energy hating the Spheroids every day.

But sometimes his anger leapt up unexpectedly. Today it might even have gotten the better of him except for the joy of piloting the *Jenner* for the first time in many weeks. He reveled in the feel of the machine under him. So much power at his command!

Even better, the Nova Cats would not be constrained by the need to use sophisticated computers and bulky 'Mech harnesses to simulate battle damage, as in previous engagements. This was live fire. That was always standard in Clan training, but till now the Dragoncats had been compelled to abide by Inner Sphere methods. Zane felt the adrenaline surge through his veins at the thought of confronting Inner Sphere 'Mechs with the full might of his weapons.

Under Star Commander Samuel, Bravo and Charlie Striker Stars of Zane's Binary were pursuing the Avengers Third Company, Second Battalion. They had managed to elude him so far, which had Zane worried. The Binary could not afford to disgrace the Nova Cats by losing the Cluster's first fight against the Second Battalion. Not with the entire Eleventh Alshain regiment on planet, watching. Anything but that. Besides, if he ever hoped to rise in rank, it was imperative he make a good showing anytime he was inside his 'Mech.

Using his right-hand joystick, Zane rotated the *Jenner*'s torso from side to side, trying to visually spot what his sensors denied. He knew the enemy was out there.

"Star One, Point Five, have you located the enemy?" Samuel's voice crackled over Zane's earpiece. Star One referred to his five 'Mechs, the first of two Stars in the Binary. Point Five referred to his position as the fifth 'Mech in Star One.

"Negative, Point One. I have no readings of any kind and no signs in the terrain that they have passed this way."

"Copy, Star One. Points Three and Four are on an approach to pass your position in another three minutes at your current speed. You have ranged far from our line. Do not proceed alone. Join your Starmates, so you will have sufficient firepower should the enemy surprise you. Quiaff?"

"Aff," Zane replied, confirming his commander's orders with the traditional response.

The minutes passed uneventfully, and soon he saw the two Nova Cat 'Mechs approaching his location.

From his left came Killian in his four-legged *Snow Fox*. It was lightly armed but lightning-fast even compared to the *Jenner*'s considerable speed. Despite that, Zane was not sure he could bring himself to pilot such a 'Mech. Walking on four legs?

Swiveling the *Jenner* to the right, he spotted Geoff and his *Arctic Wolf*, a new model 'Mech. With its back-canted legs, hunched shoulders, and head set deep into its torso, it was a strange-looking machine. The 'Mech bristled with over forty short-range missile ports, however, and was deadly in combat.

Zane had been shocked when he first learned of the presence of the *Arctic Wolf* in the Touman, for it was a design manufactured by Clan Wolf in Exile. How could the Nova Cats have any dealings with those vile outcasts? Now, only weeks after Geoff was assigned the 'Mech, Zane had actually gotten used to seeing it. In a world that produced astonishing things and events at every turn, the sight of the *Arctic Wolf* in the Nova Cat Touman simply did not register on his consciousness anymore.

"Point Five, I have visual contact," Geoff said. He leveled out of his trajectory and began loping along the same route as Zane, some fifty meters to the right.

"I also have visual contact, Point Five." That was Killian, always gruff and no-nonsense. Glancing at his monitor, Zane saw her *Snow Fox* some seventy meters to his left. Considering the relative speeds of the three 'Mechs, he knew their positions were good.

Zane opened the commline to Samuel. "Point One, I have visuals on Points Three and Four. We are now approximately two-point-three kilometers northeast of your position. We will begin a sweep in front of your current trajectory and report in two-zero minutes."

"Aff," said Samuel.

Moving faster now, the three 'Mechs began to race at the maximum speed of their slowest unit, the *Arctic Wolf*, quickly covering ground at almost one hundred-twenty kilometers per hour. Slowly swinging right, they began to climb a steep incline.

Zane was momentarily startled to see the *Arctic Wolf* wreathed in the cobalt energy of PPC fire. He almost lost his 'Mech's footing—a disastrous occurrence at such speeds. Cutting in his jump jets, he launched the *Jenner* skyward to find the source of the enemy fire.

The *Jenner* lifted high enough to give Zane a clear view of the enemy company hiding behind the hilltop. He quickly checked his secondary screens but detected no heat emanating from their 'Mechs. They had probably shut down to low power, their reactors running at the bare minimum. Knowing that the hills blocked line of sight, the Avengers had counted on the Clan scout 'Mechs becoming impatient enough to run headlong into a carefully laid trap. The four enemy 'Mechs had semi-buried themselves into the top of the hill, masked from view by the incline until it was too late.

Zane quickly called to Samuel. "Point One, we have contact with the enemy. I repeat, we have contact with the enemy at Grid A-one-point-four." He continued to maneuver the *Jenner* as he spoke, taking it into a trajectory that would put him where the enemy 'Mechs could not automatically fire on his position. Even as he did, Zane watched in horror as another volley of light smashed into the already savaged *Arctic Wolf*. This was followed by the whip of PPC fire, the strobing emerald darts of pulse lasers, and the ruby light of a large laser.

For a forty-ton 'Mech, the *Arctic Wolf* had great speed and massive firepower, but at the cost of armor. It was already mortally damaged by the previous onslaught, and this barrage sliced through the armor with ease. The dying machine lurched heavily to the right, a sure sign that the gyro was either hit or even destroyed as explosions lit it from within. The damaged armor was useless against the 'Mech's own short-range missiles exploding in both the right and left torso. Though the Cellular Ammunition Storage Equipment was intended to save the pilot from just such a catastrophe, channeling the explosions out the back, it was too little too late. The *Arctic Wolf* literally disintegrated before Zane's eyes. Every Clan warrior wished for an honorable death in combat, but Zane hoped it would not be this make-believe battle that killed Geoff.

He throttled back on his jump jets and began dropping from the sky. Warning beacons lit up his console as the enemy 'Mechs came back up to full power. Though a quick look told Zane that none of them could match his or Killian's speed, he was realistic enough to know they were in trouble. Killian's *Arctic Wolf* had died before firing a single shot, leaving the two of them outnumbered five to one, and most of those five 'Mechs were undamaged and weighed considerably more.

"Point Three, what is your location?" Zane called over the commline. He had lost Killian in the maneuvers of the last few moments, both visually and on his secondary monitor.

No answer.

"Point Three, confirm your location," he repeated, though he suddenly knew there would be no response. How could this have happened so quickly? He slammed his fist into his console three times in rapid succession until his hand began to bleed.

Zane struggled to calm his fury, which would only work against him now. He opened the command channel again. "Point One, I have a confirmed visual destruction of Point Four and cannot locate Point Three. Considering the number of enemy units, I assume Point Three has also been destroyed. Should I pull back to rendezvous with your Star or attempt to harass the enemy?"

"Point Five, confirming your report of two possible losses of Star mates. Rendezvous as quickly as possible. We will need your strength here if we are to pull victory from this situation."

"Aff, Star Commander. Will proceed." With that, Zane concentrated on running down the trough between two hills. He would have like to trigger his jump jets to gain a visual of the enemy but could not risk it. The entire company of twelve BattleMechs was surely powered up by now and moving toward his last known position. Offering his 'Mech up on a platter did not seem advisable.

A *Hunchback* moved into view, breaking over the edge of the ridge almost a hundred meters to the front and slightly to the right of Zane's current position. At fifty tons, looking humanoid except for the blocky box on its right shoulder, the *Hunchback* was ill-equipped to fight a *Jenner*, whose speed would always keep it outside the range of the squat *Hunchback*'s weapons. Unfortunately, at that moment, the *Jenner* was already in range of the massive 120mm autocannon on the *Hunchback*'s right shoulder. Its maw spit out a stream of high-velocity, depleted-uranium rounds that chewed their way across the ground on a collision course that would tear one of Zane's legs completely off.

He engaged the *Jenner*'s MASC, the only move possible short of firing his jump jets. Myomer Accelerator Signal Circuitry was specialized equipment that boosted the signals to a 'Mech's myomer leg musculature, making it contract and relax at a quicker rate. It gave the *Jenner* a burst of speed that sent it careening forward so that the autocannon would miss. Boosting the signal like that was risky. It could just as easily cause a catastrophic failure that would freeze up the entire hip and leg assembly, rendering the *Jenner* as helpless as a newborn from the canister. But it didn't, and Zane breathed a sigh of relief.

He moved his torso to the right and jerked down on the trigger of the extended-range large laser. The beam stabbed high on the *Hunchback*'s left torso, gouging a long furrow through the armor. Though the enemy warrior was attempting to track right with its autocannon, the *Jenner* was simply moving away too quickly.

Checking in front of him, Zane could see the end of his current pathway as the hills on both sides began to fall away.

The *Jenner* suddenly lurched forward, as if struck by the hammer of a god. Only long experience allowed him to keep the 'Mech upright following the transfer of that much kinetic energy to his own machine. Alarms started to sound, and red indicators flashed across multiple sections of his status monitor, showing his right rear torso armor penetrated. That was bad; the ammo for his five-pack LRM was stored there. The damage had almost completely destroyed the internal structure of that location, leaving him dangerously close to losing his entire right side. Zane began trying to zigzag back and forth, knowing he could not yet risk engaging the MASC. A glance at the lower part of his viewscreen told what was behind him.

Three 'Mechs now stood on the ridgeline; the *Hunchback*, a *Grand Dragon*, and a *Banshee*. Zane was in serious trouble, as both the *Dragon* and the *Banshee* mounted PPCs that would hold him in range for at least another ten seconds. His only hope was to try and outrun them. He slammed down on the MASC stud just as the two enemy 'Mechs fired their PPCs, the man-made lightning snapping out toward Zane.

One shot hit while the other turned the prairie grass into so much ash, but one hit was more than enough. The PPC beam tore through the previous hole in the Jenner's right rear torso, destroying the last of it and beginning to eat through the rest of its back. Surprisingly, the unleashing of so much energy did not set off the missile ammo. But even as the MASC signal-boost shot to the *Jenner*'s leg musculature, its right torso and arm were sheared clean away from its body—almost a quarter of its weight. Experiencing a burst of speed at the exact moment his 'Mech began to twist to the left, Zane tried desperately to counterbalance the move. But the *Jenner's* fragile legs literally tore themselves away from the main body, and the 'Mech slammed face first into the dirt.

As the *Jenner* went down, Zane railed inwardly at losing yet again to warriors of the Inner Sphere, even if only in mock combat. He was thrown forward and his head slammed viciously against the console. His last thought before darkness swallowed him was that he would never let them defeat him again. Never again!

15

Caunta
New Circe, Yamarovka
Irece Prefecture, Draconis Combine
15 September 3062

Seated in the back corner of this drinking hole whose exterior sign identified it only as a "bar" in crimson Japanese *kanji* letters, *Chu-sa* Palmer Yoshio sipped calmly at his sake. His was the only singly occupied table in the place, illuminated only by the flashing lights of an antiquated jukebox. The other two rickety tables were crowded in front of him, almost blocking access to his table. The bar ran the length of the right wall and two billiard tables occupied the left. Seated at the lit bar were two other fugitives from this night. Both were already far gone in their drinking.

Yoshio wondered once again why his contact had

chosen this rat hole for a meeting. It went without saying that they required a discreet location, but a Combine officer showing up in a place like this would be impossible to miss. Even dressed in nondescript clothing, he felt conspicuous. If questioned, he could say that he was out slumming. Looking to get roaring drunk. He only wished he *could* get drunk! Tonight's meeting, combined with what had happened earlier today, made him wish he could follow the bar's other two patrons into oblivion.

That morning he had merely inquire how Zane had fared after the destruction of his *Jenner* in yesterday's live-fire exercise. The warrior had lashed out with a fury that was becoming legendary among the Combine warriors. Could Zane not see that he poisoned Yoshio's men against him with such actions? Then again, maybe that was precisely Zane's intention. Yoshio had come to know many things about the young warrior in the weeks since they had met. One of them was that he nursed a pure hatred for the Inner Sphere and what he considered the corruption of his Clan in becoming part of it.

Taking another sip, Yoshio could not help a half-smile. He and Zane were much alike, despite their circumstances. Zane knew it, too, and it bothered him. It was ironic that both of them were driven by the same shame; Yoshio believed that the Combine had been sullied too. The Coordinator had sold his own son into bondage to gain maneuvering room. To have given him up for such a small price was monstrous.

As he set the small porcelain cup on the table, another similarity occurred to him. Zane had declared that he would personally try to redirect the course of his Clan back to their traditional ways. Just as Yoshio, a member of the Black Dragons, had vowed to do for the Combine. He felt a tug of empathy for Zane.

He looked up as the door opened, letting in a rush of cold air as two men entered. Both were pure Japanese and dressed in civilian clothes. They quickly scanned the bartender and patrons, evaluating their threat level. This, combined with their self-assured movements, spoke of military training. Not surprisingly, Yoshio had never seen either of them before. They walked over to Yoshio's table.

"*Komban wa*," the first one said softly, politely waiting for an invitation to sit.

"*Komban wa. Suwatte kudasai*," Yoshio replied.

The chairs scraped on the cracked linoleum as they took their seats. Then the three of them sat in silence, a waiting game.

The man Yoshio had tagged as Number One gave in first. "I hope you do not find the surroundings offensive, but we believe they are necessary," he said. This told Yoshio that the second man was only present in case any unpleasantness occurred.

"*Hai*. I do find them deplorable, and though you assure me of the necessity, I am not so certain. Regardless, we are here, and the hour grows late. I will be missed if I am away from the compound too long. Speak." Yoshio knew he was being rude, but did it really matter under the circumstances?

"The timetable has been moved up," Number One said, lowering his head slightly but otherwise giving no sign that he noticed Yoshio's rudeness.

Yoshio sat up straight, bumping the table and sending the rest of his sake sloshing over the greasy, pitted surface.

"What?" he hissed, not bothering to conceal his anger. "You cannot simply call a meeting and tell me that the date has been advanced. We have worked toward this for years, and haste will see it all undone."

The men sat looking calmly at Yoshio, who glared back. Number One spoke again. "This is not my decision, or *yours*," he said, and Yoshio bristled at the reminder. "The leader himself has issued these orders, and he is not to be disobeyed."

Yoshio wanted to lash out again, but he knew these men were only messengers. "I respect the esteemed leader and do not wish to give offense, but he has never commanded men in battle. I say again that such a matter cannot be rushed. I know that the contingency plan allowed for an earlier date, but that was a fallback only if it became absolutely necessary. Nothing has changed that we must revert to the fallback scenario."

"The warlord has also approved this change," Number One said.

Yoshio was startled to hear that. Though he still thought the decision ill-advised, he had no choice but to nod his assent. Just enough to let the men know he acknowledged delivery of their message.

Number One took a small computer disk from his side pocket. "You will find everything you need on this disk. I need not tell you that it must not fall into the wrong hands."

Those words made Yoshio want to stand up and

whip this impudent fool for thinking he could chastise a Combine officer. But Number Two sat with his hands out of sight, and Yoshio had no weapons but his own bare hands. He only nodded once more.

Without another word, the two men stood up and walked toward the door, leaving an angry and confused man the only conscious soul in the dark bar.

16

Whenever he walked through the 'Mech storage and repair bay, Zane felt as though he had been transported from the mundane world to a domain of giants—except that these giants were made of metal. The ceiling lofted fifteen meters above his head, and mammoth alcoves ran along both sides of the bay. He had seen the sight a hundred times, perhaps a thousand, but it never failed to impress him. One stroll through a place like this and he had no doubts about the reason for his own existence. He was born to be a MechWarrior, the epitome of a culture dedicated for many genetically bred generations to creating the ultimate warrior.

As he strode toward the far end of the bay, where the 'Mechs of Zeta Provisional Galaxy were housed, he thought of the last exercise against the Avengers. That his whole Binary had lost to the newly arrived Alshain unit was bad enough, but to have his *Jenner* completely destroyed was something he had never even imagined happening.

That Geoff's *Arctic Wolf* had also been destroyed was no comfort. Zane had heard of Inner Sphere MechWarriors known as the Dispossessed—warriors who no longer had a 'Mech—but it was not a concept he could truly understand. It was unthinkable that a Clan warrior would ever lack for a BattleMech. Even though he and Geoff were being assigned new 'Mechs, the thought of never having one again sent a shiver down his spine. Better to die!

Coming abreast of a four-legged *Snow Fox* swarming with technician castemen, Zane recognized Killian's machine. He knew, from yesterday's briefing, that the 'Mech had taken only light damage compared to the *Arctic Wolf* and his *Jenner*, but it had nevertheless been incapacitated. The difference was that it could be repaired and would likely be back in action before the week was out.

He wondered if the Avenger warriors were sitting around right now, drinking their sake and gloating over the Nova Cats' dismal showing. That thought made him think of his strange relationship with *Chusa* Yoshio. In some ways they were so alike, yet from different sides of the line each was attempting to hold.

In a moment that would astonish Zane for the rest of his life, he suddenly saw before him a galactic-sized mirror, with him on one side and Yoshio on the other. Both wore the exact same clothing and each was pushing against the other in the exact same manner. It was not a thought or a fantasy, but something real that he could see with his own two eyes.

He came to an abrupt halt, startled by the sight. The image went spiraling away from him, shattering into a million pieces. "What does it mean?" Zane murmured to himself.

"What?" someone asked.

Quickly looking up, he saw a technician who must have overheard him in passing and thought he was being addressed.

"Nothing, freebirth," he muttered absently. The inexplicable waking dream could not help but bring to mind his vision on the mountain, which, he realized with a start, he had not thought about in almost two full days. The destruction of his 'Mech must have affected him more than he knew.

A garnet dragon, an ebony dragon, a nova cat, and a blur of white holding a banner emblazoned with the head of a canine. He mulled over the images for the thousandth time. It was exasperating that he seemed to understand this waking dream better than the vision granted him during his Rite.

Zane knew what the garnet dragon was, and the nova cat was no mystery either. He still thought Yoshio must know something about the ebony dragon from the way he had reacted when Zane questioned him on the return voyage from Irece. Perhaps he should also have asked him about the white entity or the banner with the canine emblem. Zane resolved to probe Yoshio further the next time they met.

By now he was approaching the area where his replacement 'Mech was supposed to be berthed. Galaxy Commander Higall had already informed him that he would not be assigned another *Jenner* 2, as there were none currently available. Zane assumed he would be getting another light, maneuverable 'Mech for his usual reconnaissance role, but no other 'Mech would be as fast as the *Jenner* 2.

A MechWarrior could, technically, pilot any BattleMech, but the intricacies of each design, exacerbated by weight, speed, jump capability, armor, and weapons load-out, all combined to make the machines as individual as humans. Most MechWarriors quickly developed an affinity for one or two designs while also becoming proficient at piloting others of similar weight and movement profile. Beyond that, a MechWarrior would know the basics of getting a 'Mech from here to there and perhaps even engaging the weapons, but he would quickly fall in combat.

Zane finally came to a stop at the last four berths, each of them holding a light BattleMech bearing the crest of the Dragoncat Cluster. On his left stood a *Horned Owl* and an *Incubus*, both humanoid 'Mechs and weighing thirty-five and thirty tons, respectively. On his right was a Star League-era *Hermes* and another 'Mech he did not recognize. Until this moment Zane would have boasted of being able to make a visual identification of every known design fielded by either the Inner Sphere or the Clans. He had even studied a grainy photo of the *Tessen*, the new ComStar 'Mech being manufactured in the Draconis Combine and first fielded less than a year ago.

But the BattleMech that rose before him was none

of those. Looking to be just under nine meters tall, the machine had a slim body and slender arms that tapered to clawlike hands. Its legs seemed to be fitted with external shock absorbers built into the shin assembly. Zane guessed that was done to help alleviate the impact of an especially long-distance jump. As for weaponry, a massive gun that looked like a particle projection cannon jutted out from across the top of the right shoulder. The long-range striking power of a PPC, combined with the 'Mech's probable speed, was impressive.

"I see you have spotted our newest acquisition," a nasal voice said from behind.

Slowly turning, Zane saw a technician whose features and appearance were so nondescript that he almost seemed to blend into the background. Only the white smock he wore kept him from completely fading away.

"Yes, it is a sleek and elegant design," Zane said. "It looks as if it was designed to operate on its own for long periods without needing to rely on ammunition-fed weapons."

He was intensely curious and wanted to ask where the 'Mech had come from and what Clan produced it, but he did not intend to reveal his ignorance in front of a freebirth.

The man picked up a noteputer and began to scroll through what seemed like many pages of information. "Only those being assigned new 'Mechs ever get this far into the cave, so you must be here to collect yours."

Zane assumed that the term "cave" referred to the facility. It completely lacked natural light.

"What is your name, MechWarrior?" the tech asked, with only a hint of deference to one of higher caste. Though Zane had every right to reprimand the man's lack of respect, he held his tongue. He had better things on his mind than to argue with a freebirth.

"I am MechWarrior Zane."

"If you please, MechWarrior Zane, give me a moment."

Almost a minute passed before the technician seemed to find what he was looking for. Then he shook his head and started the process all over again. It was as though he doubted what the noteputer was telling him.

He shook his head slowly, then said, "It would appear, MechWarrior, that you have been assigned the *Pack Hunter*."

Zane's head whipped around to look at the strange machine behind him, thinking that the fierce name suited it perfectly. He walked toward the 'Mech—*his* 'Mech—and rested his hands on the cold, smooth metal of its giant right foot. He was deeply attached to his *Jenner*, and would never have thought it possible to forget the connection so quickly. Especially when he had not even sat at the controls of the *Pack Hunter* to power up the engine. Yet, he knew that as sure as the sun would rise again tomorrow he had found *his* 'Mech, the one that would carry him to greatness.

"Ah, a fine machine, Zane. A 'Mech that complements your lone ways even more than your lost *Jenner*," boomed a deep-throated voice over the din. Zane resented the interruption—it appeared as though every pure moment of his life would be contaminated by the intrustion of others—Samuel had become a good friend and one not even Zane wished to drive away.

Turning away from the 'Mech, he saw Samuel's towering form standing a respectful distance away. The incongruity of the man respecting Zane's privacy by not violating his physical space and yet speaking in that thundering voice made Zane smile slightly.

"A smile," Samuel exclaimed, spreading his arms wide and looking all around him. "But I have no witness. Our Star mates will never believe me."

Zane knew that this was Samuel's idea of a joke, and bit off a sharp retort, not wanting to spoil his own good spirits. He turned to the *Pack Hunter*, gesturing for Samuel to look up at it.

"I want to name it," he said quietly.

"You surprise me, Zane. In all the time you piloted your *Jenner*, you scorned that tradition."

"You are right, Samuel, and yet I feel this 'Mech wants a name." It was not written in the *Ways of Seeing* or any works of Nova Cat Oathmasters, but more and more Nova Cat warriors had begun to name their 'Mechs. It might have been less than a quarter who did so, but it would have been only a handful fifty years ago.

Moving backward slowly, Zane looked up until he had the entire 'Mech in his field of vision. Names began to run through his mind, and he instantly tested and discarded each one. Then, he stopped and spoke aloud the words that popped suddenly into his mind.

"Ebony Dragon," he said, astonishing even himself.

"Black Dragon," Samuel said. "A strong name, Zane, but you are filled with surprises this day. Perhaps your Rite of the Vision has changed you more than I might have thought. To choose a name so tied to the Draconis Combine . . ." His voice trailed off with uncertainty.

Zane turned to him in amazement. Instead of Ebony Dragon, Samuel had said Black Dragon. Like a door opening into another room, understanding rushed through Zane's mind. He had asked Yoshio about the *Ebony* Dragon, not the *Black* Dragon. When Yoshio said he had never heard of an Ebony Dragon, he was speaking the truth. If only Zane had phrased his question differently.

All of a sudden he felt the urge to rush out of this place and find Yoshio, demanding to know all about the Black Dragon. That was some kind of madness, however. Zane had a new 'Mech to test out. Tomorrow he would find Yoshio and discover what his dream portended. For now, the itch to be inside his *Pack Hunter*, his Ebony Dragon, overshadowed everything. He was a MechWarrior after all.

He slapped Samuel on the shoulder, forgetting any irritation Samuel's words had caused him. "It just seems like the right name, Samuel. It has no connection to the Combine, regardless of what you or others will say.

"Perhaps the Black Dragon, as you put it, is the enemy of the red dragon of House Kurita and will be the agent of its destruction."

17

Zane climbed to the top of the gantry, which brought him even with the head of the *Pack Hunter*. Then he walked across the left shoulder assembly to gain access to the cockpit hatch. The gun mounted on the 'Mech's right shoulder would make entering or exiting the 'Mech on that side difficult.

The *Pack Hunter*'s relatively short stature made it look more like a twenty-ton 'Mech than the thirty-tonner it was. The hatch alone took up most of the back of the humanoid head. As Zane wormed through the opening, he concluded that the small size was intended to cut down the 'Mech's profile in combat. Once inside, Zane sat at the controls of his Ebony Dragon for the first time.

Instantly feeling at home, he dogged the hatch and then located the reactor switch. He grabbed the large red bar with both hands, then heaved it down and locked into position, gratified to feel the thrum of the fusion reactor in the heart of the *Pack Hunter* come to life. Then he buckled himself into the five-point restraint harness that would keep him secured no matter what damage the 'Mech might take.

Reaching down to a panel concealed in the right arm of his command couch, he pulled out wires and medical monitor patches. The monitors he attached to his shoulders and the insides of his thighs. He then clipped the wire ends to the monitor patches and threaded the ends through loops in his cooling vest.

In a movement more natural and automatic to Zane than walking, he pulled a cable from the right side of his coolant vest and snapped it into a socket on his command chair. With the coolant vest activated—a sensation like grubs slithering across his chest—he knew the system was working fine, a fact of paramount importance.

All 'Mechs produced heat as the demands of movement and weapons fire pulled huge amounts of energy from the reactor. Though all of them incorporated giant radiators, known as heat sinks, to draw off the excess, most 'Mechs could generate considerably more energy than they could dissipate. This residual heat ranged from uncomfortable to deadly for the MechWarrior strapped in above the reactor. The vest, which contained coolant fluid trapped between a synthetic rubber layer on the inside and ballistic cloth on the outside, helped draw the heat away from the MechWarrior and allowed him to survive the heat levels he would experience in combat.

Next, Zane reached up behind him for his neuro-helmet, which he snugged down onto his head. Though smaller and lighter than its Inner Sphere counterpart, it served the same function—neural receptors in the helmet fed his body's natural ability to balance itself directly to the massive gyro mounted in his 'Mech's chest. It was a popular myth that a MechWarrior became part of his machine when he entered the cockpit. That was not literally true, but the neurohelmet did allow the giant machine to move with the fluidity of the MechWarrior's own movements. A 'Mech could be moved without the use of a neurohelmet, but the pilot risked a fall with every step. Zane secured the chin strap and snapped the medical monitor jacks into the bottom front of the neurohelmet.

Then he reached out and punched the button that would start the identification sequence. BattleMechs represented such a phenomenal investment of time, money, and resources that every effort was made to safeguard them from possible theft. Though it was rare among the Clans, the theft of a 'Mech did occasionally occur, usually perpetrated by a member of the exiled bandit caste. There was a two-fold safeguard against such larceny.

The first safeguard consisted of the fact that every neurohelmet was attuned to the brainwave pattern of the warrior who piloted it. Anyone who tried to connect one to a machine not his own could suffer a blinding headache, if not physical incapacitation and death, from the jolt of biofeedback when the neurohelmet reacted with a brain wave pattern it did not recognize. Nevertheless, there were ways around safeguards—illegal code-breaking devices could randomly cycle through patterns until the correct one was found. Though it took time, it would eventually crack the barrier. In Zane's case, the techs would have imported the information from his destroyed *Jenner*, bypassing the cumbersome process of calibration.

The second safeguard was virtually foolproof: the identification sequence. The first segment checked the voice pattern of the pilot against the computer's log of users, which usually consisted of only the Mech-Warrior and the technician assigned to the 'Mech. The second segment then checked a code phrase known only to the pilot. Though the technician could start the 'Mech with voice identification, he only had enough access to do repair work on the machine. Full control, including movement and weapons, was possible only with the code phrase.

A synthesized voice filled his cockpit, *"Pack Hunter 35WCSITE3 on-line. Proceed with voice identification."*

Something about the *Pack Hunter*'s serial number tugged at him, but he was too excited to pay attention. "MechWarrior Zane Nova Cat."

"Voice pattern match obtained. Working . . ."

Zane knew he would have to enter a new code phrase and then re-verify it. He had gone to sleep thinking on it and had awakened at dawn, knowing that there was only one option.

"Enter code phrase now."

"Purified in soul." Taken from his favorite passage of the *Ways of Seeing*, the words epitomized all his aspirations. Though the memory was hazy, he was fairly sure it was those words that had triggered his vision.

"Re-verify code phrase now."

"Purified in soul."

"Affirmative. Welcome aboard. Full control is now yours."

Zane smiled as the computer shunted power to his weapon systems. The primary and secondary monitors also flickered to life and his status schematic filled in, quickly showing him what the *Pack Hunter* was capable of. He was both surprised and pleased by what he saw.

The *Pack Hunter* was not as mobile as his *Jenner*, but it was still very swift. With a top speed of almost one hundred-twenty kilometers per hour and a maximum jump capacity of over two hundred meters, the 'Mech was more mobile than most Zane would encounter in combat.

He had also called the weapons array correctly—a single PPC was his only weapon. Though that was limiting, a PPC's range and firepower made it the most deadly weapon in the Clan arsenal, more powerful than anything the Inner Sphere boasted. The 'Mech was an ideal reconnaissance unit that could hold its own against much heavier 'Mechs. Assuming, of course, that the *Pack Hunter* was piloted by the right person, and he had no doubt that this one was.

What did surprise him was the relatively light armor for a 'Mech of its size. It took another moment for Zane to find the reason; there was no extra-light engine on this design. Another surprise.

The Clans manufactured two types of 'Mechs:

OmniMechs and second-line 'Mechs. OmniMechs incorporated a modular design that allowed for rapid changes of weapon configurations in the field; they were the peak of Clan technology and the backbone of most front-line Galaxies. Being the premier units of a Clan, most trueborns would pilot nothing else, and no expense was spared in equipping them with the latest technology. It was Zane's desire to prove himself a superior warrior and move from this Provisional Galaxy to a front-line Galaxy where he would have a chance to pilot an OmniMech

Second-line 'Mechs, assigned to second-line or Provisional Galaxies, were considered less important and useful. Lower-end technology was used, cutting down on the cost. After all, why provide an inferior warrior with a superior machine? Though Zane did not think often in such terms, it still burned him. After all, he was a trueborn, too!

In the past century, several Clans had begun building second-line 'Mechs that utilized the latest technology, rivaling OmniMechs. Only the Omni's adaptability in the field kept it from being overshadowed.

The fact that this 'Mech lacked cutting-edge technology should mean that it was centuries old, an easily recognizable design. Yet, Zane had never seen one before. He was intrigued and curious but still asked no questions. Besides, his desire to immediately take the *Pack Hunter* out for a test pushed all other concerns from his mind.

Opening a channel, he spoke with real excitement. "This is MechWarrior Zane. Per orders from Star Colonel Jal Steiner, I am requesting permission to remove this 'Mech from this facility." Though Nova Cat MechWarriors had no need to ask permission, they understood the importance of technicians in servicing the 'Mechs of their Touman and so observed such formalities.

The nasal quality of the technician's voice actually made its way intact through the digitization process. "Permission granted. Good hunting."

Using the foot pedals, Zane extracted the machine from its berth, with a sharp eye out for anyone careless enough to stand in the way of a moving giant. He turned toward the open doors at the far end of the bay and covered the distance quickly. Then he was through the bay doors and standing in a patch of sunlight. Using the joysticks mounted on either end of the arms of his seat, he raised the *Pack Hunter*'s arms into the air, as if the 'Mech were glorying in the feel of sunshine on its skin. Today was a good day for testing this machine.

Laughing out loud—something Zane had not done for so long he thought he had forgotten how—he walked the 'Mech past the repair bay, then brought it to a trot, then a run, and then a sprint as he pushed the throttle full-forward. The giant feet dug furrows in the sod as the *Pack Hunter* raced across the ground toward the location of the day's combat exercise. Though the moment still awaited him, today was the day Zane would defeat his Star Colonel on the field.

18

That was simply too close, Zane thought as he pushed his *Pack Hunter* through a particularly dense part of the forest. Some fifty kilometers north of New Circe, this woodland swept northward for several hundred kilometers. He had penetrated its depths, shattering limbs and tearing up trees that had been anchored to the soil for centuries as he smashed through the heavy growth.

Breaking through to the edge of the forest, where scrub began to replace the grasses of the gently rolling hills that surrounded New Circe and the Zeta Command Compound, he tried again to locate his target. Not to challenge him in traditional Clan combat, but to strike and destroy before his enemy even knew what hit him.

He shook his head, thinking how low he had descended that he would fight without honor. But he had no choice; he was under direct orders of his Star Colonel. One of the main reasons for the existence of the Dragoncat Cluster was to train in new styles of warfare against the Alshain Avengers.

Zane had heard while on Irece that Tau Galaxy was also training extensively in Inner Sphere tactics. It sickened him to know that an entire Galaxy of Nova Cat warriors was learning how to fight with deceit rather than in fearless combat. He had also heard that Tau Galaxy had been deployed to the St. Ives Compact to help it resist the aggression of a neighboring state. Yet both states were members of the Star League. How could Star League Defense Force troops be used by one member state against another? Did that not prove the Star League was a sham?

Such thoughts were distracting and had already caused a close brush when Star Colonel Steiner had ambushed his *Pack Hunter*. Piloting a *Shadow Cat*— one of the most common medium OmniMechs in the Nova Cat Touman—Jal Steiner had hidden in a particularly dense copse, waiting until Zane passed within a hundred meters before lashing out with his weapons.

Jal was piloting the Alpha configuration, which paired two extended-range large lasers with a Streak six short-range missile rack, so he should not have missed. The searing ruby beams had passed scant millimeters from the *Pack Hunter*'s chest, exploding trees a short distance away. Only the sodden condition of the vegetation, a result of the daily rain squalls, kept the errant beams from igniting a fire that would have burned out of control. The sudden onslaught, combined with the shrapnel of flying bark and leaves, had confused Zane about the direction of the attack and he had done the only thing he could think of: he kicked in his jump jets.

He recalled his nightmare about being inside the *Jenner* as it descended into a wooded terrain, but in real life the maneuver went without a hitch. With the advantage of jump jet capability greater than Jal Steiner's 'Mech, Zane had used the asset to its fullest to lose his attacker.

Now, some five minutes later, he was attempting to cautiously make his way back to the location of the ambush, hoping to reverse the trap. Jal might have guessed that Zane would try this trick and could already be lying in wait again. But Zane was hoping to catch his Star Colonel off guard by returning along the exact same route. Surely his commander would not believe he was stupid enough to do that. He smiled to himself. He was counting on his commander having a much higher opinion of him.

Zane knew he was almost to the exact spot where he had first taken fire. Slowed almost to a crawl, he kept his eyes glued to the sensors. Also keeping a close eye on the radar and Magnetic Anomaly Detector screens, he toggled his main viewscreen over to infrared. It showed him the path he had traversed only minutes before, which reassured him that he would not trip or cause irreparable damage to an ankle actuator by brushing against a low-hanging branch or stumbling over a fallen tree. Viewing the area in the infrared should also let him sight the *Shadow Cat* long before he could visually identify it through the trees. He was counting on Jal concentrating his attention in another direction, while Zane sneaked in to take him unaware.

That was the irony of 'Mech combat on the battlefields of the thirty-first century. A BattleMech's sensors ran through the whole spectrum: radar, MAG, infrared, seismic, and more. Additionally, the main viewscreen was a computer-generated image with a three hundred-sixty degree view. With all of that information, no 'Mech should be able to sneak up on another one. However, all that technology created a flood of information that was not always easy to interpret. And even though MechWarriors trained for years, they were still human.

Which was why Zane and his fellow Nova Cat warriors continued to train incessantly. And why Zane was stalking his own commander in this alien forest on a world he had yet to call home. The goal was to turn training into experience, and then transform experience into instinct. Only those who honed their skills would rise to the top of the Clan, becoming Star Colonels, Galaxy Commanders, or even one of the two Khans. It was only through superior skill that a warrior could win the right to compete in the Trial of Bloodright for one of the original eight hundred surnames of the first Clan warriors. Zane had every intention of earning the right to pilot an Omni-Mech, win a Bloodname, and rise high enough in the ranks that he could steer the Nova Cats back to their true path.

A lance of cerise energy stabbed from the same copse of woods that the *Shadow Cat* had previously occupied, finding its mark the second time around. The beam caught the *Pack Hunter*'s right arm, boiling off every last bit of armor, its residual energy blackening and cracking part of the internal structure.

"No!" Zane shouted, furious at being caught in precisely the same spot, for precisely the same reason. He'd been lost in contemplation of the future, instead of concentrating on the now. Stifling the urge to stomp down on the peddles and launch his 'Mech into the air a second time, he quickly stepped the *Pack Hunter* backward and punched at the viewscreen to switch from infrared to standard mode. Swiveling his torso to the right and tracking into the trees, he snapped off a shot. The azure beam crossed the hundred meters in an instant, exploding trees and creating a whirlwind of branches and leaves. He could not tell if he had struck his target.

There was no sense in trying to maintain distance, since the *Shadow Cat*'s weaponry had a longer range, so Zane cut to the right, drawing in closer. He slammed the throttle forward, knowing that moving with such speed through the thick timberland was a desperate gamble.

However, after several dozen meters, his new 'Mech proved more impressive than ever. The *Pack Hunter*'s light build and smaller size let it move with agility through the tangled undergrowth at a speed Zane would never have believed possible through such dense woods.

Switching back to infrared and tracking left, he caught a flash of red right where he thought it would be. He closed the distance, keeping his weapon locked onto the target, waiting for the tree cover to thin enough to give him a clean shot. Then he triggered his PPC, lashing out with an azure bolt of lightning.

Zane could not help a shout of exhilaration as his sensors registered a solid hit across the *Shadow Cat*'s lower left leg. With a combination of kinetic energy and heat that measured off the scale, the PPC slashed into the 'Mech's leg, vaporizing almost a full ton of armor into a mist that fell to the forest floor.

Confident once more, Zane stomped down on the peddles, launching the *Pack Hunter* skyward on twin plumes that vaulted him up and away from the *Shadow Cat* as it vainly attempted to twist and bring its large lasers to bear. Fighting against time, Zane cut the jump jets well before they reached full capacity, dropping quickly from the sky and then engaging them at the last moment to keep from crashing back to earth. Ruby beams sliced the sky over his head as the *Pack Hunter* fell.

He quickly put distance between himself and Jal, knowing he would work his way around again. To his astonishment, his commander's voice came over the commline. It had been standard practice for the past few weeks to forsake communication between opponents to better simulate real combat.

"Congratulations, Zane. I surprised you twice, but you salvaged the situation and managed to surprise me in turn. All of that in a machine you have never piloted before this day. Most impressive."

Knowing Jal Steiner to be a man of few words,

Zane was immediately suspicious. He waited to see where this was going.

"When Galaxy Commander Higall informed me that the Cluster had been assigned a *Pack Hunter*, I only had to see the schematic to know you were the one to pilot it. I must say, you have far exceeded even my expectations."

As Jal spoke, Zane moved to the right. He was not about to make the same mistake twice. He would continue in this direction for another few hundred meters and then cut back across his own trail, which would put him on Jal's left again. Perhaps his commander would even give something away with this uncharacteristic chatter.

"Now that I have assured myself that you and the *Pack Hunter* are indeed a perfect match, perhaps we should send a note of thanks, quiaff?"

Zane could not let that last comment go unanswered even though he had vowed to stay silent. "What do you mean? Why should we thank anyone when the 'Mech was won in a Trial of Possession?" Zane could not think how else the Nova Cats would have acquired the machine. Then he remembered his twinge over the 'Mech's serial code, and he glimpsed where Jal Steiner might be going with all this talk. He suddenly felt a sense of dread.

"A Trial of Possession?" Steiner said. "No, Zane, that was not how we acquired the *Pack Hunter*. We got it in exchange for a *Nova Cat*. You are piloting a 'Mech that our Khans thought important enough to own that we traded the pride of our Touman."

Zane could hardly believe what he was hearing. Though 'Mech trading was not unheard of among the Clans, it was rare. Besides, the Nova Cats had been Abjured from Clan space, made outcasts from Clan society. How could they trade with another Clan? MechWarrior Anton of the Dragoncat's Assault Supernova Binary fielded a *Ha Otoko*, but that was a Clan Diamond Shark design. In a mockery of the Clan way, the Diamond Shark merchant caste possessed almost as much power as the warrior caste; of course the Diamond Sharks would ignore an Abjurment.

Then he remembered hearing that the *Ursus*, a new second-line 'Mech produced by the Ghost Bears in the Inner Sphere, had also appeared in the Nova Cat Touman. Zane had assumed that it too was won in a Trial of Possession. Now he wondered if the Ghost Bears had opened relations with the Nova Cats. The Bears had barely escaped Abjurment themselves for forsaking all but their Arcadia and Strana Mechty holdings in Clan space and moving their entire population to the Inner Sphere.

Suddenly Zane knew with certainty where the *Pack Hunter* had come from. Stunned, he slowed it to a standstill and hung his head. Until now he had ignored the fact that MechWarrior Geoff of his own Bravo Striker Star fielded a 'Mech that could only have come from one source—Clan Wolf in Exile.

"Come now, Zane," he heard Jal Steiner say. "Surely you have guessed by now the origins of your 'Mech. I am sure Khan West would be happy to send a note of gratitude to Khan Kell for the *Pack Hunter*, letting him know that a MechWarrior Zane is most appreciative."

Clenching his fists so tightly that his hands ached,

Zane fought the rage that burst up from the core of his soul. He had been tricked, deliberately. Everyone knew his feelings about non-Clan 'Mechs. He had teased Geoff enough about his *Arctic Wolf*. Zane had promised himself that he would remain as pure a Clansman as possible as a reminder to others of who they were. How could it be that he was fighting in a 'Mech produced by the Wolves in Exile?

In Zane's mind, they were at least partially to blame for the sorry state of the Nova Cats. They had shattered their Clan and run off to the Inner Sphere. Zane was sure that had made enough of an impression on the previous Nova Cat Khans that they saw a precedent for allying with the Inner Sphere against their fellow Clans. They had blazed the path his Clan had blindly followed.

And now he sat in a 'Mech made by their worthless hands. He felt defiled. What made it worse was that both he and his commander knew that Zane could not give up this 'Mech. Never had he felt such an affinity for a design. Less than two hours in its cockpit and he had decided never to pilot any other 'Mech. It was a trap laid with the most exquisite care by his commander in an effort to tie Zane to the Inner Sphere.

Who would take him seriously now, knowing he piloted a 'Mech produced by the Wolves in Exile?

Zane tried to calm himself with deep, slow breathing, but it felt like he could not take in any air at all. He had to dominate his anger, must not give in to his wrath and lose the fight to his commander. His mind latched onto that thought, and it was solid enough to anchor him in the present moment.

He had to win. He had to walk away from this encounter victorious, or the entire war would be lost. He let his anger, his hate, his fury drain away, and a sense of euphoria swept over him instead. It was the same sensation he had felt while fighting *Chu-sa* Yoshio so many weeks ago.

All the tension went out of his body, and he looked calmly at his secondary monitors, trying to locate his target. Then he pushed the throttle forward with the absolute knowledge that today victory would be his.

19

"**H**ave you seen *Chu-sa* Yoshio?" Zane asked politely, trying to conceal his distaste at the sight of an entire barracks full of Combine warriors. He was the only non-Kurita in the whole building.

Thirty-some pairs of eyes turned on him, and the bantering in Japanese ceased abruptly. The mask that Zane now understood was reserved for outsiders instantly fell into place and he was looking at blank stares all around. None of this surprised him, but after scouring the entire compound looking for Yoshio, the Avengers' barracks was the last place left to check. Feeling like he was entering a snake pit, Zane had made his way through the corridors until he heard the sound of boisterous voices coming from this room. The language was different, yet the scene was not so different from a group of Clan warriors in their quarters.

The silence continued, but Zane would not be turned from his purpose. Since yesterday, the need to speak with Yoshio had become even more intense. The fight against Jal Steiner had temporarily distracted him, but not for long

He did not move and met their silence with his own, letting the minutes tick past. They probably knew who he was and how he felt about the Combine by now.

"*Sumimasen*," Zane said finally, realizing that none of them would break first. "*Chu-sa* Yoshio . . . *Kare wa doko ni imasu ka*?" Startled looks replaced the deadpan expressions of a number of them at hearing Zane's abominably accented but passable Japanese.

Zane hated revealing his burgeoning knowledge of their language, but thought it was probably the only way to get them to talk. He had begun to secretly study Japanese shortly after coming to Yamarovka, deciding he must know his enemy to find his weakness. Without a tutor or much in the way of learning materials, he had mastered only a limited vocabulary, but found he could understand a fair amount. It galled him to reveal it now because he knew that many of these warriors spoke English.

"*Chu-sa* Yoshio is not here," said the one closest to Zane. "He left early this morning and did not say where he was going."

Irritated that he had been right about their English,

Zane gave a grudging thank you. With a curt nod, he turned and left.

Leaving the building the way he came, he tried to keep from hurrying. He did not like these Combine warriors, but it would be a weakness to let them see how much. For the same reason he had not let on after learning that Yoshio was a surname—a fact that shocked him. Among the Clans the only true surnames were a limited number of Bloodnames. The right to one was reserved only for the finest warriors who had fought and defeated many others competing for the same name. Not wishing to reveal his ignorance, Zane had continued to refer to the *Chu-sa* as Yoshio.

Exiting the building, he walked out into the perpetually cloudy weather of New Circe's monsoon season. He looked up at the leaden skies and quickened his step; it would rain soon.

"Zane," someone called out, and he recognized Samuel's voice. Without slowing his step, he turned to see the giant warrior trotting in his direction. Quickly coming abreast, Samuel matched his huge stride to Zane's.

"I meant to congratulate you yesterday after the exercise, but I was unable to find you," Samuel said. "Then you were already gone this morning." He glanced over his shoulder in the direction of the barracks and raised his eyebrows slightly.

"Thank you," Zane said. He had no intention of explaining why he had gone into the Combine area.

"To defeat Star Colonel Steiner in single 'Mech combat, and piloting a 'Mech that should be inferior to his *Shadow Cat* . . .'' Samuel's voice trailed off in awe. ''Now, that is a feat worthy of praise!''

Zane was proud of it, too. He had made up his mind to beat Jal Steiner yesterday and against all odds he had done so.

''Only a handful of warriors in the entire Cluster have ever defeated him, though most of us have tried. Of course, I was a little surprised that he participated in exercises at all, but now I think I know the reason. Everyone in the Cluster now respects him, whether or not they share his point of view.''

Zane knew those final words were directed at him. He too had to admit that he respected the Star Colonel's prowess, but how could such a fine warrior support the sham Star League?

''I told you yesterday that the *Pack Hunter* felt . . . special.'' Zane had no words to explain. ''That is why I named it.'' Then he wondered whether Samuel had known all along the origins of the *Pack Hunter*. If not, he and the rest of the Cluster surely did by now.

He remembered the moment when Jal's *Shadow Cat* fell. The graceful 'Mech had unexpectedly become clumsy and ungainly after Zane destroyed its gyro. The Ebony Dragon had lost its whole right arm and taken internal structural damage in several locations, but defeating Jal Steiner was balm enough to console Zane for the damage. It was almost enough for him to ignore his commander's moral victory over him.

''You fought well and I again offer my congratulations.''

Zane was surprised to detect the slightest note of jealousy in his friend's voice. Then he realized that Samuel's loss to the Star Colonel must have been devastating. After all, Samuel piloted a ninety-ton *Supernova*, one of heaviest 'Mechs in the Dragoncat Cluster.

With incredible armor protection and mounting an unheard of six extended-range large lasers, the *Supernova* was a long-range firing platform, designed to provide fearsome support to the other members of its Star. Samuel was a superb MechWarrior who had fought in Operation Revival after the Nova Cats joined the Clan invasion of the Inner Sphere. It was also a reminder of why Star Colonel Steiner piloted an OmniMech.

Samuel, too, had wondered aloud after Jal Steiner bested him why the man was not in a front-line Galaxy. He had the talent and had already won a Bloodname, something only a handful in the entire Cluster could claim.

"I have come to invite you to join me this evening at an eating establishment in New Circe, even though you always scold me for going there," Samuel said, his tone good-humored again.

With a shake of his head, Zane was about to refuse as he had so many times before. He had no wish to eat and drink in a room filled with freebirth lowercastemen. But Samuel's next words stopped him before he could speak.

"Perhaps you might even find the person you are looking for."

Zane was surprised at the comment, yet he realized his friend might be right. He had heard Yoshio mention that he often took his meals in New Circe. Besides, Zane did not think he could sink much lower than having gone into the Avenger barracks and spoken Japanese with them.

"All right, Samuel. I would like to join you," he said.

"Excellent, my friend. I believe you will find it an edifying experience. I will meet you back in Yama at eighteen hundred hours. For now, I am on my way to meet with my technician. My *Supernova* must be repaired by tomorrow."

Zane nodded and Samuel continued on, resuming his swift gait as his long legs ate up the ground between here and the 'Mech repair facility.

Zane spent another hour attempting to locate Yoshio or learn where he had gone, but without success. Yoshio seemed to have fallen off the face of Yamarovka. Frustrated, Zane made his way back to Yama and the headquarters of the Dragoncat Cluster.

"*Domo, Tai-i,*" *Chu-sa* Palmer Yoshio said as he broke the connection. He could not help but wonder why Zane was looking for him. The news that he had not only entered the Combine barracks, but had also spoken rudimentary Japanese, was a surprise indeed. The man continued to be an enigma.

He thanked the communications officer and walked across the bridge of the DropShip *Tsuyosa* toward the hatch. Before leaving, he also thanked the DropShip's captain for the use of his comm unit.

At just over one hundred thousand kilometers from Yamarovka, the *Tsuyosa* was on its way to the system's nadir jump point, still many millions of kilometers distant. The trip to and from the jump point would take about two hundred-forty hours—just over ten days.

Yoshi's ostensible reason for making the trip was to rendezvous with an incoming Combine JumpShip to oversee the transfer of men and materiel with another Alshain Avengers regiment. The real reason was a secret meeting. Supplies and troops were indeed being exchanged, but the incoming JumpShip would also bring a visitor who was scheduled to make contact with Yoshio.

The disk Yoshio had received several days before detailed the changes to Operation *Batsu*, instructing him to travel to the jump point for a meeting with someone who would provide additional information. All the code words were solid, so he obeyed those instructions.

As he passed down the DropShip's corridor, he wondered at the fact that his subordinate thought Zane's visit important enough to notify him. Though his whereabouts were not necessarily secret, he had not wished to advertise his movements either. The scheduled arrival of the other ship had been cleared with the Nova Cats for weeks, but it was still somewhat odd for a battalion commander to oversee a routine transfer. The *Tai-i* knew how important this meeting was.

Yoshio had not wanted to spend a second longer than necessary on an open channel like that. Whatever Zane wanted, it would keep. If Yoshio was right about who he would meet with four days from now, he would need his mind sharp and clear to be ready for it.

The Dragon House
New Circe, Yamarovka
Irece Prefecture, Draconis Combine
20 September 3062

This was Zane's third night in a row dining in the restaurant known as The Dragon House, though he was not sure what kept drawing him back to New Circe. Considering that he had resisted joining Samuel for months, his change of heart was puzzling even to him.

The two of them shared a small table, Samuel towering over Zane even while seated. Zane looked around the bustling room, marveling at what to him seemed like the sheer opulence of the decor. Samuel had told him it was nothing out of the ordinary for this kind of establishment, but Zane could not truly grasp the idea of so much wealth squandered on a room where people only came to eat.

From where they sat, Zane could see the upper level of the restaurant. A long, semi-circular bar ran along one wall and a bank of gambling devices—machines that had totally baffled him on his first visit—lined the other. A colonnaded stairway swept down to the restaurant's main floor, where most of the twenty dining tables were occupied. The ceiling was all polished wood and arcing beams, and four crystalline chandeliers hung from it on impossibly thin wires.

The first time he was here, Zane had expected people to be startled at the sight of two Nova Cat warriors frequenting a lower-caste spot. Beyond a few covert looks and the sense that people were lowering their voices, however, no one seemed to act as if it was anything out of the ordinary. Zane assumed it was because so many Nova Cat warriors patronized the place it was no longer a rarity.

The server who took their order was courteous and seemed to find nothing odd about their presence, either. Zane had let Samuel order for him the first night and tried to relax once he saw that Yoshio was not present. Perhaps tomorrow, he had thought, as he sampled the alien tastes and textures of the exotic dishes. When he and Samuel got up to leave, Zane had noticed that their table was fractionally set apart from all the other tables. *The Nova Cat table.*

On the second night, he told himself that the novelty of the experience was what had drawn him back.

On the third night, that rationalization fell flat. No matter how much he enjoyed the food, that was not enough to make him want to spend his time in a den of lower-caste freebirths of the Inner Sphere.

As he looked around at those seated around him, he observed their gestures and expressions, even what they ate. Something about this place affected him, but he could not put a finger on it. It was exactly the kind of thing that had made him begin to wonder if undergoing the Rite of the Vision had been a mistake.

He was a Nova Cat, and visions were part and parcel of his Clan, but he had been almost inundated by strange, new feelings that pulled him in every direction ever since his Rite of Vision. The way he had instantly connected with his *Pack Hunter*; this compelling need to find and speak with *Chu-sa* Yoshio; a sense of . . . something about this restaurant—what had happened to him? Last night he had even woken in a sweat, the traces of a terrible nightmare vanishing in the light of consciousness, leaving him with only a memory of failure. For just a moment, staring at a noodle that looked almost alive as it slithered on his fork, he wondered if he was losing his mind.

Across from him sat two gentlemen, both Japanese, both wearing well-tailored suits. They ate delicately and spoke quietly, probably discussing some business they thought important.

To his left was a young couple—she of obvious Japanese ancestry and he looking more Caucasian, with dirty-blond hair but a surprisingly red beard. They too spoke in whispers, their hands almost touching on the table, and they ate sparingly. Though love was rare among the warrior caste, which had no need for such entanglements, it did exist among the lower castes and Zane had been instructed about the concept. Looking at this young couple, he realized it was probably love that was making them stare at each other so inanely. As far as Zane was concerned, love must be a malady of some kind if it made people behave so strangely.

Glancing over at another table, he saw a group of four people that he guessed to be what was called a family. The parents and two adolescent boys seemed so content as they ate and talked. Zane was thinking how different his life had been when he was these boys' age. Though he would still have been living in a sibko, he would already have begun to pilot a 'Mech, his whole life dedicated to becoming a warrior. He picked up snippets of their conversation about life, school, work. It all seemed so peaceful.

Zane turned back to his meal, stuffing another forkful of noodles into his mouth.

"You seem more nervous than usual," Samuel said, the concern obvious in his voice. "Is there anything I can do to help?"

Using the napkin to catch come juices that had dribbled down his chin, Zane cleared his throat. "No, Samuel, there is not. But I will tell you what I am thinking as you will only drag it out of me anyway."

Samuel smiled fleetingly, and Zane went on.

"You know as well as I how odd it is for me to come back here three nights in row," Zane said. He reached for his glass of water and took a long swallow, clearing the last of the peppery beef from his palate.

"I enjoy the food and the experience is interesting," he said. "I will even concede that I do not find the food distasteful, contrary to what I might have thought. But that is not it."

Samuel sat back and looked around the room slowly as Zane had just done, then turned back to Zane. "What do you see around you?" he asked.

Zane decided to humor Samuel. After all, other odd conversations with his wise friend had opened Zane's eyes to many things. "I see lower castemen—and some Combine warriors—having dinner. None of them are Nova Cats, probably because the lower-caste population on Yamarovka is very small."

"You automatically call them lower caste, though they are not of the Clans. Why?"

"Because that is what they are—freebirths. It does not matter that they are not Clan. They can never hold the same position as we and so must be lower. What else would I call them?"

"Yes," Samuel said, "they are lower-castemen by your definition, but they are not lower castemen in actuality—either by birth or loyalty to any Clan. Yet you see them in those terms, not simply as people of the Inner Sphere." Samuel gestured broadly, taking in the scene around them.

Zane looked around again, noticing that people at a few of the closest tables were looking over, discreetly in most cases. It was the first time anyone had ever seemed to take note of them, but he and Samuel were speaking much more than usual tonight. And his companion's tendency toward overwrought gestures was not helping any.

"Look again," Samuel demanded.

Zane did so—even making eye contact with some who looked boldly in his direction—and continued to think about it. Of course they were lower castemen. Why would they not be? He was also becoming increasingly uncomfortable under the stares of those around them. People of the Nova Cat lower castes would never have looked at Zane and Samuel in such a way.

He froze, as this thought brought him to the brink of something new in his understanding. Nova Cat lower castes . . . Then, without warning, he saw it. Comprehension flooded him as a door seemed to open in his mind, and he understood what was drawing him to this place.

The people looked different, wore strange clothing, consumed alien foods—yet they reminded him of people of his own Clan. Physically, they were as different from Zane as the philosophy of the Wardens differed from that of the Crusaders. And yet they also seemed as familiar as any freeborn Zane had known either here or in the homeworlds.

Samuel was watching him intently. "Perhaps by tomorrow you will have managed to repress the memory of this night," he said, "but it will not be banished so easily. Many other Nova Cat warriors have also begun to open to this knowledge, which I first began to understand many years ago. And though we try to explain to our brethren who have not yet gained the sight, not all will listen or are open to our words."

Again gesturing to include everyone in room, Samuel said, "After three centuries of separation, it is true that they are different from us. But they are like us as well. Each with his own hopes and fears and aspirations, just like yours or mine."

Zane closed his eyes, shutting everything out. He did not want to think of these people in that way. He was a Nova Cat warrior, destined to change the destiny of his Clan. This new understanding undermined his absolute certainty that the Nova Cats had chosen a wrong path.

Samuel tapped him on the arm. "Zane, did not The Great Father say,

"But with glory comes responsibility;
Without a pure soul we cannot give sight
To their blindness but will only blind ourselves.

"So many Clan warriors have blinded themselves to the humanity of the Inner Sphere people, seeing them only as an enemy to be conquered. But they are kinsmen to be welcomed and led. If only—"

"Stop," Zane said harshly, cutting Samuel off before he could finish. For so long he had nursed a hatred of the Inner Sphere. It had burned bright, keeping alive his fervor to change what so many thought could not be changed. But events of the past several months had cooled the bright spark that kept it aflame.

His strange connection with a hated Combine officer; his respect for a Combine warrior who had violated the sanctity of Nova Cat traditions by becoming Oathmaster; his Rite of the Vision, which seemed to have opened the door to so many strange feelings; this humble little restaurant where he had let himself see how alike were the Nova Cats and the Combine—it all threatened to overwhelm him. And then Samuel had quoted the Great Father's words that without a pure soul we are blind. To be "purified in soul" was Zane's greatest desire. He had even made it the code phrase for his Ebony Dragon. It came from his favorite passage in the Remembrance, the very words that had sparked his vision.

He stood up from the table and in his haste knocked over his chair. He did not stop to right it. His entire world, the world he had clung to so fiercely since first becoming exiled in the Inner Sphere, was on the brink of collapse. He had to get away from this place.

Purified in soul—the words echoed in his mind. Was it possible that he had been wrong all this time? He had thought the words were telling him to purify his soul that he might help bring the Nova Cats back to the true Clan way. Now, he wondered if was the other way around. Was he being called to purify his soul of the hatred that kept him from helping the people of the Inner Sphere find their way back to a truer path?

Bursting into the dark, rain-slashed street, pursued by knowledge he no longer cared to possess, Zane stumbled into the night.

=== 21 ===

DropShip *Tsuyosa*
Nadir Jump Point, Yamarovka
Irece Prefecture, Draconis Combine
22 September 3062

The *Tsuyosa* had been docked with the *Invader* Class
JumpShip for almost four hours, and still Yoshio was
waiting. After four endless days in transit, he was
impatient to meet this secret emissary. He thought
that if he had to stare at the walls of this officer's
briefing room one instant longer, he was sure to lose
his mind.

Fortunately for his sanity, the hatch opened, and
an old man entered the room. He was stooped and
withered, his hair and beard snow-white. Yoshio
could barely contain his surprise. This was not Toshimichi Uchida, Warlord of the Alshain Military District and commander of the Alshain Avengers.

It looked as though micro-gravity did not agree with the stranger. He moved haltingly toward a chair, then stopped to lean against the table, as though to catch his breath.

Yoshio was irritated. Did they let old men go wandering all over the ship, then go barging into any room? Why this man, of no apparent military rank, was a passenger on this ship in the first place was equally mysterious.

"*Sumimasen*, honored one. I do not wish to be rude, but I believe you have mistaken your way. If you would be kind enough to explain where you wish to go, it would be my honor to direct you there." Yoshio knew one should always be polite even when annoyed.

The old man abruptly stood up straight, the absent-minded look vanishing from his face so quickly that Yoshio wondered whether the snow-white beard would vanish along with it. The man was old, but there was still strength in those shoulders, and his eyes shone with intelligence and power. Yoshio was glad for the boots holding him to the deck. The change was so startling he might have taken an involuntary step backward.

"Ah, so it appears the *Tai-shu* was incorrect—there is courtesy to be found among the younger generation," the stranger said, his strong voice confirming his vitality. He smiled with a hint of cruelty.

"*Sumimasen*, father. I do not recognize you, though you seem to know me." The old man had used the word *Tai-shu*, probably referring to Warlord Uchida. He would have to be very careful. Yoshio knew that the Draconis Combine's Internal Security Force well deserved its reputation as one of the most effective and brutal intelligence agencies in the Inner Sphere.

The old man smiled broadly. "Of course I know who you are. Unlike previous fools who died because of their arrogance, I am very careful. And prudence requires learning all you can about those who can affect your plans. With your position, there is no doubt of that. You are a battalion commander, after all."

There was a twinkle in his eye, but Yoshio was not fooled by it. He took a seat at the table and secured himself in place. Even if the magnetic boots should fail, he would stay in the chair.

The old man's tone was irritating, but he had to be the emissary Yoshio had been sent to meet. He also spoke as if he had some power in the Black Dragons. Yoshio had always assumed that the ya-kuza controlled the organization, with the help of *Tai-shu* Uchida. Then again, he really did not know much about the upper reaches of the Society. It was that way for most of the members, a precaution against anyone's possible defection or capture by the dreaded ISF.

"I was told that I would receive information from *Tai-shu* Uchida that could only be entrusted to a bat-talion commander or higher," Yoshio said firmly. "*Tai-sa* Miyazaki could not be away from the regi-ment for so many days, and so I was delegated. Do you bring that information?"

"Ah, you are circumspect. I am glad to see that. However, there are times when caution must be set aside to prevent misunderstanding. Such is the case with my visit. I have risked much, traveling to all but one world where the Alshain Avengers are stationed, giving them last-minute instructions that we dare trust to no other means of communication." The old man watched Yoshio with the eyes of a hawk, perhaps to catch any wavering of attention.

Did he think Yoshio would falter now? After tying himself so closely to the Society?

The old man went on. "This, too, was something old dead fools never understood. Subordinates need to see those who command, need to glimpse the power they obey, or they can falter during the storm. For years I wore a most ostentatious uniform, which impressed the weak-minded who served under me." He paused momentarily, pulling at his beard. "Now, age has given me a different look, yet one that also demands respect in our culture." He laughed softly, and this time Yoshio thought he detected a true note of levity.

Yoshio nodded deferentially. "I acknowledge and appreciate your words, but they do not answer my original question. Who are you and what news do you bring from *Tai-shu* Uchida?"

"Ah, now there is the impatience of youth! You have no need to know who I am at this moment, though you may call me the Red Hunter." The old man continued to peer intently at Yoshio, then shook his head when he saw no reaction. Yoshio thought briefly that perhaps he was disappointed at not being recognized. Then, for no reason he could say, he did not think so. The stranger appeared to have left such vanities behind him.

"Up till now, you have not known the full degree of Operation Batsu, but some instructions must wait until the time for them is at hand. This is done to protect the entire organization. Now that time has come. You already know that the timetable has been moved up. However, you still do not know the intended target. That target is—"

Yoshio suddenly felt the pieces of the puzzle suddenly slipping into place for him. "Alshain," he said, his voice whispery with awe.

The Hunter stopped speaking, and Yoshio realized abruptly that only now was his full power revealed in that fathomless stare. Several seconds turned into a handful, and neither man moved. Hardly daring to breathe, Yoshio waited.

When the stranger looked away for a moment, it felt as though a pair of halogen searchlights had turned aside, releasing Yoshio from his paralysis. When the old man turned back again, the power of his gaze was again hidden from view. He bowed his head slightly. "You do yourself credit, though I trust you have not shared this intuition with anyone."

With sudden insight, Yoshio knew that this man calling himself the Red Hunter was a noble, perhaps one of considerable power. The slight bow of the head was that of a superior to a subordinate who had proven himself in service. His irritation washed away instantly as he realized that the man was surely a power among the Black Dragons and that he could crush Yoshio without lifting a finger. The implied threat in his words was obvious. It would be quicker and much less painful to walk out of an airlock than to anger this man.

Yoshio gave a low bow. "You humble me with your praise, but it was only as you spoke that I received such insight. The clues are there, but the audacity of it will prevent others from suspecting. I do not believe you need fear that the plans have been uncovered."

A knowing look crossed the old man's face at the sudden change in Yoshio's demeanor. With a small smile, he said, "Those are the words I wished to hear. You cannot imagine the effort that has led up to this moment. Unlike the death of the Society's previous leaders—fools all—the unraveling of this plan could well lead to destruction of the whole organization. I have tapped all of our resources to bring Operation *Batsu* to fruition, and I would be displeased to learn it had been compromised at this late date."

Yoshio repressed a shudder. "I am only here to further the cause of the Combine."

"As well you should be." The old man shifted slightly in his seat. "So, the main target of our thrust is Alshain. By all reports it is heavily defended, but it is of paramount importance that we capture that world."

"*Hai*! It is our capital."

"Yes, the capital of the Alshain Military District, which our Coordinator vowed to take back when he made Uchida Warlord of the Alshain District a decade ago. And though it was revolting to contemplate fighting alongside the Star League forces, it did rid us of the hated Smoke Jaguars and liberated many of our worlds. But most of the Alshain District, including the capital, still lies under the thumb of a barbarian Clan. Our warriors would have willingly followed Theodore against the Ghost Bears. All he needed do was lead."

The old man's voice was bitter. "It would have been a hard-fought victory—we know the Ghost Bears are a powerful Clan—but it would have been a victory nonetheless, and then all of our worlds would once again fly the Dragon banner. Perhaps such a victory would have eliminated the need for the Coordinator to tarnish Combine worlds by giving them to the Nova Cats to rule."

A look of pure disgust accompanied the allusion to the creation of the Irece Prefecture. Only a year before, Yoshio would have felt the same. But now he had spent many months training alongside Nova Cat warriors. Though the Clan had conquered many Combine worlds and killed many of its people, he could not help feeling a burgeoning respect.

His silence made the old man look at him closely, and Yoshio schooled his features to calmness, not wishing to give away his feelings to this man. He knew it would be very dangerous.

After a long moment, the Hunter spoke again. "Tell me, young man, what do you think will be the consequence of our actions?"

The question was so unexpected that Yoshio felt his composure slip momentarily. That seemed to please the old man, confirming Yoshio's impression that it was intentional. Yoshio quickly marshaled his thoughts.

"First, we will succeed. And in so doing, create pride in our actions not only to the Alshain warriors, but to all warriors of the Combine. A pride the Coordinator will not dare tarnish or try to take away. He will have no recourse but to support us. That will provide us with the reinforcements we need to hold Alshain, regardless of what the Ghost Bears do.

"Second, there is the possibility of retaliation from the Ghost Bears, but I do not believe much will come of that. They seem very content in their new home and, after a decade of acquiescence, it is unlikely our actions will stir them much. Third, other Clans might attempt to aid the Ghost Bears, though that too is unlikely. None came forward to save the Smoke Jaguars from destruction.

"Fourth, though perhaps not relevant, it is possible that there will be repercussions from the Star League Council. However, such repercussions can only take the form of words. What need have we of words, when our actions speak for us?"

Several moments passed, and then the Hunter smiled with another slight nod of his head. "Again you show exceptional intelligence. You have missed only a few minor possibilities." He paused, as though deciding whether to reveal more.

"I have every confidence that you will rise high, and I pride myself on being a good judge of character. Because of that, what I say to you now will demonstrate our resolve and my faith in you."

For a moment, Yoshio wanted to stop the old man from speaking, to hold his hands over his ears and blot out what he was about to hear. He was already bound tightly within the Society's web, but he feared that what the old man said to him now would forever cut off the possibility of disengaging himself in the future. Operation *Batsu* might be canceled tomorrow, and it would not matter that Yoshio had been involved. But if the next words were spoken, the only door out of the Black Dragon Society would be nailed shut. He told himself he must remain firm in his belief that the Dragon must be made pure, and that helped to calm him.

"The greatest threat to our plans from the Ghost Bears are their WarShips. Our intelligence on the movement of those ships is sketchy, but it appears that they rotate their vessels, giving none a permanent assignment. However, it is our belief that we will face at least one WarShip in the Alshain system."

The thought of going against a Ghost Bear WarShip with only their DropShips and aerospace fighters sent a shiver of fear down Yoshio's spine. He had assumed the Avenger regiments would use a pirate jump point to enter the Alshain system. Because gravitational forces could disrupt a jump and easily destroy an incoming JumpShip, most were made into either the zenith or nadir points above and below the system's star, far enough above the elliptical plane that gravity was effectively neutralized. However, transient points of gravitational equilibrium did exist throughout a star system. The complex gravitational interactions of a system's planets meant these points were continually moving, vanishing, and reappearing. The only way to plot a pirate point jump was with the help of a detailed and absolutely accurate map of all orbiting bodies in that system—which the Combine had, having controlled Alshain for centuries. Without that kind of detailed data, a pirate-point jump amounted to suicide.

Yet it seemed as though the old man was insinuating that even if Operation *Batsu* used a pirate point to reduce the transit time from jump point to planet, they would still encounter a WarShip. And everyone knew that the only way to fight a WarShip was with another WarShip. His eyes widened in wonder as he realized what would happen.

"I can see by your expression that you again are quick to understand," the Hunter said. "Most would dismiss it as not possible. But all things are possible, provided the right leverage is found. And with the right leverage, worlds can be moved. Or, in this case, WarShips."

The implications staggered Yoshio. The DCMS WarShip fleet was still small, but the Combine War-Ship program was a top military priority. It was also no secret that the High Command controlled their deployment rather than the Draconis Combine Admiralty. For *Tai-shu* Uchida and this man to have gained access to a WarShip . . . Yoshio could only shake his head at the implications.

The Red Hunter smiled with obvious pride and spoke in a suddenly pompous voice, as though imitating a high official within the Procurement Department, which most Combine soldiers considered a mockery. "For the safety of the realm and the protection of the Dragon's borders against possible incursion from the Ghost Bear Dominion, *Tai-shu* Uchida, Warlord of the Alshain Military District, you are given operational command of the *Dragon's Last Tear*, a *Tatsumaki* Class WarShip, the pride of the Dragon's Fleet. Use it wisely." There was no mistaking what he thought of desk-warriors.

Yoshio had heard rumors of the existence of the *Tatsumaki* Class WarShip, but that only one was in operation—*The Lair of Mighty Wyrms*. That information had come through so many secondhand sources that he had considered it completely unreliable. To realize Operation *Batsu* might have such a potent weapon when facing off with the Ghost Bears filled him with pride. He sat up taller, a sense of glory filling his heart. How fortunate he was that he would be part of this great deed.

"So, you do understand," the old man said. "It is the key to our success. For ten long years we have trained with a single goal in mind. When all four Alshain Avenger regiments drop onto Alshain with the *Dragon's Last Tear* to protect us, nothing will stand in our way. By the new year, the Alshain Military District will be reborn and back where it belongs in the realm of the Dragon."

Yoshio bowed to the Red Hunter. He could not have agreed with him more.

22

Zeta Command Compound
New Circe, Yamarovka
Irece Prefecture, Draconis Combine
28 September 3062

"I am well aware of that, Tech, but I say this is not a waste of our Clan's resources." Zane tried to keep his voice even while applying enough emphasis to remind the technician of his place. "The loss of this 'Mech and the death of its MechWarrior would be the greater waste. You are correct that the work will take some time, but such actions in the present will benefit our Clan in the future. Quiaff, Tech?"

Zane had no desire to lord it over the man, but he knew he was right. If the only way to get the modification done was to remind him that Zane was a warrior and could not be refused, then so be it.

"Aff," the tech said, his whole demeanor changing,

but Zane wondered if he might have pushed too hard. Though the man had only been his technician for a short time, he had been unwavering in his duty of keeping the Ebony Dragon in prime shape. In the past Zane might never have given the matter a second thought, but that was before his experience at The Dragon House a few nights back. Again he felt powerless over the changes being wrought within him.

"Your dedication to duty and the path is admirable," he added.

Though the man tried to conceal it, the words clearly surprised him. Then pride flooded his face. "If you will wait a moment, MechWarrior Zane, I will go and get the authorization for your signature."

Zane nodded, and the man quickly went off to fetch the document. Standing in the 'Mech bay, Zane felt, as he always did, a profound joy at being in the presence of so many mighty BattleMechs. His *Pack Hunter* was still berthed at the far end of the facility, and he always savored the long walk down the whole length of the facility.

Though the *Pack Hunter* was a superb design—undeniable even though Zane hated having to credit Clan Wolf in Exile—he wanted to correct a few of its weaknesses. For one thing, the 'Mech lacked the advanced ferro-fibrous armor, which offered more protection at less weight than standard armor. Replacing the standard armor, though costly and time-consuming, would increase that protection by some ten percent. In a light 'Mech, that was enough to make the difference between survival and destruction.

His technician had tried to tell him that the modification was not worth the expense and time—the eternal waste-not-want-not attitude of the Clans asserting itself. Zane had insisted, however, and would personally sign off on the authorization to prevent the tech suffering repercussions from his superiors, going all the way up to the Master Technician himself. If someone wanted to protest, Zane would be the one to defend the decision, not his technician.

Looking up at his machine, he patted its leg with no small amount of affection and said, "We deserve all the protection we can get, Black Dragon."

He had spoken softly, but Zane heard someone behind him sharply catch his breath in surprise. Zane snapped his head around to see a technician, stopped dead in his tracks. He felt a twinge of anger at the apparent eavesdropping, then noticed that the man had strong Asian features. He guessed that this must be a Combine man taken as *isorla*, the spoils of battle. He had proven his worth and become a member of the technician caste. Perhaps he was only surprised to come upon a MechWarrior talking to his 'Mech, but Zane guessed his reaction had something to do with hearing the words Black Dragon.

"You, come here," Zane called out in his most authoritative voice. The man seemed to shrink in size and came forward like someone trying to drag his feet through drying concrete.

"Did you hear me just now?" he demanded. The tech seemed frozen with fear and just stood there staring with wide eyes.

Zane felt his old anger bubble up, but this time he mastered it. He took a deep breath and tried again.

"You were shocked at my words, quiaff? I would

know the reason." He watched the tech carefully, hoping to catch any hint of falsehood. "Answer me, tech," he commanded.

"Yes—I mean, aff, I was startled," the man said. "I never thought I would hear those words spoken among my new . . . Clan and it caught me . . . *Sumimasen*, please, I beg your pardon for the interruption." His words were polite, and though his hesitancy gave proof of his newness to Clan ways, Zane caught no hint of deception.

"You have no need of my pardon, as it was surely a coincidence. Still, what was it I said that startled you so?"

"It is only rumors and innuendo, MechWarrior, not worthy of your time."

Zane narrowed his eyes. "I will decide what is a waste of my time."

The man looked fearful, but knew he must obey. "Again, it is only rumor, but everyone knows that the Black Dragon refers to a—" He broke off in midsentence with a jerk, realizing what he was saying. He swallowed several times, sweat beginning to bead on his forehead.

"I mean, some say that the Black Dragon Society moves against the Combine and the Coordinator. In bars and back alleys, there are those who try to recruit, saying that the Combine is no longer pure, that we have permitted enemies into our midst and hold them too close to our breast. Allowing Prince Victor to visit Luthien, his relationship with the honored Omi, the help given by the Star League forces in repulsing the Smoke Jaguars, allowing the—" He again broke off, actually beginning to wring his hands, and the sweat dripped down his face.

Zane had no doubt about what the man had been about to say. "Go on," he said, ignoring the last words.

"I have never believed such things, MechWarrior. I mean, before I joined my new Clan, I never believed such things and would not listen to traitorous talk against the Coordinator. The Dragon himself—how could they?"

Zane nodded, again sensing that the man spoke true. And the information fit into place, giving him more insight into his vision.

He dismissed the tech with a wave, his thoughts already moving on. Had Yoshio thought Zane was referring to this Black Dragon Society when he had asked about the Ebony Dragon? If Yoshio was a member of this faction within the Combine that sought to return the realm to the traditional ways practiced for centuries, it was impossible to ignore how that mirrored Zane's own deepest desire of returning the Nova Cats to their true path.

He had been driven by that idea for so long, but did he still believe it? Looking around him at the well-cared for 'Mechs in their berths and remembering the beauty of New Barcella and the Ways of Seeing Park on Irece, there was no denying that the Nova Cats were prospering in the Inner Sphere. And though his Clan was moving in ways he had previously thought anathema, was it so truly destructive? He simply could not convince himself anymore.

He leaned against his 'Mech and thought again of the Black Dragons. If they were a traitorous group within the Combine, that would explain a piece of his vision. It would be the reason the Garnet Dragon was hunting the Ebony Dragon, but where had the Black gone and why? For a moment, Zane felt as if he stood before another of those doors of sudden revelation, but the moment passed and he could not bring it back.

He wondered about *Chu-sa* Yoshio's connection to this subversive group. Was he like the technician, simply aware of the subject and startled to hear the Black Dragon name coming from the mouth of a Nova Cat? Or was there more?

It truly amazed him that a chance slip of the tongue at this precise moment had given him further understanding of his vision, but he was still far from grasping its meaning.

In a few days the entire Dragoncat Cluster would fight the full Eleventh Alshain Avengers regiment for the first time. In accord with ancient Nova Cat tradition, the Cluster would hold a Ritual of Battle the night before combat to bring them victory. Visions were known to occur in the frenzied dancing, and one might come to Zane. Perhaps he would finally see into the truth of his vision.

23

Twenty solemn drum beats echoed across the plain, paying tribute to the twenty Clans originally created by The Founder: Blood Spirit, Burrock, Cloud Cobra, Coyote, Diamond Shark first known as Sea Fox, Fire Mandrill, Ghost Bear, Goliath Scorpion, Hell's Horses, Ice Hellion, Jade Falcon, Mongoose, Nova Cat, Smoke Jaguar, Snow Raven, Star Adder, Steel Viper, Widowmaker, Wolf, and Wolverine. As the echoing reverberations gradually died away it was a sobering reminder of how many Clans had fallen in the almost three centuries since their creation. The Wolverines and Smoke Jaguars annihilated; the Widowmaker, Mongoose, and Burrock Clans absorbed into other Clans; the Wolf Clan split asunder, and the Nova Cats Abjured. Treacherous were the waters of the future and deadly to the unwary.

For the Nova Cats, cast out by the very society they had helped forge, the currents had taken them far from their starting place. Now the proud warriors of the Dragoncat Cluster of Zeta Provisional Galaxy of Clan Nova Cat stood on the Plain of Horses, dedicated to the Star League Defense Force of a united Inner Sphere and sworn to protect the Draconis Combine world from all attackers. The future could be fickle indeed.

Dressed in their ceremonial leathers, the warriors stood around a great bonfire, waiting silently as Star Colonel Jal Steiner climbed up to the wooden platform that overlooked the gathering. He strode to the center of the platform, the brightness of the flames creating eerie shadows over his face. As he raised his arms, the only sound was the snap and crackle of the blazing fire.

He began to speak in that deep voice of his, which carried easily to every warrior in the circle. "And the Nova Cat warrior received a vision. And that vision showed lightning and death stalking the Clans. And he asked the Oathmaster, what can be done? The avatar of death moves against the Clans and they know it not."

Standing among the throng, Zane began to sway slightly from side to side with the others as the fire and the darkness and the words caught them in a spell. Though such archaic speech had never been heard in any Chronicle of Battles until now, the Star Colonel's voice was mesmerizing.

"And the Oathmaster bade him find the Path to lead our Clan back to Paradise. And the warrior knew it would bring hardship beyond measure to our Clan, yet he strengthened his resolve, knowing fully that a return to Paradise demanded sacrifices. The universe would burn, but with such offerings, a remnant of his Clan would be saved. And to another warrior he showed his vision, and he also believed, giving strength for what was to come."

Jal Steiner began to slowly weave his arms in a complex pattern, while letting his voice gradually increase in volume. "And so, with the courage of a Cluster, two warriors faced the Grand Kurultai of all the Khans of all the Clans of The Founder, Nicholas Kerensky. But the others would not heed their words and dismissed the warnings. And the day came and the two warriors held their heads high with the knowledge of the truth. And these warriors followed the Path and joined the rest of humanity to bring down those who called themselves Crusader Clans. For the visions had shown that only with one Clan's aid could the avatar of death be kept from consuming all!"

As he sang out the last words, Jal Steiner dropped to his knees and covered his face with his hands. Then he ran his hands back across his head and then down either side of his body, as though splashing himself with water. His voice became softer, yet somehow rang out with even greater clarity against the flames and the darkness.

"And with the spilt life's blood did they seal their martyrdom, showing us the path of true dedication. The Path back to Paradise. Severen Leroux. Lucian

Carns. Remember! Blessed Path, warriors!" His voice seemed to vibrate in the air as he stood over the warriors, his face lifted to the black sky. Then, with a slash of his hand, he gave the signal.

A thunderous drumming filled the night, the drumbeats moving air currents that whipped the flames and shot sparks and plumes of smoke into the air. The sound had become almost physical; none could escape its claws and their hearts beat to its rhythm. The drumming began to crescendo so loud that the very ground began to shake, and the gathered warriors felt as if the beating of their hearts was now one, the rhythm and force of blood rushing through the body of a single being.

And just when it seemed that none could stand such force of beating blood, a visible incarnation of the sound's power appeared for an instant in the air above the fire, and the entire gathering gave a shout. A pure unadulterated, ululation of savagery, pride, and power that was subsumed and enfolded into the beating rhythm as it raced across the rolling grasslands. The sound could be heard almost ten kilometers away in the city of New Circe.

The drumming suddenly diminished in volume, and the warriors remembered how to breathe on their own once more. Zane, awash in the glory of the Ritual of Battle, gazed at the familiar faces around him and could not help but smile. He no longer cared that Samuel teased him for being too serious. Tonight was for acclaiming the past and anointing tomorrow for victory against their enemies. Nothing else mattered.

The gathered warriors stood within a circle marked

by a shallow trench some thirty meters in diameter, which had been dug out to create the hallowed ground for tonight's ceremonies. To Zane's left, just outside the circle, were three drums of ascending size. To his knowledge, there had never been any special significance to the drums used in Ritual of Battle. However, for the Dragoncat Cluster, that had changed forever.

Under the direction of Jal Steiner, his three Star Captains had directed the work of dozens of labor castemen deep in the forest north of the base at Yama. After several days, the laborers had cut down three different trees and transported them back to Yama. The Star Colonel found only two of them acceptable and sent out another team almost a thousand kilometers to the north, where an almost untouched coniferous forest grew native trees of truly mammoth proportions. Nothing like this had ever been done among the Nova Cats, and Zane wondered if it was some holdover from Jal Steiner's Cloud Cobra roots.

Once a third tree was judged acceptable, he ordered a four-meter section hollowed out from the base of each tree trunk. Zane thought the trunks would collapse after losing so much of their interior, but Jal Steiner assured him that the tree walls would hold up if not unduly stressed. He also explained that the addition of internal supports would drastically alter the acoustics of the instrument. Zane had stared back uncomprehendingly.

The hollowed-out tree trunks were then fitted with pieces of bovine hide—still wet from the liming and tanning process—sewn together and then stretched across the opening on one end. The hides were lashed firmly in place through small holes drilled at intervals around the trunk and allowed to dry. The trees had become enormous drums to symbolize the strength and solidity of the Dragoncat Cluster.

Zane decided it did not matter where this tradition came from. Its effect in binding the Dragoncat warriors even closer together was electrifying to see and experience. Though he had raged against the formation of this Cluster, he no longer felt the anger. This was his unit and these warriors were his comrades.

On the right side of the circle, a dozen bondsmen clothed in white, loose-fitting garments stood on another platform and played a dozen different brass and woodwind instruments. Combined with the hypnotic drumming, it produced a primal and sensual music that stirred the warriors' feet to moving.

Many were already moving back from the fire, creating an open area around it. Zane watched as several warriors stepped into the space to begin a stately and intricate dance. This was only the beginning, and it would go on for hours, the tempo building continually until it had drawn everyone present into the dance. It was an ecstasy of sound and movement during which many warriors had received visions, which they would see in the flames as they danced in celebration of past and future victories.

Zane had not yet joined the dance, a part of his mind still recalling the way Jal Steiner had opened the ritual. He had not performed a traditional Chronicle of Battles like the ones performed monthly around a bonfire at midnight after the same twenty Clan drumbeats. Those were ritualistic retellings of past battles and victories of Nova Cat warriors, inspiring those present to rise to similar greatness.

Jal Steiner had departed radically from that tradition and instead had used this ritual to praise and glorify the Nova Cat Khans who had cast the Clan's lot with the Inner Sphere. At one time that would surely have unleashed in Zane a fury that blazed as bright as the bonfire. That had not happened. Listening to Jal's words, he had instead felt gratitude and admiration for Khans Leroux and Cairns, who till now he had despised as traitors who had corrupted the Nova Cats. He clenched his fists and tried to drum up the outrage that had fired him for so long, but it was gone.

With his back to the cool darkness of the plain and the front of his body warmed by the fire, Zane realized he no longer needed his rage to justify his existence. He had entered the Inner Sphere imbued with the fierce hatred of Spheroids bred into so many Clansmen and had vowed to correct the path his Clan had chosen. He had been blind, unable to see that what he wanted, what he thought he needed, was not what was the best for the Nova Cats. A vision spoke true and most times did not give you what you wanted to see. It gave instead what you needed to see. A warrior's own free will would then decide how he would live out that truth.

Standing there, he saw that all paths must lead to the only one worthy of travel—the path that truly preserved the Clan. With calm acceptance—a serenity he had never known—Zane understood that he had wasted much of the past few years heading down what turned out to be a dead end. With no remorse—

for he had learned lessons he otherwise might not have—Zane stepped into the space filled with dancing warriors, surrendering to the rhythmic call. Whatever mountain peaks or shadowed valleys his Clan might encounter on its current path, he would be a part of it.

His feet lifted and fell as he circled the leaping fire, and he wove his arms in the complex patterns as old as Clan Nova Cat itself. He felt the past wash away, and he opened his eyes to a bright future where he would fight to strengthen his Clan rather than struggle against it.

As he circled the fire with the rest of his comrades under the starry night sky, a strange thought intruded on his mind, a thought so far from all that was happening here and now that it almost sent him stumbling out of the circle.

He caught himself before he fell, but why in the name of Kerensky he would suddenly think of Clan Ghost Bear at this sacred moment, Zane could not even guess. It was strange, but maybe no stranger than the many other things that had happened within him this night. He let it go.

His feet had not lost the rhythm of the drums. They lifted and fell, and Zane continued to circle the fire with all the other warriors of the Dragoncat Cluster, his feet moving unerringly in the dance.

══ **24** ══

Plain of Horses
New Circe, Yamarovka
Irece Prefecture, Draconis Combine
1 October 3062

"**W**hat do you mean the exercise is canceled?" Zane asked heatedly over the commline. It had not even begun yet.

"That is the order I was given," Samuel replied, sounding equally disgusted. "Star Colonel Steiner just received the order and has relayed it on. He has also received a strange report from Zeta Command Compound and is attempting to verify."

The words sent a shiver down Zane's spine. It was that same feeling of standing before a door in his mind, of hovering at the portal of some knowing.

"Samuel, what do you mean? What is going on? Is it something to do with the Avengers?"

"He did not give me any specifics. What makes you think that, Zane?"

Zane hardly knew himself. "I am not sure. Where is the Star Colonel now? I need to talk to him."

"As far as I know, he has returned to the command compound and is probably out of his 'Mech by now. We have no way to reach him."

Zane tried anyway. For more than an hour, he continued to try to raise Jal Steiner on every frequency he could think of. After what seemed like an eternity, he finally got him on the commline.

"Star Colonel, do you have information about what the Avengers are doing?" Zane asked in a rush of words.

"That is a strange question, MechWarrior Zane. What makes you ask?"

"A vision, Star Colonel," Zane said quickly. Only after the words left his mouth did he understand the urgency of his desire to know. His vision and all the questions that had formed around it were falling into place, and he understood with absolute clarity that the Avengers had something to do with the riddle.

A momentary pause signaled Jal Steiner's surprise, but visions were never taken lightly among the Nova Cats. "From what *Chu-sa* Yoshio tells me, the Avengers have been unexpectedly reassigned by the DCMS High Command. They have been ordered to leave Yamarovka immediately. Another unit will take their place within the week. They were already deployed for today's combat exercise when the new orders came. It will take most of the day for them to return to the spaceport, but their DropShips are already preparing for departure."

A flare of understanding shot through Zane's mind, bringing illumination. For whatever reason, it came with the mention of Yoshio's name. Bits and pieces began to come together, forming a complete picture that expanded and filled his inner sight. It was like seeing the sketch of a painting suddenly washed in color, and Zane was dumbstruck at what his vision had shown him.

"Zane, what is going on?"

The insistent voice of his commander interrupted Zane's spinning thoughts. How to convince Jal Steiner of what he knew? Yes, the Nova Cats prized visions, but this? Even with the clues Zane had picked up, he had just made a giant leap of logic to where his vision led. Only his belief in it allowed him to believe the Avengers were about to attempt such suicide.

"Star Colonel, I have no complex explanation to give you, only plain words. I believe that the Avengers are being moved under orders that do *not* originate with the Draconis Combine High Command and that once they leave Yamarovka, they will cross the border into the Ghost Bear Dominion and strike directly at Alshain." He finished almost breathlessly, fully aware of how improbable it all must sound.

Once again, there was a long pause, as Jal Steiner attempted to digest the statement. "That is improbable, MechWarrior Zane," he said finally.

"I understand that, OvKhan," Zane began, trying with formal words to express his earnestness. "But I did have a vision during my Rite, which Oathmaster Minoru verified. And in the past few weeks, I have begun to understand its meaning. Only moments ago, I realized its full implications and the dangers they hold for the Nova Cats."

"But there is no way to authenticate your vision." Jal sounded exasperated. "One simply cannot challenge the word of an ally. Neither can I send an HPG message to Khan West to ask that he confirm the legitimacy of the Avengers' orders."

Several more moments passed in silence as Zane fidgeted in his command couch, fully aware of the Pandora's box he might have opened. But did he have a choice? If the Avengers were on their way to attack the Ghost Bears, it could be devastating to the Nova Cats as well as the Combine. And with Yamarovka one jump from the Ghost Bear border, Zeta Galaxy would be on the leading edge of the counterassault that was sure to follow.

"We must stop them from leaving, Star Colonel," he insisted.

"So, we simply inform our esteemed allies that we do not believe that they have received legitimate orders and that we will not allow them to depart until we can corroborate their story?" The sarcasm almost dripped from the commline.

"Aff, Star Colonel. I know it sounds ludicrous. But I know what is about to happen. Even if we have to seize their DropShips to stop them, we cannot let them leave."

"You would target their DropShips?" Jal said softly as if he did not believe his ears.

"Yes. I know it is not standard doctrine for the Clans to target an enemy's DropShips. But I say again, I *know* what I saw in my vision is already under way. If we seize their DropShips and my vision is wrong, then all we have done is create a political mess that Khan West will have to fix with the Combine High Command. If I am right, however, the Avengers will attack us. I am sure their timetable does not include fighting off an attack from us."

"You severely understate the 'political mess,' as you put it, that would occur. The fallout would be disastrous, since the entire purpose of this Cluster is to train alongside Combine troops so that both sides can learn to trust and respect one another. If this program fails, it will set back our program of integration by years. If we are to survive in the Inner Sphere, it is paramount that the program succeed."

"Star Colonel, I do understand the importance of our relationship with the Combine, and I stand ready to fight and die to see it hold. But I cannot ignore my own vision."

The silence on the commline stretched out for more than a minute. Zane knew his commander was having a difficult time assimilating the surprises of this morning.

"I will speak with Galaxy Commander Higall and personally vouch for your vision," Jal Steiner said at last, then broke off the connection.

Zane was surprised at how quickly it all happened, but perhaps it was because his commander knew how vehemently Zane had opposed the Nova Cats' current path; it had been the bane of Jal Steiner's existence for many months. For Zane to suddenly make such a radical about-face must have given his words, no matter how preposterous they sounded, a conviction impossible to ignore.

Opening up his commline to Samuel, he began to explain.

"Chu-sa Yoshio, our DropShips are reporting significant 'Mech activity at Zeta Command Compound." It was *Tai-i* Logan's voice coming over the portable comm.

Startled, Yoshio looked up from the information he had been scanning on the machine's display. Already most of his battalion was on the move—slightly ahead of the other two—on their way back to their DropShips waiting at the spaceport. It would take most of the day because he'd been forced to deploy the entire Eleventh Regiment north of the Plain of Horses, despite his knowing that the engagement with the Nova Cats would never take place. It was the only way to keep the Clanners from discovering the truth. But now, after so many months of planning, Operation *Batsu* was underway and nothing could stop it.

The operation was not without risks, however. If the Ghost Bears decided to strike back, border worlds garrisoned by the Cats would surely be among the first targeted. Yoshio's respect for Zane tugged at his conscience, but he knew how to ward off those feelings. He must be pure, no matter the cost, he reminded himself forcefully.

"Do not be concerned, *Tai-i*. They know nothing."

"Hai, Chu-sa. I would not have mentioned it, but the base reports a steady stream of Nova Cat 'Mechs leaving their BattleMech storage and repair facility. The duty officer thought activity on that scale was too unusual to ignore."

Yoshio felt the hairs on the back of his neck rise. It must be a coincidence. The Nova Cats had no reason to be suspicious, no way of knowing the truth. Even if they did, it would take more than a day for them to verify the regiment's movements with their own high command. By then, the Eleventh Alshain Avengers would be long gone.

He dismissed the thought. "It is nothing, *Tai-i*," he repeated. "Ignore it."

Turning away, he began packing up the rest of the equipment from his field command post. It was time for him to get into the cockpit of his *Bishamon* and be on his way.

25

Plain of Horses
New Circe, Yamarovka
Irece Prefecture, Draconis Combine
1 October 3062

"You have to understand his position, Zane. Galaxy Commander Higall must walk a fine line with the Combine. If he does not, a mistake could have terrible consequences. For now, he will not mobilize. You understand, quiaff?"

Zane had come to meet with Jal Steiner out on the Plain of Horses, their 'Mechs waiting nearby.

"Aff, Star Colonel." He understood, but that did not mean he had to like it. The Galaxy Commander had decreed that he would not aid the Dragoncat Cluster against the Avengers in any way, but he would not hinder them either. Thus, if the Nova Cats secured the spaceport but the Avengers never attacked, the political fallout would be directed at the Dragoncat Cluster and not the whole Zeta Galaxy. And even if the Avengers did attack, it might have no connection to any subversive secret society. It would not be the first time an Alshain Avengers unit had attacked Nova Cat forces without provocation, and the capture of their DropShips might only fuel their rage. Either way, Zeta Provisional Galaxy would protect its compound and nothing else. Zane could not help feeling disgust that his Galaxy Commander was taking the safe route.

"Good," Jal Steiner said. "Then we will proceed as we have planned." He looked across the Plain of Horses, which would soon be filled with Avenger 'Mechs. "I trust in your vision, Zane, and so do the other warriors of the Cluster. Though it is a difficult thing we do, it must be done. Blessed Path, warrior." With that, he moved away toward his *Shadow Cat*.

Zane stood watching him go for a moment, surprised and moved by the Star Colonel's words. Then he turned to find his own 'Mech, feeling that his decision to recommit himself to his Clan and its leadership was the right one.

As he walked toward his *Pack Hunter*, he could see the spaceport almost a kilometer away in the distance. Knowing that the massed firepower of the dozen grounded Avenger DropShips could wipe out the Cluster before they could defend themselves, the Galaxy Commander had agreed to a plan that did not commit him to attacking.

The eight DropShips of Zeta Provisional Galaxy sat opposite the Avenger ships on the far side of the spaceport. With the ships' guns armed and locked onto the Avenger DropShips, the Nova Cat commander had called his counterpart, offering a choice between mutual destruction or agreeing not to interfere in the coming fight. It was paramount that the Dragoncat Cluster not have armed and hostile DropShips at their back. A tense hour passed before a message that the Combine commander agreed to stand down was received. If the Avengers won through to their DropShips, the Nova Cat ships would not prevent them from leaving. Until that time, the Combine ships would remain spectators of the drama that was about to unfold.

Lightning strobed the gloomy sky, followed an instant later by a long roll of thunder. Zane looked up, surprised. The sound was much closer than a few minutes ago. A storm front was moving in quickly. If there was going to be a battle, it would happen in the middle of a deluge. Zane smiled at the thought of the diminished visibility.

Normally, the superior ranges of Clan weapons would permit the Nova Cats to strike at an enemy before the enemy could strike back. In this case, the Avengers outnumbered the Cluster by more than two to one, so the advantage of range would be lost to superior numbers. With the storm front coming on so quickly, the reduced visibility would mean the Nova Cats would have to fight only a small number of Alshain 'Mechs at a time. Then they would use their speed to move on before the rest of the Alshain force could be brought to bear. Best of all, the storm would let them pull off the most daring part of their plan—the Dragoncat Cluster would strike first. Though Galaxy Commander Higall had ordered Jal

Steiner not to attack unless the Combine troops attacked first, their only chance of victory was to seize and keep the initiative.

Zane reached his *Pack Hunter* and began climbing up the retractable ladder to his cockpit as the first drops of warm rain began to fall. His hair was wet and rivulets were running down his back before he could get inside and secure the hatch against the weather. The unexpected image of the rain as blood flashed through his mind. Yes, he thought, blood would run this day.

"What?" Yoshio yelled into his commline. He was so furious his hands trembled on the *Bishamon*'s joysticks. He forced himself to breathe in deeply, trying to calm himself enough to process what he'd just heard.

"The Nova Cats have secured our DropShips at the spaceport," *Tai-sa* Myazaki repeated. "Captain Taiga has just informed me of the situation. They question our orders to redeploy and want to verify it through their own chain of command. They have politely requested that we wait outside the spaceport for a period of forty-eight hours while they corroborate our orders."

Yoshio knew that *Tai-sa* Myazaki was equally furious, but admired the way he kept his composure. Both men were aware that everything depended on keeping to the timetable. Obviously, their orders to depart Yamarovka immediately could never be confirmed by DCMS High Command because it was pure sham. If word of that reached Yamarovka before the Avengers could leave, all would be lost.

They had to depart within twenty-four hours or they would never leave at all.

"Why would they be suspicious now?" Myazaki asked. "The Nova Cats have never questioned our orders before and have been lax in allowing our JumpShips to arrive and depart from their systems. Of course, they've got their WarShips guarding every system, but why suddenly question our movements now?"

The accusation was not stated, but Yoshio knew it was there. His battalion had been on Yamarovka the longest, and it was well known that he had spent considerable time in the company of certain Nova Cat warriors, most notably MechWarrior Zane.

Maneuvering his 'Mech around a particularly rough spot of ground, Yoshio could think of no time in the past several months where a breach of security might have occurred. Everything had been routine, with absolutely nothing out of the ordinary.

"I have no idea, *Tai-sa*. As far as I am aware, complete security has been maintained. There have been no breaches."

"There is more. Captain Taiga reports that the Dragoncat Cluster is arrayed against us at the head of the Plain of Horses, while the rest of Zeta Provisional Galaxy has been deployed in a defensive position around the Zeta Command Compound. What do you make of that?"

Yoshio suddenly wondered if Zane was somehow responsible. The man had been attempting to speak with him for over a week. Though Yoshio had been off Yamarovka for much of that time, he had not wished to test his resolve to complete his mission against the strange connection he felt with Zane. Abruptly, he remembered a conversation between him and Zane on the trip back from Irece weeks ago. Zane had mentioned something about an Ebony Dragon, startling Yoshio so much that he had let it show for a moment. It hardly seemed possible that Zane could have become suspicious because of that minor slip. Nevertheless, the thought nagged at him. Why else would only the Dragoncat Cluster be preparing to prevent the regiment from getting to their DropShips?

"Again, *Tai-sa*, I know of no security breach. Why only a single Cluster? This I cannot explain."

"Neither can I. However, our timetable must not change. We could make up any lost time by making a faster burn to our JumpShips. However, whether we attack today or wait the forty-eight hours, you know as well as I what the response will be to the Nova Cat inquiry. If the Cats are foolish enough to deploy only a Cluster against us, then we will smash through them quickly and be on our way. We cannot commit our entire force all at once, as I do not trust Zeta Galaxy to maintain their neutral role. They will move—it is only a matter of predicting when they will do so. Proceed to grid Z33E for a command staff meeting. I want a working plan of attack by that time."

"*Hai*, *Tai-sa*." Switching off the commline, Yoshio stared woodenly ahead. How could they have known? Shaking his head, afraid that he would never know, he began planning a campaign to destroy warriors he had trained alongside for many months. Even for the Alshain Avengers, dedicated for the whole last decade to resisting the Clans, this would be a difficult thing. He was not the only one who had come to respect the Nova Cats.

Light strobed the darkness and rent the fabric of the universe. An expanding ball of energy formed in the nameless star system and then collapsed, revealing a *Star Lord* Class JumpShip. On its prow was the red dragon symbol of the Draconis Combine, and alongside it, still glistening with newly applied paint, was an emblem showing a fire raging under the planet Alshain.

Carrying a full complement of six DropShips, the starship had just jumped from the Courchevel system in the Albiero Prefecture into this uncharted star system on the border between the Draconis Combine and the Ghost Bear Dominion. The last jump before crossing into Ghost Bear territory would require approximately two hundred-ten hours of recharge time; the system's Class M red giant provided very little energy for recharging. The ship would remain here for almost nine days.

Light strobed the darkness and rent the fabric of the universe. An expanding ball of energy formed in the Meilen star system of Buckminster Prefecture and then collapsed, revealing a *Star Lord* Class JumpShip. On its prow, the symbol of the Draconis Combine, and alongside it, still glistening with newly applied paint, was an emblem showing a planet surrounded by a wreath of fire.

To the *Star Lord*'s portside, just over two kilometers distant, the squat frame of another ship hung suspended. It might have been mistaken for a DropShip at first glance, until it became apparent that the ship was deploying its delicate jump sail to collect the star's energy and recharge its jump drive. Though its one hundred-eighty-five meters was far less than the *Star Lord*'s immense length, the *Tatsumaki* Class WarShip massed more than twice the JumpShip's weight, and the bristling weapons that sheathed it spoke of deadly purpose. After five days of recharge, both ships would jump into a nameless system just this side of the Combine-Ghost Bear border, where they would recharge one final time for the final leap to their target.

Light strobed the darkness and rent the fabric of the universe. An expanding ball of energy formed in the Dumaring star system of the Buckminster Prefecture and then collapsed, revealing an *Invader* Class JumpShip. On its prow was the symbol of the Draconis Combine, and alongside it, still glistening with newly applied paint, an emblem showing a sword rising out of fire.

The ship immediately engaged its small station-keeping drive and began to move away from its entry point. Exactly one hour passed while the *Invader* moved to a position almost two kilometers away, and then a hole in reality was again torn as a second JumpShip, a *Merchant* Class, appeared. It bore the same two emblems. Both ships would recharge here for five days before bending space once more to jump into an uncharted star system, their last stop before crossing the border into the Ghost Bear Dominion.

It had begun.

26

Plain of Horses
New Circe, Yamarovka
Irece Prefecture, Draconis Combine
1 October 3062

Rain, driven horizontal by gale force winds, swept across the Plain of Horses. The storm had been raging for three hours, with no sign of letting up. Giant thunderheads darkened the sky, and a lightning display unlike anything either Nova Cat or Combine warrior had ever seen split the sky with continual flashes. Topsoil, loosely held by the grasses that clung to life on the plain, had turned to mud under the deluge. When the sun finally set, the plain was pitched into complete darkness, broken only by nature's strobe light.

As man and beast cowered from the violence of the storm, man's avatars of war stalked the spectral landscape, undaunted by nature's fury. With a *Raptor* in his sights, Zane fired his PPC, the supersonic beam's thunderous passage followed quickly by the equally thunderous impact against the target. Kinetic energy and terrible heat savaged the *Raptor*'s right arm, consuming it and vaporizing what little armor remained on the right torso. The already-blackened emblem of a blazing dragon vanished with the armor. Then the last of the energy bolt flicked inward, caressing the internal structure. The *Raptor* had only moments more to live, with no hope of escape.

Running parallel to the *Raptor*, Zane swung the *Pack Hunter*'s torso to the right, bringing his shoulder-mounted PPC to bear on the fleeing 'Mech. The pilot was good. Trying to put distance between himself and his pursuer, he ran the *Raptor* in a zigzag that made it more difficult to hit. But Zane felt as though his *Pack Hunter* had suddenly grown a targeting computer, so confident was he of his shot.

The green light on his console flashed ready—indicating that the weapon had recharged itself. He caressed the firing stud on his joystick, already looking toward his secondary screen for another target of opportunity. The azure beam found its target unerringly, slashing into the back of the retreating *Raptor*. The 'Mech disintegrated, the pilot dying even before he was aware his life had ended.

The soil at Zane's feet suddenly exploded, geysering into the air and splattering his 'Mech's legs with mud, which the rain quickly washed away. Stomping down on the peddles for the *Pack Hunter*'s jump jets, he tried vainly to see where the shot had come from as he was hurled into the tumultuous sky. He guessed that it had been a gauss rifle slug and that he was lucky mud was the only thing that had splattered. Propelled by a series of magnetic rings, the watermelon-sized nickel-ferrous gauss slug reached supersonic speeds, and the resulting kinetic energy transfer to the target was incredible and often terminal. The gauss rifle was one of the most powerful weapons mounted on a 'Mech, and Zane had no wish to test the *Pack Hunter*'s armor against such force.

An abrupt flash lit up the night as lightning again split the sky. The brief illumination revealed a hulking 'Mech whose two arms each ended in the gaping maw of a gauss rifle barrel. It was a *Gunslinger*, a neckless 'Mech with armor so rounded it had almost no straight lines. The *Gunslinger* was already attempting to find Zane again, aware that he had taken to the air. Luck was on Zane's side, however, as he had inadvertently jumped in the wrong direction. When he saw the eighty-five-ton behemoth, which outweighed him by almost three to one, Zane knew he would have to jump again to get out of there.

As the *Pack Hunter* was beginning to descend back toward the ground, he ignited a short burst from his jump jets to bleed off most of his speed. Then he brought the *Pack Hunter* into a light landing that few MechWarriors would have been able to achieve. Tonight, he felt as though the myths were true and he had become part of his 'Mech, firing and moving as though the thirty-ton giant were his own skin and bones. Without hesitation, he sped away into the darkness.

This was tonight's third sortie against the right flank of the oncoming Alshain Avengers, and Zane knew his Cluster had inflicted significant casualties. Striking from the darkness, applying maximum force and withdrawing before the enemy could organize, they had demonstrated that their training in Inner Sphere tactics was complete.

Twinges of conscience had plagued him during the first encounter, sorrow at the loss of honor in betraying the tradition of *zellbrigen* warring with his newfound devotion to his Cluster and Clan. The danger this Combine regiment represented was too great. Whatever the means, Zane had vowed to stop them.

During the second sortie, after joining Samuel in his *Supernova* to concentrate fire on a hapless *Javelin*, he again felt an attack of conscience. And again he steeled himself to do what he must.

By the third sortie, when he had surprised the *Raptor* pilot and destroyed him without first declaring a duel, he no longer felt any twinges. All that mattered this night was a victory for his Clan.

As he listened to the calls of the warriors of his Trinary buzzing back and forth over the commline, he noted that Star Commander Kol of Charlie Striker Star and MechWarrior Barril of Alpha Striker Star did not respond. The Dragoncats were indeed inflicting heavy casualties, but each time they lost a few of their own. And in a battle of attrition, superior numbers would always win.

Zane knew there was only one thing to do as he continued to move toward the rendezvous point. They must hold the line.

The topsoil, already weakened by the onslaught of rain, gave way beneath so much weight. Feeling the right front leg of his *Bishamon* sliding away beneath him, Yoshio canted his four-legged 'Mech back, while simultaneously crouching and lifting the offending appendage up from the ground. His piloting skills, combined with the innately superior balance of a quad 'Mech, allowed Yoshio to keep his machine upright. Testing the ground gingerly, he again set the leg down, and the *Bishamon* rose to its full height.

"*Tai-i* Sanders, repeat. I say again, repeat your last message," he called over the commline. Distracted by the sudden pitching of his 'Mech, he had missed his subordinate's final words.

"*Hai*! It would appear that the Nova Cats have again struck our right flank. *Chu-i* Takada is—"

"They appear to have attacked us again?" Yoshio interrupted. "Is there another force on this planet of which we are not aware? Perhaps the white witch has sent a regiment against us in retaliation for the Dragon taking the Lyons Thumb? Or perhaps a force of Smoke Jaguar ghosts has been summoned by this infernal storm and are now wreaking vengeance on those who sent them to their graves? Speak plainly, *Tai-i*. Exactly where, how, and what are our losses?"

"*Sumimasen, Chu-sa*. A force of Nova Cat warriors, a reinforced company—what they call a Trinary—attacked our far-right forward flank eight minutes ago. After destroying our outriders, they vanished into the storm once more. I have not confirmed, but initial reports indicate we lost five 'Mechs in the exchange. *Chu-i* Takada refrained from pursuing them, following the last disaster."

Yoshio grimaced as he listened. The disaster referred to was the loss of four 'Mechs and then another three as the woefully unprepared demi-company had raced headlong after the supposedly fleeing Nova Cats. What a mistake it had been to train the Clanners in Inner Sphere tactics. Dislodging them from the Combine world would now be a much costlier undertaking. Added to their superior technology and superlative warriors, the Nova Cats also had a whole new bag of tricks that the Smoke Jaguars had not.

Glancing to his right, he glimpsed the still-burning fuselage of a downed Clan OmniFighter. Seeing a single wing with canted tips and twin rudders, he thought it might be a *Batu*. Then he realized that the entire front portion of the craft, from just behind the canopy forward, was simply gone, torn away on impact. The fact that it could still burn under such torrential rain was astounding.

Yoshio could not help a flash of admiration as he gazed at the fighter. The pilots of Charlie Fighter Star, who had trained with his own Eleventh Alshain Aerospace, had flown into the teeth of this storm, braving weather that had grounded his own fighters. Fifteen 'Mechs had been lost to their audacity before his people had rallied enough to bring three of the fighters down. As it was, Yoshio knew only the weather had finally forced the Clan fighters from the sky. He shuddered to think how much more damage would have been done had the storm not worsened.

"Pull the outriders in closer," he said. "The Clanners are more mobile than we are, and they know our exact line of travel. They will be able to attack us from any direction. We must keep them from being able to pick off single units by presenting them a broad front. I cannot think that they would strike from the same direction a fourth time. Make sure the left flank knows they are likely to come under attack. Understand?"

"*Hai, Chu-sa.* It will be done immediately."

Yoshio pushed the throttle forward, and the spider-like *Bishamon* again stalked across the battlefield, impatient to end the stinging raids of the Nova Cats.

Five for two. The numbers told him that the Avengers would triumph in the end, but they would lose more than a battalion of 'Mechs doing so. They had already lost two full companies to a half-dozen Clan 'Mechs and three fighters. At this rate, it would be a Pyrrhic victory leaving them with nothing to use against the Ghost Bears.

A thought came unbidden to Yoshio. *Where are you, Zane?*

"Where are you, Yoshio?" Zane said softly, his voice echoing inside his neurohelmet. Though he no longer denied his inexplicable connection with the Combine officer, it would not stop him from fighting Yoshio if he must. And truth be told, he wanted that fight. In what seemed like a lifetime ago, he had felt cheated when the tide of the battle had pulled them apart in that unforgettable exercise.

He should have defeated Yoshio that day, and the warrior in him cried out for a chance to finish what he had started. Yet, he had come far enough from that day to understand that the survival of his Clan came first. Though he yearned to face off with Yoshio again, he stayed with the plan explained to him by Samuel.

Following their third sortie of an hour ago, Jal Steiner had re-formed the remaining Nova Cat warriors into new Stars. Much to Zane's surprise, his *Pack Hunter*—which had a maximum speed of almost one hundred-twenty kilometers per hour—was the slowest 'Mech in his new Star. The orders quickly illuminated the reason for this deployment. Jal wanted to strike at the Avengers from the left and right flank simultaneously. After three straight assaults on the right, he was sure the enemy would expect the next one to come from the left. The Nova Cats again struck from the right, while a Star was sent to attack from the enemy's left flank after they had turned their attention away. It was dangerous to split your forces in the face of the enemy, but the situation was desperate enough to warrant it.

The Star sent toward the Avengers' left flank consisted of Zane in his *Pack Hunter*, MechWarriors Jacqil and Jason each in an *Incubus*, MechWarrior Pela in a *Jenner* 3, and MechWarrior Killian in her repaired *Snow Fox*. With the storm continuing to shroud the landscape in a fog of rain and darkness, the five 'Mechs had sped through the night. Passing behind the rear of the enemy, they came well beyond the left flank before again turning toward New Circe. It had taken most of the hour to do it, and they were just in position as multi-colored energy beams began to light the looming clouds from within some ten kilometers in the distance. The thumping sounds of explosions and the staccato fire of autocannons soon carried to the external speakers of their 'Mechs.

Jal Steiner had given Zane command of the Star, much to his intense surprise. He would have to prove himself worthy of the rank in a Trial of Position following the battle—if he lived to see the day.

"They have engaged," Zane said even though he knew his Star mates could see the light display. The fifteen minutes they were to wait seemed to crawl by with agonizingly slowness. His entire body was tensed and ready to move the *Pack Hunter* forward. Only by keeping an iron grip on himself did Zane keep his hands from instinctively going to the throttle. The last seconds ticked off, and then it was time.

"Go!" he shouted. As his Star raced to engage the enemy's left flank, his PPC already moving to find a target, he no longer needed to hold back.

In the back of his mind one thought still persisted. *Will I fight you this night?*

27

**Plain of Horses
New Circe, Yamarovka
Irece Prefecture, Draconis Combine
2 October 3062**

Yoshio tightened the grip on his joystick, launching a flight of twenty medium-range missiles into a swarm of Elementals that had just finished off an *Owens* light OmniMech. Knowing the danger represented by these bioengineered super-infantry, he fired even while backing away from them. Though he prized his four-legged 'Mech for a number of reasons, he could only bring its weapons to bear on targets within his front arc.

The impact of the missiles shattered one Elemental's armor, pulping the human inside beyond recognition. The remaining missiles, along with the shock of the explosions, scattered the armored infantry in every direction. They almost looked like large, drunken men stumbling and wheeling in the darkness, but quickly regained their feet and began to use their jump packs to come bounding across the rain-swept hills.

Ruby beams flickered from Yoshio's left, cutting one Elemental in half and knocking several more out of the sky. He grinned in satisfaction as an Avenger *Komodo* come alongside his *Bishamon*. The hunched *Komodo* was designed specifically to counter the Clan armored infantry, and a cowling around each wrist carried five medium lasers. Yoshio continued to back away, feeling no loss of honor at leaving this job in the hands of a 'Mech designed for it.

After he had backed up several hundred meters, he took a side-step that moved him laterally and forward at the same time, a maneuver possible only in a four-legged 'Mech. From here, he could make out the spaceport just over two kilometers away. The rain was beginning to let up, and the clouds to the east glowed with the luminescence of approaching dawn. The sight of his regiment's waiting DropShips was like gazing at the Promised Land after forty years of wandering in the desert. This night had certainly *felt* like forty years, he thought darkly.

The latest assault had almost shattered his battalion, and only the arrival of First Battalion had salvaged the victory. The Nova Cats had withheld their heavy and assault 'Mechs until the final moment and then unleashed them. The Star of heavies consisted of two *Supernova*s, two *Nova Cat*s, and what Yoshio thought was a *Highlander* IIC. The five 'Mechs shattered the lance holding his front line, then drove through the sudden gap, penetrating behind the front edge of his force. Then the Clan 'Mechs had veered to the left, catching the entire right side of his line from behind. Their massed firepower amounted to more than an entire company of his own 'Mechs. He had lost another lance of 'Mechs in the first thirty seconds following the breach.

As Yoshio's right flank disintegrated, the remaining Nova Cats on that side had swung around to apply pressure to the left flank. The whole front line began to collapse, and Yoshio watched helplessly as his men died faster then he could count. For the first time during this hellish night he contemplated defeat. Then the stabbing beams of energy and flickering exhaust of hundreds of missiles descending through the brightening sky heralded the arrival of an additional two companies from First Battalion. The Nova Cat warriors fought back like demons possessed, using their legendary ability to target any location with their energy weapons to deadly effect.

Yoshio could still see the one remaining 'Mech from that assault Star as it stood in a field littered with destroyed 'Mechs. The image would stay with him to the grave. Lit from below, the *Nova Cat* was seared and pockmarked, its shattered left arm hanging low, attached only by the connective wires. A quick glance at his IR screen showed the machine glowing white-hot. Yoshio couldn't believe the warrior had even survived such heat, much less been able to keep the 'Mech functioning. It blazed away with the two lasers still mounted in its left arm. Yoshio had never faced the new heavy-type lasers fielded by the Clans, but the horrific damage the

oversized energy beams dealt could be nothing else.
The *Nova Cat* OmniMech, pride of the Nova Cat Tou-
man, seemed determined to destroy all Clan enemies.
But it had fallen in the end.

Now, as Yoshio stared at the distant spaceport, he
was again confident of victory—but at what price?
He had received reports of twenty-three Nova Cat
'Mechs confirmed destroyed. His battalion, however,
had been decimated, and the whole regiment had
lost twice that number. A Pyrrhic victory indeed.

"Did you die this night, Zane?" he whispered to
himself. Just as he was opening a commline to the
DropShips, he glimpsed a BattleMech moving among
the smoking pyres some four hundred meters to his
left. Thinking he recognized the design, he punched
up a magnification on his viewscreen.

The image of a battered *Pack Hunter* leapt up
toward him.

Zane used the *Pack Hunter*'s jump jets to get closer
to the target he had instinctively been seeking the
whole night long. He brought the 'Mech back down
to the ground some four hundred meters from the
Bishamon and opened a wide-beam channel that
would let all hear what was said. He had never imagined how this moment would transpire, but as he
faced his enemy across the death-filled landscape, he
knew there was only one true way to resolve it.

"I am MechWarrior Zane of Clan Nova Cat. I pilot
the sole *Pack Hunter* in all the Dragoncat Cluster. I
hereby invoke the ritual of *zellbrigen* and challenge
Chu-sa Yoshio, pilot of the *Bishamon*, to a duel of
warriors. In this solemn matter, let none interfere!"

Only silence greeted his announcement.

The few Combine and Nova Cat warriors still engaged were so surprised that their fighting sputtered to a halt, and all turned toward the challenger.

Staring at the defiant *Pack Hunter*, whose armor showed only minor burns and tears, Yoshio could not help but admire the other warrior. Pushing the throttle forward, he closed the distance to three hundred meters. He halted the *Bishamon* and also opened a broadband channel.

"I am Palmer Yoshio, *Chu-sa* of Third Battalion, Eleventh Alshain Avengers in the Draconis Combine Mustered Soldiery of the Draconis Combine," he said. "For five generations my family has taken up the sword in service of the Dragon, and in my thirty-one years of life, I have fought and bled on more then a dozen worlds. I accept your challenge and may none interfere."

Though it had not been a traditional samurai acceptance of a challenge, Yoshio felt his words had fit the bill.

In response he heard Zane utter a single word, "Seyla."

Facing off with this valiant warrior, Yoshio knew he would mourn the loss of him. But several moments turned into nearly a full minute as the two 'Mechs stood silently across a gap of three hundred meters. The rain had finally ceased, and the winds were beginning to push the clouds to the east. Across the plains, he saw a shimmer of golden light and knew that within minutes the sun would crest the horizon.

* * *

Zane stared across the space separating his 'Mech from Yoshio's, knowing what he had to do. Still euphoric, he was confident that Yoshio would fall to him, yet he still had not made a move. Something tugged at him, one last unanswered question.

"Yoshio, why?" he asked over the wide-band frequency.

"Why what? Why have we fought this night? I have my own question, Zane. How?"

Zane understood. Yoshio wanted to know how the Nova Cats had known about the Alshain Avengers' plan? He decided to tell the truth. "You will not accept the answer, but I will tell you anyway. Simply, it was the vision I had on Tengoku Mountain. Though it took me weeks to understand the strange images, I finally saw the meaning and realized that the Alshain Avengers would attack the Ghost Bears. And though it might cost me my life and has already claimed the lives of many of my Clansmen, we had to stop you."

His voice echoed across the field of battle, but Yoshio did not answer.

"Do you have any idea what you could have done, Yoshio? I have heard you speak of Clan Ghost Bear with respect. And yet, you take their reticence to expand their borders or involve themselves in the power struggles around them as a sign of weakness.

"Do you not understand the nature of the Bear? For months he sleeps in hibernation, but do not dare disturb him. The Bear's anger is unforgiving once provoked. The Ghost Bears did poorly in the invasion, yet look at them now. Strong and whole where others have been broken and destroyed."

"We know well the strength of Clan Ghost Bear!" Yoshio retorted angrily. "That is why we are just one of the regiments sent to take back our homeworld. We know what the Ghost Bear can do, but it does not matter. The cave they occupy was ours long before your Nicholas Kerensky was conceived! That is why we fought this night. We must return Combine worlds to Combine hands and cleanse ourselves of the Clans!"

Zane sat speechless, too stunned to fully register the vulgar slur against The Founder. The death of almost the entire Dragoncat Cluster had been for naught. The Eleventh Alshain Avengers were just one of the regiments planning to attack the Ghost Bears. How could they be so blind? An attack on Alshain would rouse the sleeping bear, and there would be blood to pay.

Yoshio's hands shook with anger. Zane's words had rekindled all his old hatred of the Clans and the shameful path down which the Coordinator had led the Combine. It no longer mattered that the Nova Cats were warriors to be admired. There was no evil in respecting one's enemy. It was his *ninjo*, his compassion, that said his relationship with Zane should matter. But Yoshio was a samurai of the Draconis Combine—the *true* Draconis Combine—and he knew his *giri*, his duty. The Combine must be washed clean of its impurities.

Abruptly, using knowledge of Clan ways that he had learned in his time among the Nova Cats, he thought of a way to walk the thin line between *ninjo* and *giri*.

"To honor the comradeship we share, I offer hegira," Yoshio said. He knew that the Clan rite of hegira permitted one's foe to withdraw from the field of battle without further combat and no loss of honor.

Would Zane see it that way?

Closing his eyes, thinking of the wasted lives of his comrades, Zane waited for the surge of wrath that should have come. But there was nothing. His mind flashed to his waking vision of himself and Yoshio as opponents, each one pushing against the same barrier blocking his path. Instead of anger, he felt sorrow. Yoshio believed, as Zane had for so long, that one's Clan could not prosper and grow unless it was purified. But that was not the way. The path lay in purifying oneself. And if that required you accept your bitterest enemy walking at your side, then that was the price and it had to be paid.

Though he knew it would change nothing, he thumbed the open commline. "I have purified myself, Palmer. Join me."

It was the first time he had ever used Yoshio's first name. Perhaps the shock of such familiarity would awaken the Combine warrior. As for Zane, he had found peace at last. This was the path.

Kashira Hohijo Goshiki's tears rolled down cheeks hot with shame. Having been raised in a staunch samurai household, he had watched with disgust as the Draconis Combine sold away its purity and honor. Becoming a member of the Alshain Avengers and joining the Black Dragon Society had seemed only natural; they all had waited long years to strike back at the inhuman Clans. The Avengers' assignment to train with the Nova Cats had been his worst nightmare, and he had spent every waking moment on this damnable world trying to keep from being tainted by the savages.

As the two sides took up arms this night, he had rejoiced at the chance to strike back at those who had taken so much from his House. But the night had held terrors he could not have imagined, and he was the only member of his company still alive. He had watched as the despicable Cats struck from hiding, killing his friends and comrades. His own *Blackjack* was missing an arm and most of its armor. The hip actuator in the right leg had frozen, and all but one of his weapons was destroyed.

Now, filled with rage, hate, and sorrow, he stared across a distance of five hundred meters at this Nova Cat warrior who stood there so arrogantly and dared challenge *Chu-sa* Yoshio to a duel.

The tears had begun at the word *hegira*. Even he knew what it meant, and he was overwhelmed that his commander would allow this subhuman to depart. In fury he lined up the HUD of his only remaining weapon on the *Pack Hunter*. Concentrating a lifetime of training on this instant, he fired.

A flame a meter and a half long shot from the barrel of his autocannon, the depleted-uranium slugs hammering into the right shoulder and tracking into the head of the Clan 'Mech. He fought the recoil with all the strength of his anger, keeping the weapon on target. He smiled when he saw the result. The headless 'Mech toppled to the ground.

Yoshio watched transfixed as the *Pack Hunter* fell. "What have you done?" he screamed. He was just turning the *Bishamon* toward the Combine 'Mech that had violated the ritual duel when voices burst over the commline.

"*Chu-sa*," his *Tai-i* said, "we have multiple readings of 'Mechs leaving the defensive perimeter of the Zeta Command Compound. There are at least two Clusters pushing past their lines toward our position. ETA is less then ten minutes. They must have been monitoring this entire engagement."

Yoshio was fully aware of what would come of this breach of the ritual of *zellbrigen*. Zeta Galaxy was on the move. He ignored the call, taking his 'Mech in a run toward the savaged *Blackjack*.

He opened a commline to the warrior piloting the 'Mech. "Fool, do you not realize we had won? What did it matter if one warrior got away?"

Without waiting for a reply, he triggered a full volley of all his weapons. The strobing green darts of pulse lasers, the searing beams of ruby light, the contrails of missiles pummeled the already wounded *Blackjack*, destroying it instantly and killing the pilot. Yoshio felt no remorse.

"All units, pull back. I repeat, pull back." Though he felt sadness over the death of Zane, his *giri* demanded that he survive the coming onslaught.

Taking his 'Mech back across the ground they had fought so hard to win, he could not help think that it was for the best. If you take an enemy as a friend, how can he be your enemy? And Yoshio knew that the Clans, no matter how they looked or what words they spoke, were the enemy.

Still, as he glanced one final time at the fallen *Pack Hunter* that looked so like a warrior in repose from this distance, a question came. *Did Zane not win?*

He did not know who had the answer.

28

The 'Mech plummeted. Buffeted by the howling winds of its passage, it fell at terminal velocity through the gloomy skies of a rain-washed afternoon on the world of Alshain. Only five kilometers distant, the ground rushed upward to crush the falling machine. Cocooned in the cockpit in the 'Mech's head—fashioned in the likeness of the mythical demon for which it was named—*Chu-sa* Jennifer Kiyaga knew fear; a pulsing, throbbing sensation that suffused her being and threatened to block out every other sensory input.

It wasn't the combat drop that frightened her. She had participated in a number of near-orbit drops in which her AKU-1X *Akuma* was jettisoned from a

DropShip. The drop pod protected it through the fiery interface with a planet's atmosphere, allowing the 'Mech to descend safely on jump jets that were either integral to its design or had been attached to it for that purpose. The maneuver was dangerous, but she was confident in her ability to bring her 'Mech to the surface of Alshain without mishap. It was what she had seen in the last several hours that had evoked her dread.

As commander of Second Battalion of the Fourteenth Alshain Avengers, she had waited for this moment with barely suppressed excitement for almost four straight weeks after leaving Courchevel. As they entered Ghost Bear territory—which she would never think of as the Ghost Bear Dominion—she knew that the exhaustive training given all the Avenger regiments would finally pay off. After ten long years, they would finally *avenge* the injustice of the Clan invasion and take back their homeworld. Knowing the terrible fight that was to come, but supremely confident of victory, Kiyaga—like all the Avenger warriors—had strained against the enforced inactivity of space travel, yearning to wreak havoc on the unsuspecting Ghost Bears.

Then the cherished dream had been twisted into a nightmare. Knowing that the Ghost Bears would have WarShips guarding both the nadir and zenith jump points, the Avengers had used their intimate knowledge of the Alshain system to plot a pirate point. What would normally have been a transit time of nine days from jump point to planet was reduced to a scant two days from the pirate point. Having synchronized their arrivals, all the Avenger regiments should have arrived within hours of each other.

The first shock occurred when the Eleventh Alshain Avengers did not arrive as scheduled at the rendezvous point. When three more hours passed without any word or sign of the regiment, the other three could no longer risk detection and began their high-speed run toward Alshain.

With an aerospace fighter escort composed of a full regiment of some one hundred fighters and the inspiring sight of the *Tatsumaki* Class WarShip *The Dragon's Last Tear*, the three combined-arms regiments had pulled a punishing two gravities to make planetfall as quickly as possible.

The invading Combine troops were surprised when the Ghost Bears did not respond to the attack with a batchall, the challenge of combat required by the Clan rules of warfare. Either the Ghost Bears had renounced the Clan way, which was unlikely, or Alshain was simply too important for such niceties. The doubts had begun.

As they neared the planet, swarms of aerospace fighters pushed through the atmosphere to meet the incoming invaders in the deathlike silence of space. Following close behind were Clan DropShips, bringing more fighters and their own weapons to the fray. The *Tatsumaki* was unable to target ships as small as the aerospace fighters, but it made short work of the DropShips, which scattered like minnows before a whale.

The second shock of the day appeared on the far horizon of Alshain. Cocooned in her 'Mech's drop pod, Kiyaga and all the other battalion commanders had been patched in to visual feeds of the attacking DropShips. Magnification brought a sight like nothing she had ever seen, and silence filled the commline for a full minute, broken only by distant explosions muffled by the DropShip's hull.

Where before there had been no naval shipyard, one now floated above the world of Alshain. Massive in proportion, it was easily as large as the Combine's Wakazashi Enterprises shipyards at Chatham. It was not so much the size of the facility that struck dumb the invading fleet, but the ship berthed in the unpressurized repair facility that spanned the length of the shipyard.

The open metal latticework of the facility looked like the rib cage of some monstrous mechanical beast, each rib thicker then the largest of the incoming aerospace fighters and some thicker than a DropShip. The Alshain warriors were given an unobstructed view of the largest WarShip the human race had ever constructed. There had been rumors and speculation about the *Leviathan* Class, of which only two were said to exist, but the WarShip stretched a mind-numbing one point six kilometers in length. Even more terrifying was its mass. The ISF had been unable to obtain complete reports except that the *Leviathan* was rumored to mass almost two million four hundred thousand tons. Now it was more than rumor, and the rumors were true.

Staring at the behemoth, Kiyaga was stunned by the colossal technological edge and military advantages of such a vessel. The *Tatsumaki*, the pride of the Combine fleet, was insignificant beside such magnificence.

What finally broke through the battalion commanders' stupor was the realization that massive sections of armor were absent all along the side that was visible, giving a glimpse into the cavernous interior. This ship would not be used against them. Why such a new vessel would need an extensive overhaul so soon Kiyaga couldn't even imagine.

Then the view of the naval yards was suddenly blocked by another WarShip, this one much closer and moving at all speed toward the invading Combine ships. Turning toward it, *The Dragon's Last Tear* positioned itself between the approaching vessel and the Avenger DropShips.

Watching her screen closely as the DropShip captain punched up the magnification on the approaching WarShip, Kiyaga's heart sank. Unlike the *Leviathan*, which no one in the Combine had seen until this moment, the approaching WarShip was known. The *Nightlord* Class was more than double the size of the *Tatsumaki*, and Kiyaga knew this fight could have only one outcome. She prayed that the *Tatsumaki*'s valiant stand would buy the DropShips the final minutes they needed to begin the combat drop.

The Fifteenth Alshain reached the drop zone first and began to jettison 'Mech drop pods as quickly as possible. Exactly three minutes later, Kiyaga's own Fourteenth began their drop. Completely cut off from the outside world for another handful of minutes, she was deaf, dumb, and blind, impotent to affect the unfolding battle.

When her *Akuma* finally passed through the upper atmosphere, it emerged from the exploding drop pod into a scene from some infernal nightmare. All around, Clan fighters dove at the descending Alshain 'Mechs, destroying many still in their pods. Though the Avenger aerospace fighters were making a heroic attempt to hold the Clan OmniFighters at bay, her trained eye estimated that the Ghost Bears would have air superiority in less then an hour.

The final shock was the thunderous and fiery entry of *The Dragon's Last Tear* into Alshain's atmosphere. She had known that the *Tatsumaki* was simply and completely outclassed in this clash of titans. But seeing the graceful ship plummet out of control into the atmosphere that began to tear it apart, she mourned the loss of it and the two hundred-forty warriors who had given their lives trying to take this planet back from the Ghost Bears.

It hurt even more knowing that they had given their lives in vain. Kiyaga, only a fair MechWarrior at best, had been given her command and made executive officer of the Fourteenth Alshain Avengers because of her skill at high-level strategy. Several of her suggestions to the original plan of Operation *Batsu* had, in fact, been implemented.

Now, as she fell through a sky filled with fire and death, she knew they had gravely underestimated the importance of Alshain to the Ghost Bears. With a shipyard like that and WarShip protection, she had no doubt that an entire Galaxy, possibly two, of elite Ghost Bear MechWarriors awaited them.

Together, all four Alshain regiments just might have plucked victory from the jaws of defeat. But with the unexplained absence of the Eleventh and half of the Eighth destroyed in their DropShips by the *Nightlord* before they could drop, there would be no victory this day.

Still, she would fight and die like the samurai she was. If today brought her death, then she would take as many Ghost Bears with her as she could. She only hoped this defeat would not result in a disastrous reprisal against House Kurita.

Clearing her mind, *Chu-sa* Jennifer Kiyaga freed herself of all fear by composing a death haiku. In the cockpit of her *Akuma*, she spoke the words aloud as they came to her:

> Blue-white cold engulfs
> Dragon slumbers in twilight
> Rouse, fury unbound

Then she smiled. Perhaps this day would be the start of a great awakening. Once the ultimate sacrifice by the Alshain Avengers became known, perhaps other warriors of the Combine would remember that it was the Dragon's destiny to rule the entire Inner Sphere.

Yes, she would die like a samurai.

29

Unity Palace
Imperial City, Luthien
Kagoshima Prefecture, Draconis Combine
1 November 3062

Theodore Kurita, Coordinator of the Draconis Combine and First Lord of the resurrected Star League, found himself forced into actions beyond his control for the second time this year; it was a feeling he despised. Standing in the Black Room deep inside Unity Palace, he stared at a holoprojection of the Draconis Combine, seeing the blue-white lines reaching from the Ghost Bear Dominion to envelop almost every Combine world along the border. He did not understand how this could be happening. It had only been three years since the end of Operation Bulldog, and already the Combine was again at war with a Clan! It was too soon.

"How can this have occurred, Ninyu?" he demanded.

It was not just that worlds were in danger of being lost and that numerous units were on the edge of annihilation—this was also a political catastrophe. Theodore had played each of his warlords against the others in order to give the Nova Cats a home within the Combine without another bloody war that neither his military nor his people could afford. He had even managed to rein in the impetuous warlords who had insisted that the Combine attack the Ghost Bear to win back occupied worlds. He wondered why it seemed that he was the only one who could see how disastrous a war would be for the Combine right now, much less a war against the awesome might of the Ghost Bears. His warlords argued that the Combine should never have tried to co-exist in peace with the Clans, and they were using the Ghost Bear invasion as an excuse to stoke the fires of discontent over his alliance with the Nova Cats.

When the Clans had invaded in 3050, none had deployed more then five Galaxies against the Inner Sphere, and yet they had swept all before them with their superior technology. Many of his warlords argued that the advances in Inner Sphere military technology over the past decade had closed the gap with the Clans. Now was the time to strike.

What his warlords failed to recognize or outright ignored was the ISF's report that the Ghost Bears had abandoned almost all of their holdings in Clan space and had moved their entire population and military to the Inner Sphere. The might of the Ghost Bear measured some thirteen Galaxies. Thirteen Galaxies! And now, the Bear had been roused from sleep.

"As you know," Ninyu said, "we received a priority HPG message early this month from Khan West of the Nova Cats, asking confirmation that the Eleventh Alshain Avengers were being re-deployed off Yamarovka. He reported that the Avengers claimed they had received new orders requiring them to leave immediately. For reasons that are not yet clear, the Dragoncat Cluster would not allow the Avengers to depart and fighting broke out. In the end the entire Zeta Provisional Galaxy was drawn into the conflict. Reports are still sketchy, but I understand that both sides took heavy casualties and that the remnants of the Eleventh are currently fighting guerilla actions."

"This I know," Theodore interrupted impatiently. "These actions have also added fuel to the fire over the Nova Cat situation among my warlords. I have already ordered Takura Migaki to apply the full force of the Voice of the Dragon in painting this disaster in the best possible light. Can I assume the reason you give me news of what I already know is that we have learned what happened with the rest of the Alshain regiments? Did you verify that those Alshain regiments were the ones that attacked the Ghost Bears?"

"*Hai, Tomo.* In fact, my own agents buried within the Dominion say all three regiments attacked Alshain."

Theodore shook his head in dismay. Not only had the Avengers betrayed the Combine, they had attacked the very capital of the Dominion. No wonder the Ghost Bears were retaliating in full!

"How could that happen?"

"*Tai-shu* Toshimichi Uchida signed the orders."

Theodore fixed Ninyu with a steady stare. If there was something more, he wanted to hear it.

Ninyu bowed his head slightly, then went on. "I do not believe Uchida had the resources or manpower to initiate such an operation and keep it secret for so long. Our warlords have immense autonomy in such matters, but something would have been discovered if he had been acting on his own."

Ninyu paused again, as though ordering his thoughts. "There is strong evidence pointing to Black Dragon involvement. In fact, it now seems obvious that *Tai-shu* Uchida and a good portion of the Avengers were members of the Society. I am also certain that high-level, non-military aid was arranged. There is no other explanation for how four DCMS regiments could turn traitor and attack a foreign power without our knowledge."

Theodore continued to gaze fixedly at his most trusted advisor as several scenarios occurred to him. "Duke Ricol," he said finally.

"*Hai.*"

"You believe he has become a member of the Black Dragon Society?"

"We both know his past. He only holds his current position as Duke of the Alshain District because he gave the Combine the Gray Death memory core to get it. Considering his aspirations of the past, it is highly like that he assumed a leadership position."

"Is there evidence?" Theodore asked, knowing the answer. The Red Hunter had always been a careful one.

"*Iie*, Tomo. Nothing that links him to any of this."

"Then we must let him be for now." Theodore turned back to the holoprojection. "*Tai-shu* Uchida is another matter. Have we been able to verify whether he actually participated in the fighting?"

"*Iie*."

"He is to be found and exiled. He must not be allowed to die in combat or commit seppuku. That would only make him a martyr to the Black Dragon cause. As for the Alshain regiments, there is no way to know how deeply they have been contaminated. If any of the three regiments that attacked Alshain directly survived, they must all die now."

Theodore's voice was hard and cold. It was a brutal decision, the kind his father would have made without a second thought. But these traitorous events threatened his entire realm and that could not be tolerated. The injured parts must be cut out to save the body.

"Is this projection accurate?" he asked. "Have all these worlds been attacked?

"As far as we have been able to verify, the Najha, Kiesen, Meilen, Dumaring, Kiamba, Mualang, Courchevel, Schuyler, Nykvarn, Idlewind, and Richmond systems are under attack. It is also my belief that the systems of Yamarovka, Itabaina, Labrea, and Caripare in the Irece Prefecture will also be attacked before the week is up. Those systems are still more than a single jump to reach from the Dominion."

"Do you believe the Bears will content themselves with only those worlds, or will they expand?"

"I can give you my opinion, Tomo, but I am not a military specialist. Perhaps one of your other advi-

sors can provide you with a more accurate as̶
ment of this invasion."

"*Hai*, you are correct," Theodore said. "However, I do not need my advisors to tell me that we lack sufficient forces on that border to hold back a full-scale invasion. In our efforts to give aid to Victor along our FedCom border, we have weakened ourselves, perhaps disastrously so."

Gazing intently at the projections of the hundreds Combine worlds, *his* worlds, Theodore knew there was only one response.

"I must order the redeployment of the Ghost Regiments back toward the Dominion border and hope they can get there quickly enough. I will provide Victor whatever support I can in the Star League Council, but I must look to the safety my own realm. I have a feeling this war has only just begun."

It saddened Theodore that he would not be able to fortify Victor Davion, who had become his friend, as much as he would have wished. Young Davion would surely need all the help he could get in the difficult days to come. Theodore wished him all possible success, but it looked like the Prince of the Federated Commonwealth would have to win back his throne by himself.

Many light years distant from the palace on Luthien, and even farther away from the Combine worlds under attack by the Ghost Bears, the old man sat peacefully on his favorite bench in Peace Park on Dieron. Before him, the ivory tokens of *shogi* were spread out on a red and black duraplast checkerboard inlaid into a gray, mushroom-shaped table. He stroked his trimmed white beard while casually studying the board. Around him, the blossoming trees, manicured lawns, and the topiary shrubbery of the Peace Park were a safe and tranquil refuge from the world outside.

Staring at the board, he saw that most of his tiles were gone, while his opponent still retained most of his pieces. That did not distress him. He had been at this game too long to let anger over the loss of his tiles disturb his serenity. He picked up several *Fu* pieces from the pile and held them in his hand as though weighing them.

As he closed his fingers around the *Fu* pieces, he knew that the people around him were also pawns. He understood, as did his opponent, that the game never ended and that new pawns could always be found.

A smile tugged at his lips. The challenge of overcoming defeat after so much has been lost was always the most gratifying.

A new phase of the game had begun.

Epilogue

Ways of Seeing
New Barcella, Irece
Irece Prefecture, Draconis Combine
20 December 3062

Long minutes had passed since the opening twenty drumbeats of the Chronicle of Battles had died away. The bonfire snapped and leapt with fury, and still Minoru Nova Cat made no move to ascend the platform mounted over the roaring fire. The dry brush used to ignite it was rapidly consumed in a flash of heat and light, lofting large flakes of fiery ash through the air, threatening to set the surrounding grass ablaze.

Minoru's place was here, but his thoughts had wandered far. It did not matter that he had fiercely walled off the part of himself that used to be Minoru Kurita; the shocking events of the past few months had broken through his carefully constructed walls as easily as a sapper defeated walls of solid stone.

Behind him he felt the immensity of the Nova Cat

genetic repository and around him the synergy of
Clan warriors gathered together as one mind. Minoru
was ashamed to be distracted by concern for the
Combine, but he saw that a long road still lay ahead.
He had become a member of Clan Nova Cat and
driven himself relentlessly for four years to reach the
goal of Oathmaster. Now he realized it was only a
plateau, a resting point. The mountain still rose
above him, its heights hidden in the haze of the
future.

Minoru had become a living link in the alliance
between the Nova Cats and the Combine, but his
work was not done. The Dragon needed the Clan's
strength to survive the present moment, and if it required that Minoru sacrifice all that he knew and all
that he was, so be it.

He continued to gaze into the fire, yet the flame
he saw was the one within his own heart. It showed
him suddenly what he must do. He had been
adopted into the Nova Cats, then allowed to become
a member of their warrior caste, but he would never
be truly accepted among them without a bloodname.

Becoming Oathmaster was not enough, and it had
only been possible because the Nova Cats were one
of the few Clans that allowed a non-bloodnamed
warrior to hold the post. Winning a bloodname
would not vanquish all resistance to his presence in
the Clan, but it would go a long way. And he would
do it without the backing of any high-ranking member of the Clan, the final proof of his legitimacy as a
Nova Cat.

Now that the full fury of the Ghost Bear had been
aroused, there would be abundant opportunities to

win a bloodname. Already the Bear had conquer.
many of the Combine worlds they had attacked the
month before and had expanded their operations.

The Nova Cats had also lost a world to the Ghost
Bears. Yamarovka, whose defenses had been weakened by Zeta Provisional Galaxy's battle to extermi-
nate the last of the Eleventh Alshain Avengers, fell
easily to a force composed of units from the Ghost
Bear Sigma and Omega Galaxies. They had not offered the Zeta survivors hegira, forcing what was left
of them to retreat off world without honor. Once
again, the Abjurment reared its ugly head. Like the
other Clans, the Bears apparently intended to offer
no quarter.

Yet, old loyalties asserted themselves even as Minoru pondered these dark thoughts. His mind should
be on the future of his Clan, but he could not help
fearing for the Combine.

Just this week news had arrived via Khan West
that Arthur Steiner-Davion had been assassinated.
Tensions between Steiner loyalists and Davionist
units had been heating up for months, and Arthur's
murder could well be the spark that finally set off
the conflagration of civil war. There had been rumors
and reports of rebellions and battles between Steiner
and Davionist units on a number of worlds ever since
fighting broke out in the streets of Solaris City last
summer.

Though many hard-liners in the Combine would
rejoice at this turn of events, it was no secret that
Arthur had harbored anti-Combine sentiments. The
young man had been expressing just those sentiments in a speech at the moment he was cut down.

Except for the last ten years, the Federated Suns and the Draconis Combine had been at war for centuries. Even the alliance forged to defeat the Clans had not been enough to heal that festering wound. In the chaos of a FedCom civil war, there would be Draconis March units that would see Arthur's murder as justification for launching retaliatory raids against their old enemy. And with the Combine moving the lion's share of its forces toward the Ghost Bear Dominion border, that would be devastating. It would be many weeks, if not many months, before any significant forces could be diverted to deal with FedCom attacks. At the moment, the Ghost Bears represented a much greater danger to the integrity of the Combine.

The piercing shriek of a peregrine cut through the night like a blade, snapping Minoru back to the present moment. He heard the crackling fire, smelled the heady scent of burning wood, felt the cool night air touching his bare skin where his ceremonial leathers did not cover. All around him the throng of warriors awaited his ascent to the platform to begin the ritual retelling of Nova Cat battles and victories.

And still, his mind wandered. The dancing shadows of the bonfire carried him back to another dark night when Minoru had gone to the top of a lonely mountain to meet an angry and confused warrior. Having cast off his past and accepted the need to become both more and less than what he had once been, Minoru had believed himself superior to that young warrior. And yet, he had sensed a spark deep in the other man that might one day let him see beyond his narrow vision.

From the reports of the fighting on Yamarovka,

MechWarrior Zane had indeed come to accept and embrace the path of his Clan. He had done everything in his power and beyond to prevent a war with the Ghost Bears. Though he had failed to stop the Alshain Avengers' attack on the Ghost Bears, Zane had achieved something even greater. It was a victory that the Oathmaster of the Nova Cats would forge into a legacy to bind up the wounds within the Clan so they might achieve the purpose of preserving the fragile Star League and protecting the Inner Sphere from predation.

With sudden energy, Minoru strode to the base of the platform and began to ascend the wooden stairs. Zane, who had lived every horror the Nova Cat Abjurment could offer, had triumphed over his own doubts and fears. Minoru would make sure that all the Nova Cats knew it, especially those who still questioned the wisdom of the Clan's current path.

Zane was not a Bloodnamed warrior and his genetic legacy would never be honored by becoming part of the Nova Cat breeding program. Minoru vowed, however, that Zane would achieve a victory over death far more real than even the Clan breeding program offered. He would be immortalized in the Remembrance as the hero he was and all Nova Cats till the end of time would know that Zane had found his path of glory.

Reaching the top of the platform, feeling the heat of the great bonfire, Minoru believed that he had found the key to help reunite the Clan of the Nova Cats, thus preserving the Dragon. Drawing in a breath so deep that it momentarily seared his lungs, he began to speak.

About the Author

Randall N. Bills was born in Kingston, Jamaica, but quickly moved through several states before finding "home" in Arizona just before starting high school. It was about that time that he discovered science-fiction/fantasy literature and adventure gaming, both of which he has spent inordinate amounts of time exploring with many good friends.

Upon graduation from high school, he spent two years on an LDS mission in Guatemala. After returning, he held various jobs before he was presented with the opportunity to actually make money based on all those years of gaming; he was offered a job in the gaming industry. A long-held dream, he now helps develop FASA's BattleTech line, while providing additional creative input for FASA's Shadowrun line and other game lines. Though he has written scenarios and co-authored several source books for BattleTech, this is the first of Randall's hopefully many novels, fulfilling another lifelong dream.

He currently lives in the Windy City with his wife, Tara—who, much to his delight, actually joins in with most of his gaming and puts up with a husband who never leaves work behind—and his son, Bryn—who makes any day bright and of course also wants to play with Daddy's "toys"—and a seven-foot, red-tailed boa called Jak o' the Shadows.

You've played the game—now experience even more drama and excitement as you follow the lives of the men and women who fight bravely on the front lines of the MechWarrior ranks.

A MechWarrior struggles to save his people from annihilation in *Ghost of Winter*. . . .

A ragtag group of Clan warriors are ordered into a battle they cannot win in *Roar of Honor*. . . .

To avenge his brother, one brave MechWarrior will face his greatest enemy in *By Blood Betrayed*. . . .

All the action of BattleTech. With the heart of a MechWarrior.

An excerpt from *Ghost of Winter* by Stephen Kenson follows!

Kore
The Periphery
11 April 3060

The sensors screamed a warning as the missiles arced in. Sturm Kintaro pulled hard on the control stick, spinning his 'Mech as quickly as possible into an evasive turn while trying to maintain top speed across Kore's icy terrain. The fifty-ton *Centurion*'s servos whined as its internal gyroscope fought to keep it upright through the maneuver. The missiles roared past, missing by barely a meter, impacting on the ground nearby and sending up a cloud of dirt, snow, and pulverized rock. Sturm fought against the shock wave of the near miss and managed to keep the 'Mech upright, spinning toward the new attacker.

He used the dust and dirt kicked up by the missile attack as cover and quickly took stock of the newcomer. It was a Clan 'Mech, of course, one the Inner Sphere had dubbed the *Uller*, after the Norse god of archery, though *Kit Fox* was the Clan name for it. This particular *Uller* looked like an alternate configuration, equipped with long-range missile packs. The enemy 'Mech was hunched and crablike compared to the sleek humanoid form of the *Centurion*.

At thirty tons, the *Uller* was smaller than Sturm's *Centurion*, but it was faster and more maneuverable. Its missile packs also gave it the advantage at longer range. The *Centurion* was armed with an autocannon and a single LRM 10-pack. If Sturm kept his distance from the *Uller*, he would probably get pounded into scrap by missile fire while the faster 'Mech evaded his attacks. He decided to close the distance and put his 'Mech superior size and close-range firepower to work.

All this happened in an instant of recognition. Battle-trained reflexes took over and, a split-second after the *Uller* glowed to life on his display, Sturm was slamming the control stick forward. The *Centurion* accelerated toward the enemy 'Mech at near top speed, almost sixty kilometers per hour across the frozen tundra.

Sturm thumbed the firing stud for the *Centurion*'s own LRMs as he closed in, sending a wave of missiles trailing white smoke screaming out from his 'Mech's chest toward the *Uller*. As he expected, the *Uller*'s pilot was quick enough to get his 'Mech out of the way of the incoming missiles: Inner Sphere missile systems were often unguided, and relied far more on skill and luck than electronics to hit their target.

Sturm took advantage of the frozen ground, covered in a white blanket of snow that was rapidly being churned into gray-brown muck by the pounding tread of the metal giants. There was a danger of slipping and losing traction on the icy ground, but this time, Sturm was counting on just that. Fighting to keep control of the joystick and relying on his 'Mech's gyroscopic stabilizers, he slid the remaining distance between the *Centurion* and the *Uller* like a ball player sliding into home plate. It was a maneuver intended to catch the *Uller* pilot off-guard, and it worked.

The *Centurion*'s legs collided with the *Uller*'s left leg with a shriek of protesting metal and the crash of armor. Flashing red lights on the damage schematic indicated some minor harm to the *Centurion*'s leg armor, but no significant damage to its internal systems. The steel-titanium alloy skeleton of the giant war machine was stable. The *Uller*, on the other hand, flailed its arms in a very human, almost comical, gesture before falling over with a thunderous crash, muffled by the sound systems inside the *Centurion*'s cockpit.

Sturm didn't waste any time enjoying the sight of the *Uller* lying on its back like a turtle flipped over by a mischievous child. He gripped the controls tightly and maneuvered the *Centurion* into a firing position as quickly as possible, bringing the humanoid 'Mech back up on one knee so he could bring its weapons to bear. The *Uller* pilot fought to do the same, but non-humanoid 'Mechs often had trouble righting themselves from a prone position.

The *Uller* pilot brought up his 'Mech's right arm,

trying to bring its LRMs to bear on the *Centurion*. Sturm grinned savagely. LRMs were notoriously inaccurate at such close range, and the enemy warrior would be lucky to hit the broad side of a planet.

The LRMs roared and streaked toward the *Centurion* on trails of fire. Several slammed into its left arm and torso. Warning indicators screamed of damage to the *Centurion*'s own missile system. The firing mechanism was badly damaged and off-line. Damn!

Sturm growled a curse and raised his 'Mech's right arm, bringing the heavy Luxor-series autocannon to bear on the *Uller*'s underside. With his other hand he trained the floating cross hairs of the *Centurion*'s medium laser over the center of the enemy 'Mech. He punched down hard on the firing buttons.

A dull roaring filled the cockpit as the autocannon spat fire and a stream of heavy 80mm shells that shredded and tore the composite armor of the *Uller*. At the same time, a lance of emerald light blazed from the medium laser, vaporizing armor in clouds of superheated smoke, cutting into the *Uller*'s vital internal systems.

A bright light blossomed in the depths of the *Uller* as Sturm's laser found the other 'Mech's fusion reactor. Sturm pulled the *Centurion* to its feet and backed away as quickly as possible as the *Uller*'s damaged reactor began to go super-critical. There was a dull *wumph* from the damaged 'Mech as the pilot attempted to bail out. Sturm couldn't tell from his position whether the enemy pilot was able to eject from the crippled 'Mech or not. The *Uller* flared up like a miniature sun and its reactor melted its internal systems, leaving only a blackened hole and molten slag as it began to dim and fade.

But Sturm didn't get a chance to enjoy his victory. Just as he checked the *Centurion*'s damage again and began to sweep the battlefield for signs of other enemy 'Mechs, he got one. The sensors barely had time to shriek a warning before a flight of missiles slammed into the *Centurion*. The wireframe schematic lit up to show armor blown away by the impact along the 'Mech's right side. The missile warheads were followed by twin crimson lances as lasers seared and melted armor off the *Centurion*'s torso and arm. Sturm spun toward his new adversary, bringing all his available weapons to bear, and froze.

It was a *Mad Cat*, one of the deadliest Clan 'Mechs in existence. At seventy-five tons of state-of-the-art weapons and armor, it outweighed the medium *Centurion* by fifty percent. It had a hunched-over design similar to the *Uller*'s, but looked far more ominous. The *Mad Cat* packed heavy and medium lasers in each of its clublike arms, a long-range missile rack on each shoulder, and a row of heavy machine guns and lasers under its long, pointed "chin." Its wide, splay-footed legs pawed at the frozen ground, almost like a predatory bird.

Sturm hesitated only an instant before letting loose at the *Mad Cat* with everything he had. The *Centurion*'s autocannon roared and its medium laser lanced out. Autocannon shells smashed against heavy ferro-fibrous composite armor, and the laser left a blackened scar along the *Mad Cat*'s right leg, but the heavier 'Mech kept on coming, firing its own weapons as it lumbered forward. The *Centurion* tried to move, but too late.

Damn it! Sturm thought, not only is that thing bigger than me, it's faster, too. The *Mad Cat*'s ruby lasers slashed across the *Centurion* like red-hot blades, slicing away chunks of armor and laying bare myomer muscle and delicate internal structures. Another wall of missiles screamed in and slammed into the 'Mech's leg, sending red indicators flaring to proclaim the loss of vital armor in that area. The damage wasn't critical . . . yet, but there was no doubt that the *Centurion* couldn't take much more of that kind of pounding.

The cockpit of the *Centurion* was stifling and Sturm's body—clad only in boots, shorts, and a coolant vest—was drenched in sweat, making the controls slick under his hands. He pressed his head forward slightly against the inside of his neurohelmet and quickly considered his options.

Thing is, he thought, if I turn my back on this guy, I'm definitely a dead man. The *Centurion* was one of the few 'Mechs that mounted rear-firing weapons, but Sturm seriously doubted that a single medium laser would do any significant damage to the *Mad Cat*. In the meantime, the Clan 'Mech's weapons could cut through his light back armor in an instant and make hash of its internal systems, much like Sturm did to the *Uller* just moments before. He also couldn't back away from the *Mad Cat*, not on such treacherous ground and with the *Mad Cat* moving as quickly as it was. He immediately decided that his only chance was to try and outflank the bigger 'Mech; do an end run around it and run like hell before the _Mad Cat_ could recoup enough to wipe him out.

Sturm dodged his 'Mech to the left as another storm of missile fire came in, missing him narrowly. He gritted his teeth and slammed the control stick forward, pushing the _Centurion_ up to top speed as he ran almost directly toward the _Mad Cat_ on a zig-zag path intended to give him the most chance of avoiding any incoming attacks. The _Mad Cat_ pilot never even wavered at the sight of the fifty-ton _Centurion_ rushing at him, continuing forward in the same almost casual gait.

Sturm triggered the _Centurion_'s autocannon, stitching a line of fire along the _Mad Cat_'s left leg and torso as he charged forward, evading the incoming missiles and laser fire. A medium laser cut across his already damaged left torso, and the wireframe schematic lit up with some internal structural damage.

"C'mon, baby, hang together," Sturm muttered under his breath as the _Mad Cat_ swelled in his viewscreen and the distance indicator in his heads-up display dwindled. Damn, but it was big. Only a few more meters . . .

As the _Centurion_ neared the massive Clan war machine, Sturm shifted the control stick hard to the left and changed direction. Almost like a bullfighter waving his cape, the _Mad Cat_ swiveled its torso and swung one of its massive arms like a club. Sturm saw it move, but he couldn't react fast enough to do anything about it. The giant metal arm filled his entire viewscreen as it rushed it toward him.

There was a deafening "CLANG!" that shook the

cockpit as the impact sent the *Centurion* tumbling out of control. Sturm fought the controls to keep it upright, but gravity held the fifty tons of BattleMech in its relentless grip, and the *Centurion* toppled over onto the ground like a punch-drunk prize fighter. Sturm got the wind knocked out of him as the cockpit rattled, its shock-absorption systems strained to their utmost.

Still, Sturm wasn't about to give up. Almost by reflex he threw the *Centurion* into a roll to the side, trying to avoid the strike he knew was coming next. Instead of swinging its other arm, however, the *Mad Cat* kicked with its clawed foot instead. The impact boomed through the cockpit as the kick smashed armor and internal systems, lighting up flashing red indicators on the damage display. As Sturm tried to bring his autocannon to bear on his enemy, he looked up at the viewscreen and saw the *Mad Cat* point its massive arms downward at his 'Mech. As he grabbed for the controls, a hellish red light filled the screen, the heat in the cabin skyrocketed, and then everything went dark.

Batu

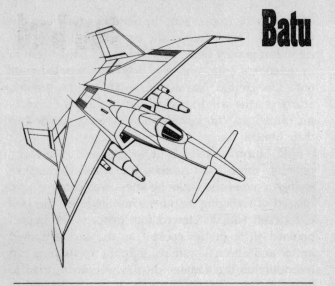

Noruff

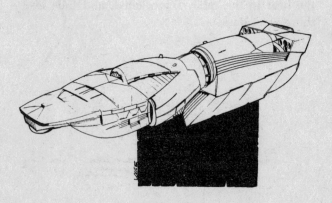

Star Lord

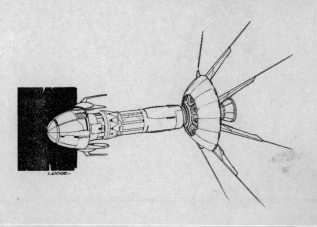

Bishamon

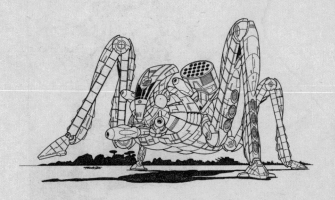

Elemental

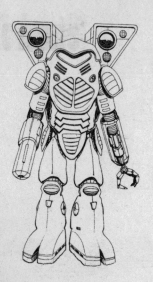

Shadow Cat

Jenner IIC

Pack Hunter